實用商業美語
——實況模擬
Vol. III. —進階篇—

杉田敏　著　　張錦源　校譯

三民書局 印行

國家圖書館出版品預行編目資料

實用商業美語 III——實況模擬／杉田
敏著，張錦源校譯.--初版.--臺北
市：三民，民86
　　面；　　公分
ISBN 957-14-2577-X (平裝)

1.英國語言-讀本

805.18　　　　　　　　　　　86003020

國際網路位址　http://sanmin.com.tw

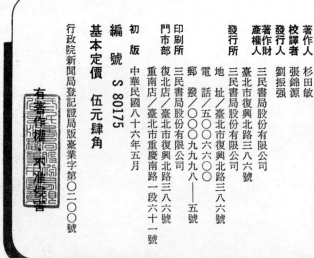

© 實用商業美語 (III) ——實況模擬

著作人　杉田敏
校譯者　張錦源
發行人　劉振強
著作財產權人　三民書局股份有限公司
發行所　三民書局股份有限公司
　　　　地址／臺北市復興北路三八六號
　　　　電話／五○○六六○○
　　　　郵撥／○○○○九九九八——五號
印刷所　三民書局股份有限公司
門市部　復北店／臺北市復興北路三八六號
　　　　重南店／臺北市重慶南路一段六十一號
初版　　中華民國八十六年五月
編號　　S 80175
基本定價　伍元肆角
行政院新聞局登記證局版臺業字第○二○○號

有著作權・不准侵害

ISBN 957-14-2577-X (第三冊：平裝)

序

　　主角澤崎昭一從國際食品公司轉至 ABC 食品公司，雖然經歷了各式各樣的挑戰，但他卻是樂在其中，每天都像工作狂般地勤奮。而上司的眼睛也是雪亮的，在器重他之餘，更向上推薦，把他調任至紐約總公司。本書即敘述了一些澤崎在紐約所發生的事。

　　幾乎書中所有的故事情節，都是作者所親身經歷，要不就是發生在作者周遭的事。而作者也盡可能以實際商務狀況為考量，並融入人情味，使之以通情合理的會話風貌再次呈現出來。

　　作者一直很用心地要把故事情節寫得實際且饒富趣味，還要能具有話題性。因此，此系列節目在播出之後就不斷有聽眾來信說，「故事情節的戲劇性發展相當吸引我。」

　　然而，語言的學習本來就是件極為辛苦且嚴肅的事。若有人說「英文能力可以在享受學習之樂中，不知不覺地進步」，那定然是個神話。

　　英文有句俗諺說，"All things are difficult before they are easy." 意思就是說，「事情要先難而後易」。萬事起頭難，但熟悉之後就能上手。

　　學習英語亦然。只要基礎打好了，臨場便可脫口而出。但在達到那樣的程度之前，「困難」與「考驗」是免不了的。若為了好逸惡勞而總找「容易」的著手，則永無登峰造極的一日。

　　人類的潛能是無限的，願諸位都能持之以恆，往成功之路邁進。

杉田　敏

本書的使用方法

　　要想用英語跟老外「暢所欲言」並不容易。即使你買了幾本會話書籍，且一字不漏地背誦下來，但你接下來卻會面臨到無法「照本宣科」的問題，因你無法掌握實際談話內容。在本書中，會有各種狀況的模擬，告訴你要如何在不同的情境中與人展開對話。本書更以商場上的實際對話為例，引導讀者去思索學習會話之道。

預習

　　先仔細閱讀「課文內容」，並將概要記住。若要使用另售的錄音帶，則一開始盡量不要看課本，試著用耳朵專注地聽。Sentences 是故事中所使用句子的採樣，這也是大腦的暖身操。

課文‧翻譯

　　試著閱讀完「狀況」之後，在心中描摹該場景。若是配合錄音帶使用，則先不要看劇情內容，嘗試用耳朵聽。如果覺得會話速度太快而無法理解，千萬不要立刻放棄，可以多聽幾次。

字彙

　　基本上，只要有初步的字彙能力，便足以應付大部分的商務英語會話了。但若自己需要遊走多國，則應該要背誦基本商務用語的廣義解釋及其正確發音。在 Vocabulary Building 中則藉由例句來學習活用法。並請讀者參考本書末了的單字表。

習題

　　每個例句都各有四個劃線部分，其中一個的文法有誤，請將之選出。

簡短對話

與內文的說法和談話進行方向不同的對話。

總結

會話應盡量具有實用性，且能反映國際商業環境。所以每一課在總結的地方都會有異國文化的應對之道、社會語言學知識、以及各種重要的商業情報。

CONTENTS

■■■■■ 《實用商業美語》Vol. I, II 的內容 ■■■■■

P R O F I L E

～故事中出現的主要人物～

● **Shoichi Sawasaki**/澤崎昭一(38歲)

本系列的主角，在合併後的尼爾森ABC
食品公司中被調至公司位於芝加哥的
總部，擔任行銷聯絡部門的一員。在如
此的企業環境中，他更是積極地向工
作挑戰。

● **Gil Parker**/吉爾・帕克(45歲)

英國人。他總理各個行銷部門，也是公
司副總。

● **Bradley Winchell**/布雷得利・溫謝爾(38歲)

昭一的同事。與昭一同時調至芝加哥
總公司，是昭一商談的良伴。

● **Sally Egler**/莎莉・艾格勒(34歲)

昭一在芝加哥總公司的同事，是個活
潑的美國女性。

● **Peter Swarbrick**/彼得・史瓦布利克(39歲)

昭一在芝加哥總公司的同事，為維護
其「自尊心」而決定離職。

● **Maria Cortez**/瑪莉亞・古岱茲(29歲)

昭一以前在紐約的同事，是個有波多
黎各血統的美國人。現在與先生共同在
芝加哥經營小眾市場行銷顧問公司。

● **Alex DeMarco**/亞力士・迪馬哥(44歲)

尼爾森ABC食品公司的總裁。外界評
為「冷酷無情」，是位天才型的經營
者。

Lesson 32

Professional Luncheon
（午餐會）

◆ Lesson 32 的內容 ◆

在合併後新公司 ── 尼爾森 ABC 食品公司 ── 的芝加哥總部，澤崎和溫謝爾被調派至行銷連絡小組。這是一個集合了該領域的菁英，以推廣銷售為出發點的作戰部隊。負責統籌者則為首席副總裁，英國籍的吉爾·帕克。

今天，歷史悠久的芝加哥行銷俱樂部特地邀請了尼爾森 ABC 食品公司的總裁亞力士·迪馬哥，在他們的年度大會上發表演說。尼爾森的該組成員因此有機會列席此次餐會。當日會場盛況空前，還有不少人被婉拒在外。這次演說的主題是迪馬哥的經營理念 ── 「扁平的金字塔」。

And it's a decent wine, too. Would you care for some, Shoichi?

Professional Luncheon (1) (午餐會)

●預習 —Sentences

· You're the last one from our group to show up.
· I must say this is quite an event.
· They've got a turn-away crowd at the entrance.
· Did you have any trouble getting here?
· The CEOs still like to huddle together.

●Vignette

Winchell: Hello, everyone. Is this seat for me?

Sawasaki: Yes, Brad. You're the last one from our group to show up. That other empty chair is for Peter. He's running around here somewhere.

Winchell: I must say this is quite an event. They've got a turn-away crowd at the entrance.

Parker: Did you have any trouble getting here?

Winchell: No, I just got lost after I came into the building. Actually, I took a cab. I still haven't tried to use the El. On the way here, my taxi was stuck in traffic so bad it took five lights to get through a single intersection. What happened to all that decentralization of industry I was hearing about a few years ago— spreading out production sites, letting people work at home and things like that?

Parker: Oh, industry is decentralizing, but the head offices aren't. The CEOs still like to huddle together. They don't trust any technology newer than the telephone or the fax machine.

Sawasaki: Actually, the fax machine is a good argument for telecommuting, Gil.

Winchell: Sure. We could all live and work miles from here and come once a week for a conference. If we all had personal computers and faxes, we wouldn't need to actually be in the same building.

　　午餐會即將開始，溫謝爾總算及時趕到。他說是因為搭乘計程車碰上塞車之故。

溫謝爾：　大家好。這個座位是給我的嗎？

澤崎：　是的，布雷。你是我們組裡到得最晚的人了。還有一張空著的椅子是彼得的。他還在這棟樓的某個地方跑來跑去。

溫謝爾：　我得說，這真是件大事。進門的地方有一大群人被擋在門外不能進來。

帕克：　你在來到這裡的路上，有沒有甚麼問題？

溫謝爾：　沒有。我是進到這棟大樓之後才迷路的。事實上，我還是沒有搭乘高架火車，我坐計程車來的。路上，我搭的那輛計程車被卡在車陣當中，動彈不得。每過一個十字路口，都要等燈號變了五次才過得去。我們前幾年不是還聽過產業要分散嗎？要把生產點分散開來，讓大家可以在家上班甚麼的。現在到底怎麼回事？

帕克：　噢，產業是在分散沒錯，不過總公司可沒有。那些執行長還是喜歡聚在一起。通訊科技的發達對他們而言也僅止於電話和傳真機，他們不信任其後的任何發明。

澤崎：　吉爾，事實上，傳真機的發明更叫人有理由在家上班(採取遠距離上班)。

溫謝爾：　那是當然。我們儘可以都住得遠遠地，工作地點也相距好幾十哩，然後一週來開一次會。如果大家都有個人電腦和傳真機，我們實際上並不需要在同一棟大廈內上班。

Lesson 32 Professional Luncheon (1)

Words and Phrases

show up 出現	head office 總公司
El (<elevated railroad) 高架鐵路	CEO (chief executive officer)
intersection 十字路口; 交叉口	執行長; 最高經營主管
things like that 像那類的事情等的	fax machine 傳真機

Vocabulary Building

- **turn-away** *adj.* 被拒入場的 *v.* 拒絕; 謝絕
  cf. The politician just said, "No comment," and turned away all reporters.
  (那個政客只說了一句:「不予置評。」然後就把所有的記者擋掉了。)

- **be stuck in traffic** 被卡在車陣中
  Now that I have a cellular phone in my car, I can keep in touch with clients even when I'm stuck in traffic.
  (自從我車上有了行動電話之後, 即使我因為交通阻塞而被卡在半路, 仍可與客戶保持聯絡。)

- **decentralization** 疏散; 分散 (化)
  Decentralization has resulted in less face-to-face contact in our business.
  (產業分散化的結果是, 公司裡的人愈來愈少有面對面接觸的機會了。)

- **huddle** 群聚在一起
  cf. The labor representatives went into a huddle before accepting the new union contract.
  (在決定要接受新的工會合約之前, 勞工代表們祕密地聚在一起會商。)

12

1. An examination committee <u>informed to</u> <u>the</u> students who <u>failed</u> the
   　　　　　　　　　　　　　　　　A　　　　　B　　　　　　　　　C

   <u>exam</u>.
   　D

2. Having <u>forgot</u> his <u>notes</u>, Jim <u>winged</u> his presentation <u>to</u> management.
   　　　　　　A　　　　　B　　　　　　C　　　　　　　　　　　D

3. Not <u>until</u> Ned's wife <u>left</u> him, <u>he realized</u> how much he <u>loved</u> her.
   　　　　A　　　　　　　　B　　　　　　　C　　　　　　　　　　D

◆◆◆◆◆◆◆◆◆◆◆◆◆◆ 簡短對話 ◆◆◆◆◆◆◆◆◆◆◆◆◆◆

Parker: Didn't you see the sign at the entrance that said where the meeting
was?

Winchell: Was there a sign at the entrance? No, I missed that entirely. I
was afraid I was going to be late, so I just came barreling in and asked the
first official-looking person I saw.

Parker: Did they give you the wrong directions?

Winchell: Not exactly. This person told me where the meeting was, but
when I got there, I discovered it was a different group. I think he probably
didn't hear me right.

Parker: You were probably talking too fast. Sounds like a case of "haste
makes waste."

---

barrel 快速進入　　**give someone the wrong directions** 給某人指錯路了
Haste makes waste. 欲速則不達。

Lesson 32

Professional Luncheon (2) （午餐會）

●預習 — *Sentences*

- There's not much we can do to decentralize.
- Why did Nelson establish his headquarters in Chicago?
- Chicago was right at the center of American agriculture.
- This is still the breadbasket of North America.
- Alex rarely gives speeches, so Peter was delighted.

●*Vignette*

Parker: Wait a minute, gentlemen. You can decentralize information systems and put your auto factories in the suburbs but if you're in the food business, you're not in the production business, you're in the shipping business. And low shipping prices demand bulk, so businesses tend to cluster around the ports and railheads. In our case, there's not much we can do to decentralize.

Sawasaki: Why did Nelson establish his headquarters in Chicago, though, instead of some other distribution center?

Winchell: Well, during the Depression in the '30s, a lot of the country's food production shifted to California, but before that, Chicago was right at the center of American agriculture. There was an enormous amount of shipping on the Great Lakes, and all these Midwestern states, along with southern Canada, were just one big farm. Of course, this is still the breadbasket of North America.

Parker: Oh, here comes Peter. He's very proud of himself, you know. It was his idea for Alex to address this annual meeting of the Chicago Marketing Club. Alex rarely gives speeches, so Peter was delighted when he gave his OK.

Sawasaki: I hate to admit this, Peter, but I've never paid much attention to these professional groups. What do they do?

Swarbrick: Well, for the most part the purpose is to let you share ideas and information and give you an opportunity to meet other marketing and communication people.

　　大家的話題轉到了在家上班方面。帕克適時提出了他對目前情況的解釋：「即使是把資訊系統分散，若要食品業也看齊，仍有其條件上的限制。」

帕克：　先生們，先打住一下。你們是可以把資訊系統分散，把汽車工廠搬到市郊，但如果你們所在的是食品業這一行，那就不再是製造業的問題，而是貨運業。運費若要低廉，就得採取大宗輸運，所以這一行多偏向集中在港口和鐵路輸運中心附近。以我們的例子而言，能作產業分散的不多。

澤崎：　如果是這樣，為什麼尼爾森要把總公司設在芝加哥，而不是在其他的物流中心？

溫謝爾：　你之所以這麼想，是因為在30年代的大蕭條時期，國內很多食品生產都轉移到了加州，不過在此之前，芝加哥卻正好位於美國的農產中心。那時在五大湖區，每天來往輸運的貨物極多。而所有這些中西部的州，加上加拿大南部，合起來正是一個巨大的農場。當然了，它現在也仍是北美的穀倉。

帕克：　噢，彼得來了。你們可知道他這回相當自傲。因為亞力士之所以會在這個芝加哥行銷俱樂部的年度會議中發表談話，全是彼得出的主意。亞力士極少發表演說，但這次他同意了，彼得可高興得很。

澤崎：　彼得，我不得不說，我從沒重視過這些所謂的專業小組。他們有什麼功用呢？

史瓦布利克：　這個嘛，大部分是用來讓你表達意見，同時也獲得資訊。在這裡你會有機會看到其他負責行銷和連絡的人物。

Lesson 32 Professional Luncheon (2)

Words and Phrases

auto factory	汽車工廠	Great Lakes	北美五大湖區
cluster around	在…附近集結	Midwestern	中西部的
railhead	鐵路輸運的終站(或起站)	address *v.*	向人發表演說

Vocabulary Building

● **bulk**　大量; 大部分

The bulk of our sales are to repeat customers.

(我們大部分的銷售額都是來自於重複訂單的客戶。)

● **distribution center**　物流中心

We have a corporate network of eight distribution centers nationwide.

(我們公司在全國共有八個物流中心,以構成一個銷售網。)

● **(the) Depression**　(1930年代的)大蕭條

Having grown up during the Great Depression, Joe hated to see people wasting things.

(喬是在大蕭條時期長大的,所以他恨惡看到別人浪費東西。)

● **breadbasket**　穀倉

Iowa is breadbasket of the United States.

(愛荷華是美國的穀倉。)

在下列例句中，每句各有四個劃線部分，
其中一個的文法有誤，請將之選出。　　(解答見261頁)

1. To <u>balance</u> this year's <u>budget</u>, the task force proposed <u>laying off</u> half the
　　　A　　　　　　　B　　　　　　　　　　　C

　<u>personnels</u>.
　　D

2. I thought <u>living in</u> a city would be rather <u>excited</u> but now I am <u>completely</u>
　　　　　　A　　　　　　　　　　　　　B　　　　　　　　C

　<u>fed up</u>.
　　D

3. There were quite a few people <u>that</u> could <u>make themselves</u> <u>understood</u>
　　　　　　　　　　　　　　　　A　　　　　　B　　　　　C

　<u>in</u> Chinese.
　　D

◆◆◆◆◆◆◆◆◆◆◆◆◆ 簡短對話 ◆◆◆◆◆◆◆◆◆◆◆◆◆◆

Sawasaki: By the way, I thought Sally said she was coming today.
Parker: She was planning to, but she called in sick this morning.
Sawasaki: Nothing serious, I hope.
Parker: Well, she said she was running a temperature and had a sore throat
　and aching muscles.
Sawasaki: Sounds like it could be the flu.
Parker: Yeah. I told her to forget about work and concentrate on getting
　better.

---

call in sick 打電話來說生病了　　**run a temperature** 發燒　　**sore throat**
喉嚨痛　　**aching muscles** 肌肉痛　　**flu** (<influenza) 感冒

Professional Luncheon (3) (午餐會)

●預習 — *Sentences*

- Tell me, what's Alex going to be talking about?
- It's basically about his management style.
- Is that one of his newest slogans?
- We know how Alex feels about that.
- He says it's the management style of the '90s.

●*Vignette*

Swarbrick: By the way, you ought to look into membership, Shoichi and Brad. The company will foot the bill and you can learn a lot from your fellow professionals.

Sawasaki: Sounds interesting.

Winchell: Tell me, Peter, what's Alex going to be talking about?

Swarbrick: His topic today is the "flattened pyramid." It's basically about his management style. You know the lean and agile style.

Sawasaki: Is that one of his newest slogans?

Parker: It's not really a new idea. Picture a business as a pyramid, with the president or owner at the top, and bigger and bigger layers of management until you hit the shop floor. Getting top management closer to the troops has always been given lip service, but when times are good, the layers of management expand and the pyramid gets taller.

Swarbrick: And we know how Alex feels about that. He'd like to make our pyramid even flatter than it already is.

Parker: That's true. And he will. He says it's the management style of the '90s.

Sawasaki: I have a problem with the word "style." Isn't he just trying to cut fat and make the company more efficient?

Parker: No, it's much more than that.

迪馬哥確信，90年代經營哲學的主流，在於盡可能縮短階級上的金字塔。換言之，就是要創造出一種上層與作業現場間距離縮短，沒有人事贅肉的靈巧風格。

史瓦布利克： 順帶一提，我說布雷和昭一啊，你們應該研究一下，看要不要加入，成為會員。公司會付會費甚麼的，而你們又能從其他同是專家的同伴身上學到很多東西。

澤崎： 聽起來蠻有趣的。

溫謝爾： 彼得，告訴我亞力士今天要說些甚麼。

史瓦利克： 他今天的主題是：「扁平了的金字塔」。基本上是一些有關他管理風格上的東西。你們也知道那種風格：一個沒有贅肉的公司，機能才會靈活。

澤崎： 那是他最新的口號之一嗎？

帕克： 這概念其實不新了。它是把事業想像成一個金字塔，最上層是總裁或所有者，接下來是一層又一層愈來愈龐大的管理階層，最下面才是實際的作業現場。常有人在說要拉近最高管理階層與生產線員工間的距離，但都只是說說而已；一旦景氣好起來，管理階層又會膨脹，結果，金字塔就愈來愈高了。

史瓦布利克： 而且我們知道亞力士對此深有所感。我們現在的金字塔已經比從前矮了不少，但他還要再砍掉一些。

帕克： 沒錯，而且他會做到的。他說這是90年代的管理風格。

澤崎： 我對「風格」這個字有點感冒。他不就是做人事減肥，好使公司運作更有效率嗎？

帕克： 不，那還只是小意思呢！

Lesson 32 **Professional Luncheon (3)**

Words and Phrases

membership   會員的資格   活自如

fellow professional   其他同為專家   layer   層

   的夥伴   cut fat   切掉肥肉

flattened pyramid   扁平了的金字塔   It's much more than that.   還不

lean and agile   沒有贅肉，活動靈   只是那樣呢!

Vocabulary Building

- **foot the bill**   付帳

  I refuse to foot the bill for my children's extravagances.

  (對於我的孩子們買的奢侈品，我拒絕為它們付帳。)

- **picture** *v.*   想像

  Just picture in your mind a fully automated automotive plant.

  (在你心中想像一下，一個完全自動化的汽車工廠。)

- **shop floor**   工廠的作業現場

  Few of today's manufacturing executives have shop-floor experience.

  (今天大多數的製造業經營主管都沒有工廠作業的經驗。)

- **troops** *usu. pl.*   軍隊；部屬

  Go back to your workplace and tell the troops to cut down on private phone calls. They're costing the company a pretty penny.

  (回到你的工作崗位，告訴你下面的人，私人電話不要打那麼多。公司已經付掉不少電話費了。)

在下列例句中，每句各有四個劃線部分，其中一個的文法有誤，請將之選出。 （解答見 261 頁）

1. You must <u>wash</u> a wool sweater <u>by squeeze</u> water <u>through</u> <u>it</u>.
            A   B   C   D

2. Not <u>having given</u> instructions, the demonstrator was <u>unsure</u> <u>how to</u> <u>handle</u>
           A   B   C   D

   the new car.

3. There <u>was</u> <u>many</u> confusion <u>among</u> the people who <u>lost</u> their houses in
          A   B   C   D

   the earthquake.

◆◆◆◆◆◆◆◆◆◆◆◆◆◆ 簡短對話 ◆◆◆◆◆◆◆◆◆◆◆◆◆◆

Parker: According to Alex, Japanese companies make do with fewer layers of management than companies in this country, and that's one of the reasons they're so competitive. Is that true, Shoichi?

Sawasaki: Well, I can't claim to be an expert on Japanese organizations, but as a general observation I'd say that's correct, especially in manufacturing.

Parker: It's funny in a way, because we tend to think of the Orient as a place of rigid hierarchies. You know, with Confucianism and all that.

Sawasaki: I can't speak for the other countries in Asia, but in Japan it's really not that rigid. That may be partly due to American influence after the war.

---

make do with 能靠…而應付得了　　**layer of management** 管理階層　　**general observation** 一般的觀察　　**rigid** 嚴格的　　**hierarchy** 階級制度　　**Confucianism** 儒家思想

Lesson 32

Professional Luncheon (4) (午餐會)

預習 —Sentences

- You don't let them look for scapegoats.
- That sounds pretty tough on the unit heads.
- He's attracted a lot of entrepreneurs.
- He asked to skip his entree.
- I haven't had a bite to eat so far all day.

Vignette

Parker: The idea is that you don't order people from the top; you lead them. Each unit of the company is treated as a business in itself and a strong executive is chosen to head it. If he or she gets in trouble, you don't tell them what to do and you don't let them look for scapegoats. You give them vision and try to help them.

Winchell: That sounds pretty tough on the unit heads.

Parker: Yes, but it has its up side too. Alex has a lot of highly motivated people working for him, because he gives them lots of responsibility and self-confidence. He's attracted a lot of entrepreneurs.

Winchell: I see Alex is not eating but working on his speech.

Swarbrick: Yeah. He asked to skip his entree. He'll probably just have a few bites of salad. He says lunch slows him down before a speech.

Winchell: What's this? Is wine included with the lunch?

Swarbrick: Each table has a couple of bottles. They were donated by a California winery for this occasion.

Sawasaki: That was a good marketing ploy to take advantage of this high-powered crowd.

Swarbrick: And it's a decent wine, too. Would you care for some, Shoichi?

Sawasaki: Maybe later. I haven't had a bite to eat so far all day and it wouldn't do to get smashed in front of my boss, at the company table, while my company president is addressing a conference.

Parker: Let's quiet down, everybody. It looks like they're about to introduce Alex.

　　迪馬哥雖然作風強悍，但也由於他願意交付他人重任，使人有充分的自信，所以對主動性高的創業型員工來說，可說是魅力十足。

帕克：　它所考量的是，你不是從最上層下達命令，而是引導下屬。公司的每一個單位都要被視作一個獨立的事業，而且要選一位有能力的主管來全權負責。假如這位主管在某些地方出了差錯，有麻煩了，不會有人告訴他該怎麼做，他也不能找人頂罪。在上位的要使這些主管對事情有洞察力，並試著從旁協助他們。

溫謝爾：　這樣聽起來，這些單位主管的日子不會好過了。

帕克：　沒錯，但這樣做也是有優點的。亞力士旗下有很多主動性很強的人，這是因為他給與他們很多的責任和自信。他吸引了不少企業家到他身邊。

溫謝爾：　我沒看到亞力士在吃東西，他一直在準備他的講稿。

史瓦布利克：　是啊，他說過正餐不用預備他的分。他可能只吃一兩口沙拉就不吃了。他說，演說前吃午餐會使他變得遲鈍。

溫謝爾：　這是什麼東西？酒也包括在我們的午餐內嗎？

史瓦布利克：　每張桌子上都有幾瓶酒。這是加州一家釀酒廠特別為這個場合贈送的。

澤崎：　這倒是一個相當不錯的行銷策略。因為與會者都是很活躍的人物，可以好好利用一下。

史瓦布利克：　而且這酒還相當不錯。昭一，你要來一點嗎？

澤崎：　可能等一下吧！我今天一直到現在什麼都沒吃，喝了可能會醉倒。當著老闆的面，醉倒在公司桌上，前面又正好有公司總裁在發表談話，我可不敢想像那種狀況。

帕克：　各位，我們安靜一下，他們好像要介紹亞力士了。

Lesson 32　Professional Luncheon (4)

Words and Phrases

get in trouble	有麻煩了	winery	釀酒廠
be tough on	對…而言是艱難的	take advantage of	利用…
motivated	受到激發的	decent	還不錯的
entrepreneur	企業家；興業家	get smashed	醉倒
skip	省掉；略過	quiet down	安靜下來
entree	主菜		

Vocabulary Building

- **scapegoat**　代罪羔羊；替罪者
  Don't try to make me a scapegoat for your own failures.
  （你自己的失敗可不要找我作替罪羔羊。）

- **up side**　正面
  cf. The investors decided against the investment since the downside risk was too great.
  （由於這個投資的負面風險太大，投資者決定縮手不進。）

- **ploy**　策略
  The expensive German car was part of the ploy used by the con artists to swindle money out of their innocent victims.
  （昂貴的德國車是那些騙子用以詐騙無辜消費者的策略之一。）

- **high-powered**　活躍的
  The new president brought in a team of high-powered consultants to revamp the organization.
  （那位新任總裁引進了一個活躍的顧問小組，要對整個公司組織做番改革。）

(解答見 261 頁)

▶**Exercises** 在下列例句中，每句各有四個劃線部分，
其中一個的文法有誤，請將之選出。

1. When Bill was in grammar school, he dreamed to be a doctor.
   A   B   C   D

2. The audience should listen to Lisa's lecture in quiet so as to show
                          A   B   C   D

   respect.

3. Few persons showed any interest in playing on the market.
   A   B   C   D

◆◆◆◆◆◆◆◆◆◆◆◆◆ 簡短對話 ◆◆◆◆◆◆◆◆◆◆◆◆◆

Sawasaki: How about you, Brad? Can I offer you some of this wine?
Winchell: Er, I guess not, thanks.
Swarbrick: Relax, and have a glass. I can assure you that it's not going to
   go down as a black mark in your file somewhere.
Winchell: Well, if you insist . . .
Swarbrick: That's the spirit.

---

go down 被記錄下來   **black mark** 污點   **if you insist** 假如你堅持的話
That's the spirit. 這就對了。

Professional Luncheon — 總結

∎ ∎ ∎

餐會接近尾聲時，澤崎技巧地以「今天沒吃甚麼東西」為由，婉拒敬酒。

一般認為要觀察一個人的感受性及禮貌，餐桌是最適合的地方，甚至有公司在徵募外勤人員時，也會把用餐時的 job interview 列入甄試項目之一。

在吃歐式自助餐時，如果裝得太滿又沒吃完，那是很令人反感的。當然，喝湯不出聲，吃東西不說話，更是不需贅言的基本常識。但如果需要拿取離自己較遠的鹽或胡椒，切忌彎腰探身，應該要禮貌地說，"Would you please pass me the salt?" 來請別人代勞；相反地，如果東西在自己身邊，就不要等到對方開口，而該主動詢問，"Would you like salt and pepper?"

在歐美家庭，若有女孩到了約會年齡，家人(特別是兄長)會教導她們約會時不可點太貴的東西。商業便餐也是一樣，如果此時點的是昂貴菜肴、進口葡萄酒或甜酒等的，會讓人以為是趁火打劫。如果是真的很想品嚐，最好事先徵詢對方意見： I hear lobsters in this area are very good. If you don't mind, I'd like to try this dish. (聽說這裡的龍蝦非常可口，可以的話我想嚐嚐看)。不過如此一來，最好就不要再點其他湯類，若再點選其他菜肴時就要盡量選擇便宜一點的了。

然而，只點便宜的東西，也有可能被誤解成輕看對方，所以，根據 yardstick (判斷的大原則)，點選中等價位才是上策。至於用餐的速度，最好配合對方，太快或太慢都不適合。

Lesson 33

Environmentalism

（環境保護主義）

◆ Lesson 33 的內容 ◆

　　有人說，環境問題是 90 年代人類最大的課題。而企業也已開始正視淨化環境的責任，著手進行防止環境破壞的活動。尼爾森 ABC 食品公司亦對環境問題深表關切，並發表了要在西元 2000 年前植滿一百萬棵樹的計畫。此外，全球廠長紅利考核的重點之一，也包括了他們有否提供任何建設性的建議給公司，以協助生產無污染、無公害的產品。

So it's good business to be responsible about the environment.

Lesson 33

Environmentalism (1) (環境保護主義)

●預習 — *Sentences*

- Environment is the key word for us in this decade.
- That would have seemed almost antibusiness to me.
- There's so much damage everywhere you look.
- Pollution knows no boundaries and favors no ideologies.
- Africa is becoming the least habitable continent.

●*Vignette*

Sawasaki: I see in the management newsletter that Nelson ABC Foods has promised to plant a million trees by the year 2000.

Parker: That's right. Environment is the key word for us in this decade. In fact, the bonuses of our plant managers around the world are now based in part on the generation of ideas to make our products ecologically safe. A few years ago that would have seemed, well, almost antibusiness to me.

Egler: I'm very proud of the fact that our company is so aggressive in the battle to save the planet, because there's so much damage everywhere you look. It was a real shocker to learn about the terrible environmental devastation in Eastern Europe that came to light after the collapse of the communist regimes there.

Swarbrick: It only shows that pollution knows no boundaries and favors no ideologies.

Parker: In the U.S., people complain about algae caused by pollution interfering with marine sports. But in other countries it's a matter of life or death. Africa is becoming the least habitable continent with the damage caused by desertification. Mexico City has severe air pollution problems and a lot of the Amazon rain forests have been wiped out.

　　如果說80年代的風潮是「苗條」、「低卡路里」，那麼90年代的關鍵字就是「綠色」與「環境」。目前世界各地正受公害肆虐，引發種種嚴重的後遺症。

澤崎：　我從管理簡訊上得知尼爾森 ABC 食品公司承諾要在西元 2000 年以前種一百萬棵樹。

帕克：　沒錯。對我們來說，環保是這個時代重要的關鍵辭彙。事實上，公司會考量我們在全球各地的廠長對於生產無公害產品所提出來的構想，以決定他們的部分紅利。要是再早幾年，這種觀念在我看來簡直就是違反商業利益。

艾格勒：　看到我們公司在這場地球保衛戰中如此積極的表現，我覺得十分驕傲，因為你不管往那兒看，到處都是災情慘重。自從東歐共產政權解體以來，當地嚴重的環境污染頓見天日，真是令人震驚。

史瓦布利克：　這意謂著污染沒有疆界之分，也不會去管你當地的意識型態是甚麼。

帕克：　在美國，有些人抱怨說，因污染而孳生的藻類干擾了他們的海上運動。但對其他國家而言，這可是事關生死。由於沙漠化造成的災害，非洲已逐漸成為最不適於人類居住的大陸。墨西哥市的空氣污染相當嚴重，而亞馬遜河雨林也有一大部分被砍伐殆盡。

Lesson 33 Environmentalism (1)

Words and Phrases

environmentalism	環境保護主義	regime	政權
ecologically safe	無害生態環境的	algae [ˈældʒi]	藻類
antibusiness	反商業利益	interfere with	干擾…
battle to save the planet	地球保衛戰	habitable	適於人居住的
environmental devastation	環境破壞	desertification	沙漠化
		rain forest	熱帶雨林
collapse	崩解	be wiped out	砍伐殆盡

Vocabulary Building

- **in part**　部分

  There's no question that I was a diligent worker, but my success, if you can call it that, is owing in part to luck.

  (毫無疑問，我工作是很勤奮，但我的成功（如果你能如此稱之）有部分是歸因於運氣好。)

- **come to light**　敗露；被揭露

  A case of massive fraud came to light in the course of the audit.

  (一場規模龐大的舞弊案在稽核的過程中被發現了。)

- **know no boundaries**　沒有國界之分

  cf. Diseases know no boundaries of class or wealth.

  (疾病是不分階級或貧富的。)

- **matter of life or death**　攸關生死的問題

  Trade is a matter of life or death for the economies of most modern nations.

  (對多數的現代國家而言，貿易乃是攸關其經濟存亡的問題。)

1. <u>What</u> we have to have <u>at camp</u> is fire for cooking, water for <u>drinking</u>,
     A   B   C

   and tents for <u>sheltering</u>.
                    D

2. The <u>management</u> had to <u>cut</u> the budget <u>in order not</u> to <u>layoff</u> workers.
         A   B   C   D

3. The high school soccer <u>tournament</u> will <u>be held</u> every day <u>even if</u> it
                              A   B   C

   is rainy weather.
        D

◆◆◆◆◆◆◆◆◆◆◆◆◆◆ 簡短對話 ◆◆◆◆◆◆◆◆◆◆◆◆◆◆◆◆

Sawasaki: Do you know who came up with this million-tree idea?
Parker: What I heard was that Alex himself suggested it out of the blue at an executive board meeting a few weeks ago.
Sawasaki: I didn't realize that he was personally interested in the environment issue. Somehow it doesn't quite fit my image of him as an executive with his eye constantly on the bottom line.
Parker: Well, for one thing, he probably sees it as a way of generating some favorable publicity.
Sawasaki: It should certainly do that.
Parker: Also, I do believe he's recently developed a sincere concern for environmental affairs.

---

out of the blue 出乎意料; 晴天霹靂   **environment** 環境   **bottom line** 利益   **for one thing** 先舉一例   **generate** 引起; 產生

Lesson 33

Environmentalism (2) (環境保護主義)

●預習 — *Sentences*

- What kind of program are you talking about?
- Miles of beach front have been polluted by oil spills.
- This is something that all of us are in together.
- We've even managed to put a hole in the ozone layer.
- Business is just starting to really get involved.

●*Vignette*

Swarbrick: And those debt-for-nature swap programs never picked up real momentum either.

Sawasaki: Sorry, Peter, what kind of program are you talking about?

Swarbrick: It's a system that's designed to grant debt relief to developing nations in exchange for steps to protect rain forests and other natural resources.

Egler: Meanwhile, back here at home, miles of beach front in Alaska, California, and Texas have been polluted by oil spills. And 75 percent of our landfills are expected to be full within a decade. This is truly something that all of us are in together.

Sawasaki: There's been an amazing amount of press coverage on the subject.

Parker: Yes, but at the same time there's some skepticism as to whether we're even starting to make a dent in the problem. Half the world's environmental damage is said to have occurred in the last 30 years. We've even managed to put a hole in the ozone layer. I grant you, people are certainly starting to move toward minimizing pollution. But there's a lot more that can be done and eventually is going to *have* to be done.

Egler: Business is just starting to really get involved.

　　一般認為，世界環境的破壞，有一半是在過去三十年間所累積下來的。儘管現在有不少人在大聲疾呼要遏止公害的產生，但要想真正解決這些問題，似乎仍是遙遙無期。

史瓦布利克： 而那些「自然保護與債務的交換計畫」也從未被認真推動過。

澤崎： 抱歉，彼得，你說的是甚麼計畫？

史瓦布利克： 這是為開發中國家所設計的，只要他們願意採取措施來保護自身的雨林和其他自然資源，那他們就可以得到債務救濟。

艾格勒： 同時我們反觀國內，在阿拉斯加、加州以及德州，有好幾英里的海岸線都受到石油外洩的污染。而且在未來十年內，國內有 75% 的垃圾掩埋場將達飽和程度。這就真是我們得共同面對的問題了。

澤崎： 關於這個課題，媒體上的報導多到會令你嚇一跳。

帕克： 是啊，不過同時也有人在懷疑，我們真的有開始要解決問題了嗎？據說，全球的環境污染始於過去這三十年間。人類甚至還想過要在臭氧層上打個洞。我是同意你的說法，大家當然都開始在朝減低污染的方向邁進了。但是，目前可以做的還有很多，而且這些到頭來都非做不可。

艾格勒： 企業界才正開始要共襄此舉呢！

Lesson 33 Environmentalism (2)

Words and Phrases

debt-for-nature swap program 　自然保護與債務交換計畫	beach front　　海岸線
	landfill　　垃圾掩埋場
debt relief　　債務救濟	skepticism　　懷疑論
developing nation　　開發中國家	ozone layer　　臭氧層
natural resources　　自然資源	minimize　　使最小化

Vocabulary Building

- **pick up momentum**　得到發展助力
  The crusade against smoking has picked up a lot of momentum in the last few years.
  (禁菸運動在過去數年間得到相當大的發展助力。)

- **press coverage**　媒體報導
  Our active stance on the environment has generated a lot of favorable press coverage for us.
  (我們對環保議題所採取的積極態度，使得各方媒體在報導上對我們都廣為讚揚。)

- **make a dent**　大幅降低；使減少
  So far I haven't even made a dent in the stack of work that accumulated over my vacation.
  (到目前為止，我甚至都還沒能去處理那些在我休假期間堆積如山的工作。)

- **I grant you**　我同意你的看法
  I grant you that nobody's perfect, but George's less perfect than most.
  (我同意你的看法，的確，沒有人是完美的，可是比起多數不完美的人，喬治還要來得更糟。)

1. Can you <u>point</u> the <u>exact</u> spot <u>on</u> the map <u>where you live</u>?
　　　　A　　　B　　　　　C　　　　　　　D

2. Our new design <u>softwares</u> <u>enabled</u> us to create the <u>graphs</u> for the next
　　　　　　　　　　A　　　　B　　　　　　　　　　　C
week's presentation in just <u>under</u> an hour.
　　　　　　　　　　　　D

3. Tomiko wanted to <u>go to abroad</u> <u>so</u> she <u>could</u> practice <u>speaking</u> English.
　　　　　　　　　A　　　　　B　　　C　　　　　　D

◆◆◆◆◆◆◆◆◆◆◆◆◆ 簡短對話 ◆◆◆◆◆◆◆◆◆◆◆◆◆◆◆◆

Sawasaki: The depletion of the ozone layer is really scary.
Egler: You can say that again.
Sawasaki: I understand it may lead to higher rates of skin cancer.
Egler: It's true, but actually that may be the least of our worries.
Sawasaki: How so?
Egler: We human beings can always cover up or use a good sunscreen when
we're outside. The real problem is the damage that the ultraviolet rays
may do to other plant and animal life. It could end up destabilizing the
entire ecosystem.

---

depletion 枯竭; 減少　　**ozone layer** 臭氧層　　**You can say that again.** 你說
得沒錯。　　**skin cancer** 皮膚癌　　**ultraviolet rays** 紫外線　　**destabilize**
使不安定　　**ecosystem** 生態系統

Lesson 33

Environmentalism (3) (環境保護主義)

●預習 — *Sentences*

- It's business's responsibility to clean up the environment.
- People push for stronger controls.
- Newer and tougher regulations are inevitable.
- Potential liability is escalating too.
- After all, you're paying for the packaging that you don't need.

●*Vignette*

Swarbrick: Nowadays there are a number of good reasons why businesses can't afford not to get involved. Most important, people have made it clear that they're not going to put up with toxic emissions and irresponsible use of the earth's natural resources.

Parker: Something like 75 percent of Americans think that it's business's responsibility to clean up the environment.

Egler: That's becoming very evident as people push for stronger controls. Newer and tougher regulations are inevitable.

Swarbrick: It's in a company's best interest to design new factories so that they meet the regulations of the future rather than having to pay for expensive restructuring when new laws come into effect.

Parker: Potential liability is escalating too. Taking steps early, like our new lighter, environment-friendly packaging may also help our industry to avoid or at least stall regulation.

Egler: An increasing number of our customers are writing to us to suggest that we use less packaging. After all, you're paying for the packaging that you don't need—and then you're paying again to have it towed away to the dump.

多數美國人認為，淨化環境是企業的責任。因此，今後的法規將日趨嚴格，而罰金也有增加的傾向。這些潛在的法律責任觀念，正逐漸深入人心。

史瓦布利克： 現今倒是有許多充分理由，可以解釋何以企業界非關心環保不可。最重要的一點是，人們已清楚表態，他們不再忍受有毒排放物，以及任何不負責任地取用地球自然資源的行為。

帕克： 有大約 75% 的美國民眾認為，企業必須負起淨化環境的責任。

艾格勒： 當人們在為更強硬的法令催生時，他們的態度是相當明顯的。未來不免會有新法公布施行，而且要求也絕對會嚴格得多。

史瓦布利克： 最符合公司利益的作法是，設計符合未來法規的新工廠，不要等到新法令生效後，才又花上大筆的改建費用。

帕克： 潛在的法律責任也在升高之中。若能早點採取因應措施，像是公司新推出的輕型環保包裝，也許會對我們這一行有所幫助，能使我們避免觸犯法規，或至少不要那麼快就碰到法律問題。

艾格勒： 有愈來愈多的顧客寫信到公司，建議我們減少包裝。畢竟，你是在為無謂的包裝付費 —— 然後又要花錢讓人運去丟掉。

Lesson 33 Environmentalism (3)

Words and Phrases

toxic emissions	有毒排放物	restructuring	重新改造
clean up	清除	potential liability	潛在的法律責任
evident	明顯的		

Vocabulary Building

- **something like**　約
  The outstanding bills amount to something like $500,000.
  (未付清的帳單大約還有五十萬元。)

- **push for**　推動
  The animal rights group is pushing for a total ban on animal testing.
  (動物權利保護團體正在推動法令的制定，要全面禁止用動物來作任何測試。)

- **escalate**　昇高; 擴大
  What started out as a minor border skirmish quickly escalated into a full-fledged war.
  (這件事開始時原本只是邊境的一點小衝突，之後迅速擴大成為一場正式的戰爭。)

- **environment-friendly**　符合環保要求的
  Consumers are showing a clear preference for environment-friendly products.
  (消費者明顯偏好符合環保要求的產品。)

1. Even when <u>driving</u> carefully, the motorcycle <u>is</u> a very dangerous <u>mode</u>
             A   B   C
  of <u>transportation.</u>
          D

2. If you <u>had spent</u> less money <u>on</u> cards, you <u>would</u> <u>have</u> gotten in trouble.
          A   B   C   D

3. "I <u>want you</u> to know I cannot <u>be bought off</u>," Andy said refusing to
         A   B
  <u>accepting</u> the <u>bribe.</u>
     C   D

◆◆◆◆◆◆◆◆◆◆◆◆◆ 簡短對話 ◆◆◆◆◆◆◆◆◆◆◆◆◆◆◆

Sawasaki: Sally, you sound like a really committed environmentalist.

Egler: Actually, I'm involved in a volunteer group that's trying to raise people's awareness of the problems.

Sawasaki: You know, I really admire people like you who get involved in activities like that. I don't know how you manage to find the time with your heavy workload.

Egler: Basically it's a question of priorities. If you decide that something's really important to you, somehow or other you manage to make time for it.

---

committed 致力的；獻身的　　**environmentalist** 環境保護主義者；環保人士
manage to 成功地（辦到某事）　　**workload** 工作量　　**priorities** 優先順序
somehow or other 不管怎樣

Environmentalism (4) (環境保護主義)

預習 — *Sentences*

- It also costs us less to make and less to ship.
- It's turned out to be a big cost-cutter in our business.
- Pollution abatement is more than just a way to save money.
- It's now a $100 billion industry.
- Hordes of companies are starting waste management divisions.

Vignette

Parker: And businesses know that for everyone who writes letters, there are many more who feel the same way but didn't write.

Sawasaki: I notice that a lot of detergents and other consumer goods are now being offered in thin plastic refill bags so you can refill your own containers. The lighter packaging is not only better for the environment; it also costs us less to make and less to ship.

Swarbrick: True. Many things that companies do to make a product more ecologically sound can save money. Take recycling, for example. It's turned out to be a big cost-cutter in our business. And designing plants to minimize toxic emissions also saves money in resources, fuel, and waste disposal.

Sawasaki: So it's good business to be responsible about the environment.

Parker: Pollution abatement is more than just a way to save money. It's now a $100 billion industry and it's growing at more than ten percent a year. Hordes of companies are starting waste management or pollution clean-up divisions.

Swarbrick: The fact that we're being given financial incentives to minimize pollution shows us where the company stands. Nelson ABC Foods wants its managers to perform well in this area.

現在多數的消費性商品都有塑膠袋包裝的補充包，可以改裝在自家的容器內。輕巧的包裝不僅對環境有貢獻，在製造和運輸的費用上也相對節省了公司不少錢。

帕克： 而公司也知道，還有不少人跟這些來信者有同感，他們只是沒有提筆罷了。

澤崎： 我注意到現在有許多清潔劑和其他消費性商品都供應有薄層塑膠袋包裝的補充包，你可以將之倒入自家的容器裡。輕型的包裝不僅對環境有利，而且在製造和輸運的成本上也比較低廉。

史瓦布利克： 沒錯。公司為使所生產的產品能無害生態環境，其所做的許多努力都能收省錢之效。就拿資源回收來講好了。這麼做的結果反為公司省下一大筆成本。還有，若能設計出可將有毒排放物降至最低的工廠，那在資源、燃料和廢棄物的處理上也會省下一筆開銷。

澤崎： 這麼說來，負起環保責任並不是件虧本生意囉！

帕克： 減低污染還不只可以省錢而已，它現在可是個擁有千億身價的事業，而且每年還在以超過百分之十的速度成長著。好多公司都開始在成立廢料處理和污染清理部門了。

史瓦布利克： 而看到公司用金錢來誘使我們將污染減至最低，我們也可以想見公司的立場。尼爾森 ABC 食品公司希望旗下的主管們在這個領域內都能有好的表現。

Lesson 33 Environmentalism (4)

Words and Phrases

hordes of	許多…	waste management	廢棄物管理

Vocabulary Building

- **save money**　　儲蓄；省錢

  cf. You should save up money before you have children.

  （你在生小孩之前，該先存個一筆錢。）

- **cost-cutter**　　削減成本的東西

  The new inventory control system has proved to be a major cost-cutter for our company.

  （事實證明，新的存貨管制系統成為公司削減成本的主力。）

- **pollution abatement**　　減輕污染

  Pollution-abatement equipment will be coming into demand because the local government is about to adopt a stringent clear air bill.

  （由於地方政府將要採行嚴格的空氣淨化法案，所以，能夠降低污染的設備將會大為搶手。）

- **financial incentive**　　金錢誘因；金錢獎勵

  Financial incentives aren't the only thing that motivates people. Recognition by their superiors and peers is also important.

  （金錢誘因並非唯一能策勵人心的方法。上司與同儕的認同也很重要。）

▶**Exercises**   在下列例句中，每句各有四個劃線部分，   （解答見262頁）
其中一個的文法有誤，請將之選出。

1. People <u>spend</u> more <u>times</u> at the office these days <u>than</u> they did <u>in the past</u>.
        A   B   C   D

2. Times <u>have</u> changed— and <u>times</u> <u>fly</u> like <u>an</u> arrow.
        A   B   C   D

3. Please <u>come</u> to my house <u>on</u> Sunday for <u>surprise birthday party</u> <u>for</u>
        A   B   C   D

   James.

◆◆◆◆◆◆◆◆◆◆◆◆◆ 簡短對話 ◆◆◆◆◆◆◆◆◆◆◆◆◆◆

Sawasaki: So I suppose you must be quite pleased about the tree-planting campaign?

Egler: Oh, yes, very. I mean, by itself it may not make that much of a difference, but it's important for every individual and organization to do what they can.

Sawasaki: When the problem is too big, it can be easy to feel helpless and decide that you're powerless to do anything about it.

Egler: I know. That's the sort of attitude we're trying to fight in our volunteer group.

I mean　我的意思是　　　**by itself**　事情本身　　　**that much of**　那麼多的…
attitude　態度

Environmentalism — 總結

＊　＊　＊

環保是 90 年代最大的課題，而其關鍵字之一就是「綠色」。一提到綠色，總讓人聯想到草木，但它也是「成長」的象徵。事實上，green 與 grow 的字源是同一個。

環境保護主義 (environmentalism) 在 60 年代是個社會問題，但它今天的角色不一樣了。在以往，environmentalism 被視做 social activism 的一環，其地位等同於民權運動或是反越戰運動。但在今日的美國人當中，四個裡面就有三個自認為是 environmentalist。

由於事態已相當嚴重，所以一些對於社會動向較敏感的企業，早就有了危機意識。有不少公司採行尼爾森的作法，由公司提撥獎金，發給提出建設性意見的人，就是為了將公害減至最低；而倡導植樹運動的企業也不在少數。

每年製造出數億英磅廢紙及塑膠垃圾的某大速食連鎖店，就正積極推動資源回收運動。而一些電力公司也和環境保護團體合作，共同提出有效利用能源的相關計畫。在美國，越來越多的超級市場在其商品外包裝上，標示 Ozone Safe, Environmentally Friendly, Packaged in Recycled Paper 等的文字。最近還出現 green marketing 這個新字，意指銷售具有環保概念，外包裝少，或是屬於再生製品 (recycled or recyclable products) 等的商品。這個行銷策略由美國一家超市率先引進，現已推廣至英國及加拿大等地。

以往傳統的 marketing mix 只包含產品、地點、行銷、價格等要素，但現在應該還要加入「公害防治」。畢竟，環境保護工作已不再只是消極的事後淨化而已，乃是要在事情發生前，就積極主動地防治。

Lesson 34

Modern Etiquette

（現代禮儀）

◆ **Lesson 34 的內容** ◆

　　最近幾年，美國的禮儀經歷了大幅的調整。其中最根本的就是「女士優先」這一觀念的轉變。以往，大家總是覺得凡事要讓女性優先，像是男士為女士開門、上樓梯時讓女士先上，下樓則女士後下，以及男士為女士點菸等的。然而，令澤崎吃驚的是，這些禮儀並不見得都能得到女性的認同。這是因為在婦女解放運動之後，女性不僅否認自己是「弱者」，更希望能得到與男性同等的對待，所以她們覺得這些行為是多餘的。不過，喜歡這種傳統禮儀的女性仍是大有人在。

It's still "ladies first" but many of these courtesies have been gradually falling by the wayside.

Modern Etiquette (1) （現代禮儀）

●預習 — *Sentences*

- You look a little miffed.
- He didn't bother to show.
- I'd tip the waiter $5 to $10 and leave.
- I'll remember that in case it happens again.
- What kinds of things do the books cover?

●*Vignette*

Egler: Shoichi, you look a little miffed. I take it the lunch with Conradsen didn't go well?

Sawasaki: It didn't go at all. He didn't bother to show.

Egler: Didn't show? That's frustrating, isn't it?

Sawasaki: You can say that again. You know, one of the most difficult things about living in a foreign country is understanding the rules of etiquette. Take this case for example. What should you do if a business partner doesn't show up to a lunch he's invited you to?

Egler: Well, I'd say that you're supposed to wait at the table but not have anything to eat or drink. My own time limit is 20 minutes. If the other person hasn't shown up by then, I'd tip the waiter $5 to $10 and leave.

Sawasaki: Thanks. I'll remember that in case it happens again.

Egler: Being courteous in America is getting difficult even for the natives. In the last few years there has been much ado about etiquette. Lots of books have been published on the subject, including some on executive manners specifically.

Sawasaki: What kinds of things do the books cover?

Egler: Oh, everything from how to politely fire an employee to how to get fired without causing too much mental damage to your sense of self-respect.

　　這天發生了一件令澤崎相當不悅的事。邀他吃午飯的人居然放他鴿子。更糟的是，碰到這種狀況，澤崎一點兒也不知道該如何應變。

艾格勒： 昭一，你看起來有點兒不高興。我猜你和康拉德生的午餐約會進行地不太順利？

澤崎： 根本沒有甚麼午餐約會。他連人都沒來。

艾格勒： 沒來？那可真令人喪氣，是吧？

澤崎： 妳說得一點兒沒錯。妳知道，在異鄉生活裡，最困難之處便是去瞭解當地的禮節規矩。就拿今天的事來說吧！如果有個工作上的夥伴邀你吃午飯，可是他人卻沒有出現，那妳該怎麼辦？

艾格勒： 我會建議你先在桌邊等他，不過別點任何吃的或喝的。我自己的極限是二十分鐘。如果到時對方還未出現，我會給服務生五至十元的小費，然後離開。

澤崎： 謝謝。如果再發生這樣的事，我會記住妳這些話。

艾格勒： 現在在美國即使是本地人也很難做到彬彬有禮。過去幾年間，禮儀成了人們大肆談論的話題。相關的出版品也不在少數，其中還包括了專門針對主管級人員的禮節所寫的書。

澤崎： 這些書都談些甚麼呢？

艾格勒： 噢，從如何禮貌地請員工走路，到自己在面臨遣散一途時，如何不使自尊心太過受傷等，鉅細靡遺。

Words and Phrases

miff	使惱怒	rules of etiquette	禮儀的規範
frustrating	令人沮喪的	courteous	有禮貌的

Vocabulary Building

- **show**　出現

  cf. The airlines take more reservations than they have seats, because they expect a certain percentage of no-shows.

  (航空公司在原有機位預定一空後，還會接受超額訂位，因為他們預估會有一定比例的訂位者不會出現。)

- **You can say that again.**　你說得一點兒也沒錯。

  "Time flies." — "You can say that again."

  (「光陰似箭。」「你說得一點兒也沒錯。」)

- **much ado about**　大驚小怪；白忙一場

  All the commotion about the impending takeover turned out to be much ado about nothing. It was just rumors.

  (有消息說公司即將遭到購併，引發了種種騷動，但這些都只是虛驚一場，不過是謠言罷了。)

- **self-respect**　自尊心

  cf. No self-respecting person will put up with that kind of abuse.

  (任何有自尊心的人都沒辦法忍受那種差辱。)

▶ *Exercises*

在下列例句中，每句各有四個劃線部分，
其中一個的文法有誤，請將之選出。

（解答見 262 頁）

1. Some teenagers do not <u>respect for</u> the elderly and <u>behave</u> <u>rudely</u> <u>toward</u>
                            A   B   C   D
them.

2. Most people think that <u>the Chinese</u> is a very <u>difficult</u> language <u>to master</u>
                               A   B   C
because it has <u>a great many</u> hard-to-remember characters.
                          D

3. Mozart <u>is</u> one of the <u>most greatest</u> composers who <u>ever</u> <u>lived</u>.
     A   B   C   D

◆◆◆◆◆◆◆◆◆◆◆◆◆◆ 簡短對話 ◆◆◆◆◆◆◆◆◆◆◆◆◆◆◆◆

Sawasaki: But isn't standing somebody up considered to be a serious breach
    of etiquette here?

Egler: Of course it is. And really, it doesn't happen that often in a business
    context.

Sawasaki: I suppose I should give Conradsen the benefit of the doubt. He
    may have had some good excuse for not showing up.

Egler: Maybe, but at least he could have phoned the restaurant and had you
    paged.

Sawasaki: That's exactly what I thought while I was sitting there.

Egler: Anyway, he'll probably call you any minute now with his apologies.

---

stand somebody up 放某人鴿子　　**breach of etiquette** 違反禮儀規範　　**give**
someone the benefit of the doubt　（在未發現證據之前）假設某人無辜　　**show**
up 出現　　**page** 用廣播呼叫　　**apology** 道歉

Lesson 34

Modern Etiquette (2)（現代禮儀）

●預習 — *Sentences*

· What am I supposed to do if someone does that?
· "No thanks, that's not my brand of poison."
· Drugs aren't used frequently in the food industry.
· I feel a little unsure of how to handle myself.
· Etiquette has become rather confusing.

●*Vignette*

Egler: And in between there are things like what to say and not to say to businesswomen, why you should not take business calls at the table in nice restaurants, how to address your boss on the golf course and how to react if someone offers you cocaine.

Sawasaki: Wonderful. What am I supposed to do if someone does that?

Egler: The trick is to refuse politely without making the person feel uncomfortable. Say something like, "No thanks, that's not my brand of poison."

Sawasaki: So the other person really isn't sure whether you take drugs or not.

Egler: Exactly, but I should let you know that the top executives here are drug-free and drugs aren't used frequently in the food industry the way they are in, say, the music business, so I wouldn't worry too much about getting an offer like that.

Sawasaki: That's a relief, but I still feel a little unsure of how to handle myself in certain situations—like dealing with women executives.

Egler: Right. Since women have taken a more prominent role in American society, etiquette has become rather confusing. Some women prefer to follow the traditional rules of etiquette between men and women and others don't.

Sawasaki: So what's a guy supposed to do?

Egler: Good question.

在宴會進行當中，如果有人請你吸古柯鹼，該作何反應呢？艾格勒教了澤崎一招可以婉拒對方好意又不會令人起反感的萬全之策。

艾格勒： 而且之間它還會告訴你一些事情，像是說，面對商場上的女性，有哪些話可說，哪些話不能說；為何不該在高級餐廳中的餐桌上接聽商務電話；若在打高爾夫球時碰上老闆，該如何稱呼；以及如果有人請你吸古柯鹼，該作何反應。

澤崎： 真不可思議。如果有人這麼做，那我該怎麼辦？

艾格勒： 祕訣就在於要禮貌地拒絕對方，而不令人覺得不高興。你可以像這樣說：「不了，謝謝，我用的毒品不是這個牌子。」

澤崎： 那麼對方也就無法確定你到底吸不吸毒了。

艾格勒： 就是這樣，不過，我該讓你曉得，這兒的高層主管都不吸毒的。而且毒品在食品業界的使用情形也不像是在，比方說音樂界，那樣的頻繁，所以我也不會太過擔心有人要請我來一點。

澤崎： 那我就放心多了，可是在某些場合，像是在跟女性主管應對的時候，我還是有點不太確知該如何自處。

艾格勒： 是啊，由於女性在美國社會所扮演的角色愈加重要，所以在禮儀方面也變得令人無所適從。有些女性喜歡遵從傳統男女之間的禮儀，有些則不然。

澤崎： 那麼男士該怎麼做呢？

艾格勒： 問得好。

Words and Phrases

cocaine	古柯鹼	drug-free	不吸毒的

Vocabulary Building

- **address** *v.*   稱呼

There's no simple set of rules governing terms of address in today's America.

（在今日美國，並沒有一套簡單的規則可以告訴你稱呼他人時的用語。）

- **Wonderful.**   真不可思議。［反語］

cf. That's all I need.

（我所需要的就是這些了。）［帶有諷刺意味的反語］

- **trick**   祕訣; 技巧

cf. Turning down an offer of drugs can be a tricky business.

（要拒絕送上門來的毒品可說是件相當棘手的事。）

- **prominent**   顯赫的; 重要的

A group of prominent business executives signed an open letter to the government about tax reform.

（一群重要的企業主管共同簽署了一封關於稅務改革的公開信給政府。）

(解答見 262 頁)

▶ *Exercises*

在下列例句中，每句各有四個劃線部分，
其中一個的文法有誤，請將之選出。

1. The zoo fire was a <u>terrible</u> <u>tragedy</u>. A number of <u>exotic</u> and rare animals
A   B   C

<u>had been died</u>.
D

2. Yoshiro <u>suicided</u> in the traditional Japanese <u>fashion</u> <u>by</u> disemboweling
A   B   C

<u>himself</u>.
D

3. I try to <u>tailor</u> my <u>remarks</u> to suit the <u>particular</u> audience I'm <u>speaking</u>.
A   B   C   D

◆◆◆◆◆◆◆◆◆◆◆◆◆ 簡短對話 ◆◆◆◆◆◆◆◆◆◆◆◆◆◆

Sawasaki: When I was transferred to New York, they showed me a video about the drug problem. I had no idea it was so serious.

Egler: It is, and the incidence of drug-related violence is simply appalling.

Sawasaki: The worst part to my mind is the number of innocent bystanders who get caught in shoot-outs.

Egler: I know. Even small children have been getting killed.

Sawasaki: You'd think the government would have taken more serious action by now, like imposing strict controls on guns.

Egler: Unfortunately, the gun lobby has a lot of clout on Capitol Hill.

---

incidence 發生率　　**drug-related** 與毒品有關的　　**appalling** 可怕的；驚悚的　　**innocent** 無辜的　　**bystander** 旁觀者　　**shoot-out** 槍戰　　**clout** 政治權力；影響力　　**Capitol Hill** 國會山莊 (美國國會所在地之山丘)；美國國會 (亦稱 the Hill)

Modern Etiquette (3)（現代禮儀）

預習 — *Sentences*

- Men used to open doors for women.
- Is that because of women's liberation?
- She'd probably think he was trying to steal her purse.
- People just aren't friendly to strangers anymore.
- Assertiveness is just another word for being pushy.

Vignette

Egler: American manners changed so much over the last quarter century that for a while most of us didn't really know what we should do in certain situations. Men used to open doors for women, stood up when women entered a room, went down the stairs before them, up the stairs after them, lit their cigarettes, and picked up all of the restaurant tabs. It's still "ladies first" but many of these courtesies have been gradually falling by the wayside.

Sawasaki: Is that because of women's liberation?

Egler: That and other reasons like crime, for example. When I was young, Boy Scouts were told to help little old ladies cross the street as their good deed for the day. But if a young boy took a woman's arm nowadays, she'd probably think he was trying to steal her purse. People just aren't friendly to strangers anymore. They can't afford to be. The '70s had a lot to do with it too. You know, the "me decade." People went from flower power to looking out for No. 1. Bookstores were flooded with manuals on how to be more assertive. And assertiveness seminars blossomed.

Sawasaki: Don't Americans regard being assertive as a positive thing?

Egler: The majority do, especially those who were young in the '70s, but to many older people assertiveness is just another word for being pushy. Anyway, besides that, there were other social changes that modified the American sense of propriety even within the family.

Sawasaki: In what way?

犯罪率的增加也是使傳統禮儀改觀的主要原因之一。童子軍的「日行一善」運動因此愈來愈難落實了。

艾格勒： 過去廿五年來，美國的禮節改變了許多，有一陣子，我們大多數的人都不太曉得在某些狀況下要怎麼做。過去，男士習慣要為女士開門，有女士進入室內時要起身致意，下樓時走在她們前面，上樓時則走在後面，要替她們點菸，吃飯時要付帳。現在也仍是「女士優先」，但這些禮儀有很多都慢慢地被淘汰了。

澤崎： 這是因為婦女解放運動的關係嗎？

艾格勒： 這是原因之一，還有其它因素，比方說像是犯罪。在我還小的時候，童軍所受到的教導是，要幫忙帶老婦人過街，以作為他們的日行一善。可是今天若有個小男生要去扶某位女士的手臂，那她可能會認為這男孩想要扒她的錢包。大家對陌生人都不再友善了，因為他們承擔不起受騙後的損失。70年代對於這種現象的形成也有很大的關係。你也知道的，就是「自我中心的十年」。但現在人們的想法已從「權力歸花朵」轉到凡事都要爭取第一。書店裡充斥著教人如何能更肯定自我的手冊。而關於自我肯定的研討會更是如雨後春筍般地出現。

澤崎： 難道美國人不認為自我肯定是件正面的事嗎？

艾格勒： 大部分人都抱持肯定態度，特別是那些在70年代長大的人，但對許多年紀較長的人來說，自我肯定就是獨斷獨行，不過換種說法而已。此外，其他社會上的變遷也重新調整了美國人對禮節的觀感，甚至連在家庭裡都會受到影響。

澤崎： 在哪方面呢？

Words and Phrases

restaurant tab　餐廳帳單	"me decade"　「以自我為中心的
"ladies first"　「女士優先」	十年」(70 年代的口號)
women's liberation　婦女解放	assertiveness seminars　討論自我
purse　錢包	肯定的研討會
flower power　權力歸花朵 (60 年	blossom　興盛
代由嬉痞所號召的和平運動，愛情與	majority　大多數；大部分
非暴力為其訴求)	modify　修改

Vocabulary Building

● **fall by the wayside**　半途而廢；中途退出；被擱置一邊

Some of the people we considered top prospects when we hired them have since fallen by the wayside.

(有些人在我們初雇用時，其前景是相當為我們看好的，但他們之中有一部分的人卻在這之後就開始不濟事了。)

● **assertive** *adj.*　自我肯定的

Being assertive is fine up to a point, but Margaret carries it to extremes.

(在某種程度上，自我肯定是蠻不錯的一件事，可是瑪格麗特卻表現得過火了。)

● **another word for**　另一種說法

cf. "I'd love to, but . . . " is another way of saying "No thanks."

(「謝謝您，不用了」的另一種說法是「我很願意，但…」。)

● **sense of**　…的感覺；…感

Tim has no sense of responsibility. He's usually the first one to leave the office even when his team members are up to their ears with work.

(提姆一點兒責任感也沒有。即使其他的同事都還忙得焦頭爛額，他也總是第一個離開辦公室。)

▶ **Exercises**   在下列例句中，每句各有四個劃線部分，
其中一個的文法有誤，請將之選出。   （解答見 262 頁）

1. The <u>best</u> <u>way</u> to find yourself is to <u>lose</u> <u>oneself</u> in our hotspring.
　　　A　　B　　　　　　　　　　　　C　　　D

2. You just don't <u>have to be</u> perfect. Just <u>do</u> your best and you <u>will</u> improve
　　　　　　　　A　　　　　　　　　B　　　　　　　　　C

   <u>gradual</u>.
　　D

3. Almond and vanilla are natural <u>essences</u> available <u>at</u> most <u>healthy</u> food
　　　　　　　　　　　　　　A　　　　　　　　B　　　　C

   shops <u>throughout</u> the nation.
　　　　D

◆◆◆◆◆◆◆◆◆◆◆◆◆ 簡短對話 ◆◆◆◆◆◆◆◆◆◆◆◆◆

Sawasaki: What's your personal preference as to things like having the door held open for you?

Egler: Well, I understand the feminist position that it's insulting to women, because it implies that we're too weak to do things for ourselves. But personally I consider it rude to refuse a favor like that, though I certainly don't think men should feel obliged to do it.

Sawasaki: It would make life simpler if everybody would be that flexible in their thinking.

Egler: I quite agree. There are a lot more important things for us to worry about.

---

personal preference 個人偏好　　**feminist** 女性主義者　　**insulting** 侮辱
的　　**imply** 意味; 暗示　　**rude** 無禮的　　**flexible** 有彈性的　　**I quite
agree.** 我深表贊同。

Modern Etiquette (4) （現代禮儀）

●預習 — *Sentences*

- He's not a fiancé or a husband.
- "Roommate" or "friend" sounds a bit too platonic.
- So what do you call someone like that?
- I think most people just use the word "boyfriend."
- How do you keep on top of it, Sally?

●*Vignette*

Egler: Well, the high divorce rate and the new kinds of living arrangements people are involved in these days—like couples who live together before marriage and gay couples—all make things a bit more complicated. They raise questions like whether or not you should invite dad's new wife to the children's weddings or how to refer to the man your daughter lives with when introducing him to your friends. He's not a fiancé or a husband, so you can't use those words, but "roommate" or "friend" sounds a bit too platonic.

Sawasaki: So what do you call someone like that?

Egler: I think most people just use the word "boyfriend," and hope that their friends assume the couple date in the traditional manner and don't live with each other. But anyway, things are turning around a bit. I'd say that the trend now is a return to the traditional. Clothes, parties, wedding ceremonies, and even manners seem to be reverting back to an older style.

Sawasaki: You mean just when I'm starting to understand the new system it's all going to change again?

Egler: Sure, like anything else.

Sawasaki: How do you keep on top of it, Sally?

Egler: I read those etiquette books like everyone else. And if I run into a situation that I'm unsure of, I wing it. I'll lend you my guide to executive manners but the key to etiquette is to be gracious and considerate of others. On that count, Shoichi, I'd say you're a model for all of us.

「要怎麼做才合乎禮儀？」或許各種禮儀書籍對此的定義都不盡相同。不過，艾格勒認為，關鍵在於高雅並能體貼人心。

艾格勒： 嗯，高離婚率以及最近人們採行的新生活型態 —— 像是婚前同居，和同性戀伴侶 —— 都使事情變得更複雜。而這產生了一些問題，像是該不該邀請父親的新婚妻子去參加小孩的婚禮，或是該如何向人介紹女兒的同居男友。他不是未婚夫，也不是丈夫，所以這些稱謂都不能用，但「室友」或「朋友」聽起來又太純潔了一點。

澤崎： 那像這樣子你要怎麼稱呼？

艾格勒： 我想大多數人就用「男朋友」這個字，希望說他們的朋友會認為這對情人是以傳統的方式在約會，而且也沒有住在一起。但無論如何，事情有點在走回頭路了。我認為現在的潮流又開始回歸傳統。服飾、宴會、婚禮、甚至是禮貌似乎都在復古。

澤崎： 你是說我才剛開始要瞭解這種新的模式，它又要再大搬風了？

艾格勒： 沒錯，事事皆如此啊！

澤崎： 莎莉，那妳如何掌握這一切呢？

艾格勒： 我也像大家一樣讀禮儀方面的書。如果遇到我不確定的情況時，我就隨機應變。我可以借你我的主管禮儀手冊，不過，禮儀的關鍵就在於高雅並能體貼人心。昭一，就這方面說，我會說你是我們所有人的榜樣。

Lesson 34 Modern Etiquette (4)

Words and Phrases

divorce rate	離婚率	fiancé	未婚夫
living arrangement	生活形態	platonic	柏拉圖式的; 精神層面的
gay	男同性戀者	gracious	親切有禮的

Vocabulary Building

- **revert**　回復原狀

  Sally's husband was a teetotaler for almost ten years, but then he suddenly reverted to his old drinking ways.

  (莎莉的先生曾經有幾乎十年的時間都滴酒不沾, 但後來又突然回復他喝酒的老習慣了。)

- **keep on top of it**　掌握; 走在前端

  cf. I try to keep on top of developments in my field by reading a lot and attending key conventions and seminars.

  (我會閱讀大量書籍, 參與重要會議及研討會, 以藉此掌握所學領域內最新的發展狀況。)

- **wing it**　臨場發揮

  You should never try to wing it in an important presentation.

  (在重要的簡報場合, 絕對不可以臨場發揮。)

- **on that count**　就這方面來說

  cf. On account of bad weather, the company outing was canceled at the last minute.

  (由於天候惡劣的關係, 公司旅遊活動在出發前一刻取消了。)

1. The Japanese have refined the art of living in a small world. Everything
        A   B

   can be at your fingertip.
           C   D

2. It is the best to store flour in the bag in which it is sold, and keep it in
        A   B   C   D

   a cool, dry spot.

3. Students of English should listen to much as authentic English language
      A   B   C

   as possible.
       D

◆◆◆◆◆◆◆◆◆◆◆◆◆ 簡短對話 ◆◆◆◆◆◆◆◆◆◆◆◆◆◆

Egler: Have you had the same sort of changes in Japan?

Sawasaki: Certainly not to the degree that they've occurred here. It is true that our divorce rate has gone up fairly sharply in recent years. All in all, though, the nuclear family is fairly solid in Japan, I'd say.

Egler: How about homosexuality?

Sawasaki: It does exist, but it's certainly not highly visible the way it is here.

---

to the degree　到…程度　　**divorce rate**　離婚率　　**all in all**　總而言之
nuclear family　核心家庭；小家庭　　**solid**　穩固的　　**homosexuality**　同性
戀　　**visible**　可見的

Lesson 34

Modern Etiquette —— 總結

■ ■ ■

甚麼才是正確的禮儀呢？自婦女解放運動 (women's liberation movement) 以來，禮儀這個問題在美國又變得更加微妙了。

在各國報刊上常有連載的 Ann Landers 專欄，偶爾會談到這個問題。有一次，她接到一個問題說，如果寫信給某公司，salutation (開頭敬稱) 用 Gentlemen 是否恰當？Ann 的回答是，Surely you know "Gentlemen" is no longer acceptable. "Ladies/Gentlemen" sounds like a unisex bathroom. The best of the lot is "Dear Sir or Madam."

也就是說，用 "Gentlemen" 不妥，而 "Ladies/Gentlemen" 聽起來又像是個「男女共用的洗手間」，所以，最好是用 "Dear Sir or Madam"。不過，Ann 後面又加了一句 "unless somone out there can come up with something better. Any suggestion?" 看來，她也不是很確定。

該封信函是於 1983 年 5 月刊載的。但在那以後，並沒有人提出足以取代 Dear Sir or Madam (或 Dear Sir/Madam) 的 salutation。

據說，Ms. (複數為 Mses.) 這個敬稱 (title of respect) 是從 50 年代開始使用的。其快速普及則是因著 70 年代初期的婦女解放運動。

這個敬稱的源起是，對男性只要用 Mr. 就可「一網打盡」，但對女性卻有 Miss 和 Mrs. 的分別，這是很不合理的。

但由於涉及婦女解放運動，所以還是有些女性無法接受此一稱呼，而堅持使用 Miss 和 Mrs.。至於新聞媒體的用法，則有一律不採用敬稱的趨勢，對於首次出現 (first reference) 的人物用 full name (連名帶姓)，第二次以後則只用姓氏來稱呼。

至於日常禮儀，有些女性基於男女平等的原則，不願被視為「弱者」，要求男性給予公平待遇。她們認為，不管是搭乘電梯或是走樓梯，不該有所謂的「女士優先」，應該「循序」前進才對。但也仍然有人謹守男女之間的傳統禮儀。看來，禮儀真是個「知難行也難」的問題。

Lesson 35

Stressed Out

（精疲力盡）

◆ Lesson 35 的內容 ◆

　　已經快下午兩點了，但澤崎居然還沒有吃午餐。或者應該說，他最近因為工作壓力太大，有點食慾不振，根本不想吃午餐。墨菲實在看不下去了，所以就半強迫地邀澤崎到員工餐廳去。澤崎似乎是得了名之為「壓力」的文明病。艾格勒正好也在場，他們便談到了一些克服壓力的辦法。

The company actually sponsors our membership in the fitness center.

Stressed Out (1)（精疲力盡）

●預習 — *Sentences*

· Try to reach the sales manager at the hotel.
· Here are some messages for you.
· How do you work with them?
· When can I see the final report then?
· It won't happen again.

●*Vignette*

Murphy: Shoichi, the National Restaurant Association convention canceled our hotel reservations by mistake, and now the hotel has no room for our hospitality suite. What shall I do?

Sawasaki: Oh, no! Try to reach the sales manager at the hotel and tell him what happened. We do a lot of business with them. If he can't help you, put him through to me.

Murphy: Here are some messages for you. Two phone calls from the Tokyo office. Finance wants to see you about your moving expenses. Your Realtor wants to talk to you about plumbing in your new apartment. And, oh, International Market Research wants to postpone the focus group discussion till next week, and I told them to talk to you directly.

Sawasaki: Ugh! This is the second time, Patti. Thanks.

[*Phone rings*]

Sawasaki: Sawasaki. Gil. Yes, well, no, IMR just postponed again. Sorry. How do you work with them? Uh-huh. Their work may be excellent, but when? OK, sorry again. I'll let you know.

Murphy: [*On extension*] Shoichi, it's Mike Fields from IMR on line 2.

Sawasaki: Mike, what's going on?

Fields: I'm sorry, Shoichi, but we have to delay the focus groups for three days. We couldn't find enough qualified people for the demographic sample you wanted and I don't—

Sawasaki: Excuse me, but when can I see the final report then?

Fields: I promise you'll get it before the end of this month. Honest.

Sawasaki: Mike, we're counting on you.

Fields: Don't worry, Shoichi. It won't happen again. Sorry.

* * *

　　澤崎才離開一個鐘頭去開個會，就發生了諸多事情，最令他覺得血壓暴升的就是討論小組的會議要延到下禮拜的事，因為這已經是第二次延期了。

墨菲：　昭一，全國餐飲協會代表大會不小心取消了我們的旅館訂房，而旅館現在已經沒有房間可以給我們作招待套房了。我該怎麼辦？

澤崎：　真糟糕！妳現在試著打電話給旅館的業務經理，告訴他發生了甚麼事。公司跟他們有很多生意上的往來。如果他無法幫妳，就把電話接給我。

墨菲：　這兒有些你的留言。東京辦事處來了兩通電話。財務部想跟你談談你搬家的費用。你的房地產經紀人要跟你談一下關於你新公寓配管的事。還有，噢，國際市場調查公司想要把討論小組的會議延到下禮拜，我要他們直接跟你說。

澤崎：　哎呀！派蒂，這已經是他們第二次延期了。謝謝。

[電話鈴響]

澤崎：　我是澤崎。吉爾。是啊，嗯，沒有，國際市調公司又給我們延期了。抱歉。你都怎麼跟他們合作的？哦，是這樣。他們事情也許辦得很好，但要甚麼時候？好吧，再跟你說聲抱歉。我會讓你知道的。

墨菲：　[在分機上] 昭一，國際市調的麥可・菲爾德斯在第二號分機。

澤崎：　麥可，怎麼樣？

菲爾德斯：　昭一，我很抱歉，可是這個討論小組非得再延個三天不可。因為我們找不到夠多條件符合的人來做你們所要的人口統計學樣本，而且我沒有——

澤崎：　打個岔，那我要甚麼時候才可以看到最後的報告？

菲爾德斯：　我保證這個月底前就可以給你。一定。

澤崎：　麥可，我們就指望你了。

菲爾德斯：　昭一，別擔心。這種事不會再發生了。對不起。

＊　　　＊　　　＊

Words and Phrases

hospitality suite　招待客戶用的旅館套房	Boards 的會員)
	plumbing　配管
put someone through　(電話用語)把某人的電話接到…	ugh　(表示厭惡的聲音)哎;呀;啊
	postpone　延期
moving expenses　搬家的花費	what's going on　怎麼了
Realtor　〔美〕房地產業者　(National Association of Real Estate	qualified　資格符合的
	demographic　人口統計學的

Vocabulary Building

● **by mistake**　不小心;失誤
Jim erased the disk by mistake when he pushed a wrong key.
(吉姆不小心按錯鍵,把磁片的檔案都殺掉了。)

● **do business with**　與…做生意
I refuse to do business with your new sales rep. He's incompetent and he has no manners.
(我拒絕與貴公司的新業務員做生意。他不但能力不夠,而且沒有禮貌。)

● **focus group discussion**　(銷售)討論小組會議〈從潛在的消費者中選出一些人來組成討論小組,然後由一位市調人員主導討論會的進行,目的是要令與會者能發表其對公司、產品、以及宣傳廣告的感覺和看法〉
Before we test-market the new shampoo, I suggest we should hold a series of focus group discussions to gauge consumer reaction to the product.
(在進行新洗髮精的市場測試之前,我建議先舉行一系列的銷售討論小組會議,以評估消費者對產品的反應。)

● **count on**　依靠;依賴
Of all the salesmen in my department, you can count on the oldest one in any slack month.
(在我部門所有的業務員當中,最資深的那一位是你不管在任何景氣蕭條的月份都可以信賴的。)

1. "What a great idea!" Arthur told to his secretary, who was helping him
   　　　　　　　　　　　　　A　　　　　　　　　B　　　　　　C
   write the script.
   D

2. Dave cooked the muffins from scratch, but most people now use a com-
   　　　A　　　　　　　　　B　　　　　　　C
   mercially prepared mix.
   　　　　　　　　　D

3. The experts say that the health benefits of body massage is numerous.
   　　A　　　B　　　　　　　　　　　　　　　　　　　C　　　D

◆◆◆◆◆◆◆◆◆◆◆◆◆ 簡短對話 ◆◆◆◆◆◆◆◆◆◆◆◆◆◆◆

Murphy: Several faxes also came in. I left them on your desk.

Sawasaki: Fine. [*Looks through faxes*] Er, Patti?

Murphy: Yes?

Sawasaki: You're so good about filtering out junk mail and preparing answers to routine correspondence. Could you try to do the same for incoming faxes from now on? Not all of these have to come straight to
me.

Murphy: I'm sorry. I've tended to assume that anything that comes in by fax
must be an urgent communication.

Sawasaki: Sometimes it is, but there are times when it can go into the
circular file.

---

filter out 過濾 (不要的東西)；濾除　　**junk mail** 垃圾郵件 (如廣告單等不重
要的信件)　　**routine correspondence** 日常業務例行的信件　　**incoming** 進
來的　　**assume** 猜想；假設　　**circular file** 傳閱檔案

Lesson 35

Stressed Out (2)（精疲力盡）

● 預習 ─ *Sentences*

· Have you had your lunch yet?
· I only had coffee for breakfast.
· We may be a bit underdressed.
· How do you handle the stress and maintain sanity?
· Have a sense of humor.

● *Vignette* ───────────────

Murphy: Shoichi, have you had your lunch yet?

Sawasaki: Lunch? I forgot such a thing existed. No, I only had coffee for breakfast. [*Sighs*] Sorry, Patti. I'm just . . .

Murphy: Oh, Shoichi! Allow me to escort you, sir, to our elegant gourmet restaurant, the Nelson ABC Foods cafeteria. We may be a bit underdressed but I know the maitre d'.

*   *   *

Murphy: One boss I had used to give vent to his frustration by throwing things.

Sawasaki: Like pencils and files?

Murphy: No, like typewriters and ashtrays. We got him one of those little basketball backboards for his trash can. He'd wad up paper balls and fire away.

Sawasaki: Seriously, Patti, don't you think this is a stressful work environment? How do you handle the stress and maintain sanity?

Murphy: Have a sense of humor—not take all of this work too seriously. There's life before death, you know. But you obviously aren't the only one who feels that way. I read in the paper the other day that three quarters of Americans say their jobs cause them stress. Hang loose.

　　墨菲把澤崎帶到員工餐廳去吃個飯，放鬆一下。而澤崎則一本正經地問道：「妳難道不覺得這裡的工作壓力很大嗎？妳都怎麼處理這樣的壓力，而不讓自己發瘋？」

墨菲：　昭一，你吃過午飯了沒？

澤崎：　午飯？我都忘了還有這回事。還沒，我早餐也只喝了杯咖啡。[嘆氣] 抱歉，派蒂，我只是…

墨菲：　噢，昭一！先生，讓我護送你到我們漂亮的美食餐廳 —— 尼爾森 ABC 食品公司員工餐廳。我們穿的可能有點隨便，不過我認得那兒的經理。

＊　　＊　　＊

墨菲：　我以前有一個老闆，他在遭受挫敗的時候總是藉著丟東西來發洩。

澤崎：　像是鉛筆和檔案嗎？

墨菲：　不對，是打字機和菸灰缸之類的。我們給他的垃圾桶裝了個小小的籃板。他會把紙揉成一團然後射籃。

澤崎：　派蒂，說正經的，難道妳不覺得這裡的工作壓力很大嗎？妳都怎麼處理這樣的壓力，而不讓自己發瘋？

墨菲：　要有幽默感 —— 別把工作看得太嚴重了。你也知道的，只要還有口氣，日子總是要過。不過，顯然你也不是唯一有這種感覺的人。我前幾天看到報紙上說，有四分之三的美國人覺得他們的工作使他們覺得有壓力。放輕鬆點。

Lesson 35　Stressed Out (2)

Words and Phrases

escort　護送; 護衛	wad　揉成一團
gourmet [ˈgʊrme]　美食家	fire away　投射; 投籃
underdressed　穿著簡單的; 樸素的	sanity　理性; 理智
maitre d' [ˌmetrəˈdi]　服務生領班	sense of humor　幽默感

Vocabulary Building

● **give vent to**　發洩 (脾氣)
cf. David let off steam by pacing around the room.
(大衛在房內踱步, 藉以消氣。)

● **handle**　處理
I'm afraid I can't handle this work load by myself.
(我擔心我自己一個人無法處理這樣的工作量。)

● **There's life before death.**　人只要還沒死, 日子總是得過。〈與 life after death
(死後) 相對應, 是特意要表示幽默的講法。一般較常使用 There's life after . . .
的形態。例如: There's life after work. (下班後還有生活要過。) There's life
after Nelson ABC Foods. (無論是從尼爾森 ABC 食品公司退休或是被解雇,
人生還是要繼續下去) 等〉
cf. Is there life after death?
(死後還有生命存在嗎?)

● **hang loose**　放輕鬆
cf. The union hung tough in the negotiations.
(工會在談判時的態度十分強硬。)

(解答見 263 頁)

▶ **Exercises**   在下列例句中，每句各有四個劃線部分，
其中一個的文法有誤，請將之選出。

1. Do you think <u>can we</u> get <u>away</u> with that scene?   <u>Won't</u> the censors
        A   B   C

   <u>object</u>?
     D

2. <u>Whenever</u> I was baffled <u>by</u> a reader's <u>complicating</u> inquiry, Rosemary
         A   B   C

   always <u>came</u> to the rescue.
            D

3. Although <u>numerous</u> mosquitoes <u>buzzing</u> <u>around</u> him, Bob slept like a
                A   B   C

   <u>log</u>.
     D

◆◆◆◆◆◆◆◆◆◆◆◆◆◆ 簡短對話 ◆◆◆◆◆◆◆◆◆◆◆◆◆◆

Murphy: You know what I find so remarkable about you, Shoichi?

Sawasaki: What is it?

Murphy: I'm impressed how you manage never to fly off the handle even
when everything seems to be going wrong.

Sawasaki: Fly off the handle?

Murphy: Lose your temper, I mean.

Sawasaki: Actually, I have a very short temper, but I've learned that losing
it rarely produces any good results. Still, I feel the anger inside, believe
me.

---

fly off the handle   勃然大怒   **lose one's temper**   發脾氣   **short temper**
脾氣不好

Stressed Out (3) (精疲力盡)

預習 — Sentences

- I have to deliver the goods before the end of my stint.
- You have to take real good care of yourself.
- You're right and I know what's good for me.
- That's why I'm feeling so stressed out.
- You may just be feeling the effects of all these life changes.

Vignette

Sawasaki: But I have to <u>deliver the goods</u> before the end of my three-year <u>stint</u>. I've got to produce results.

Murphy: So you have to take real good care of yourself, Shoichi. Do you eat breakfast?

Sawasaki: Not usually.

Murphy: Only have time for coffee? Too much caffeine isn't good for you. A good meal in the morning gives you <u>energy</u> for the rest of the day. Eat right and don't take anything that comes wrapped in cellophane, ever.

Sawasaki: You're right and I know what's good for me — fresh, light, low-fat foods.

Murphy: The trick is to eat what you know you should.

Sawasaki: Maybe that's why I'm feeling so <u>stressed out</u>.

Egler: Excuse me, Shoichi, but you may just be feeling the effects of all these life changes.

Sawasaki: Oh, hi, Sally.

Egler: Hi. Ever heard of the scale for rating stressful events in your life, like an operation, a divorce, or a death in the family?

墨菲對於澤崎愛喝咖啡和飲食不當的習慣覺得頗為擔心，她懇切地勸告澤崎：「太多咖啡因對身體不好，而且絕對不要吃用玻璃紙包裝的東西。」

澤崎： 但我必須要在這三年的任期結束之前對公司有所交待。我得做出點東西來。

墨菲： 昭一，所以你更得要好好照顧自己。你平常吃早餐嗎？

澤崎： 不常。

墨菲： 時間只夠用來喝咖啡？太多咖啡因對身體不好。早上好好吃一頓會使你一整天都有活力。要吃得正確，而且絕對不要吃用玻璃紙包裝的東西。

澤崎： 妳說的沒錯，我也知道甚麼對自己有益 —— 新鮮、清淡、低脂的食物。

墨菲： 而祕訣就在於要吃你所知道自己該吃的東西。

澤崎： 也許這就是我會覺得自己如此疲憊不堪的原因。

艾格勒： 打個岔，昭一，不過你可能是因為才剛剛感受到生活上種種變動所帶來的影響。

澤崎： 噢，嗨，莎莉。

艾格勒： 嗨。你有沒有聽過一種測定尺度？那是專門用來測知生活中各種會給人帶來壓力的事件，像是動手術、離婚、或是親人過世等的。

Lesson 35   Stressed Out (3)

Words and Phrases

caffeine [ˈkæfiɪn]	咖啡因	trick	訣竅
cellophane [ˈsɛləˌfen]	玻璃紙	scale	標準
low-fat	低脂肪的	divorce	離婚

Vocabulary Building

- **deliver the goods**   履行義務；履約；不負所望
  cf. People complain that George never delivers on his promises.
  (大家都抱怨喬治從不信守諾言。)

- **stint**   任期
  After a brief stint in an ad agency, Mitchell decided to go back to college and study business.
  (在廣告公司任職了一小段時間後，密契爾決定再回到學校去唸商學。)

- **energy**   精力
  Don't waste your energy on this project. You have more important things to do.
  (別把精力浪費在這項計畫上。你還有更重要的事得做。)

- **stressed out**   精疲力盡
  cf. Ned used to feel excited about his career, but now he's completely burned out.
  (奈德從前對他的事業一直是興致勃勃，不過他現在整個人都累垮了。)

(解答見 263 頁)

► **Exercises** 在下列例句中，每句各有四個劃線部分，
其中一個的文法有誤，請將之選出。

1. I accepted the position in Ethiopia, but I am beginning to have second
    ‾‾‾‾‾‾‾   ‾‾‾‾‾‾‾‾‾‾‾‾‾
       A   B

   thought about it.
   ‾‾‾‾‾‾‾ ‾‾‾‾‾
      C   D

2. Just when we were about to give up, we began to see the light at the
                                   ‾‾‾‾‾‾‾   ‾‾‾‾‾   ‾‾‾
                                      A   B   C

   ending of the tunnel.
   ‾‾‾‾‾‾
      D

3. Shortly after arriving in Buenos Aires, Alice wondered what she had
                ‾‾‾‾‾‾‾‾ ‾‾   ‾‾‾
                   A   B   C

   come to.
        ‾‾
        D

◆◆◆◆◆◆◆◆◆◆◆◆◆◆ 簡短對話 ◆◆◆◆◆◆◆◆◆◆◆◆◆◆◆

Murphy: Another suggestion I would make is about your lunchtime habits.
Unless you have something special on your schedule, I've noticed that you
tend to gulp down a sandwich or something at your desk and keep working
the whole time.

Sawasaki: I do that because it's one of the few times during the day that I
can work without constant interruptions.

Murphy: I realize that, and I know you have a lot to do but I still think
you'd be in better condition for the afternoon if you allowed yourself a bit
of a break in the middle of the day.

Sawasaki: I'll keep that in mind.

---

gulp down 狼吞虎嚥 **interruption** 中斷 **I'll keep that in mind.** 我會
銘記在心的。

Lesson 35

Stressed Out (4) (精疲力盡)

●預習 — *Sentences*

· Is getting fired one of the events?
· Sometimes I meditate or read.
· It can put a new perspective on those problems.
· I used to get a massage and do aerobics in Tokyo.
· Maybe I should look into that.

●*Vignette*

Sawasaki: Is getting fired one of the events?

Egler: Yes, of course, but in your case, you moved to a new city and to a new position. Now, they are probably the most traumatic social adjustments you can ever make.

Murphy: Give yourself a break, Shoichi. Allow some time for the dust to settle before you demand so much of yourself. Take some time to relax. I play the piano and sing in the choir at church.

Egler: Sometimes I meditate or read.

Murphy: Or take a walk. A walk is one of the most effective stress management tools. Take a little walk when you sense the pressure mounting and feel like you want to strangle somebody. It can put a new perspective on those problems.

Sawasaki: I used to get a massage and do aerobics in Tokyo.

Egler: Oh, is that right? Well, if there's only one thing you do to manage your stress, let it be exercise. You should join a workout class at the Apple Sports Center. Aerobics, weights, the pool—get the blood pumping.

Murphy: The company actually sponsors our membership in the fitness center.

Sawasaki: Oh, yeah? Maybe I should look into that.

消除壓力的方式不勝枚舉，但最好的方式應該是運動吧！澤崎倒是對那個由公司補助入會的健身中心蠻感興趣的。

澤崎： 被炒魷魚也算嗎？

艾格勒： 算啊，當然算，不過以你的例子來看，你搬到了一個新城市，換了個新職務。這可能是你目前所遭遇到最具精神衝擊的社會調適問題。

墨菲： 昭一，放你自己一馬吧！在要求自己做這許多事之前，先緩一緩，讓事情有塵埃落定的機會。找時間放鬆一下自己。我都在教堂的唱詩班彈琴唱詩。

艾格勒： 我有時候會做點冥想或閱讀。

墨菲： 散個步也不錯。散步是疏解精神壓力最有效的方法之一。當你覺得壓力愈來愈大，有種想要掐死某人的念頭時，就去走走。這可以使你對所面臨的問題有個新的看法。

澤崎： 我以前在東京時常常會去做做按摩或是有氧運動。

艾格勒： 哦，真的嗎？嗯，如果你用以疏解壓力的方式只有一種，那就運動吧！你應該加入蘋果運動中心的健身班。裡頭有有氧運動、舉重、游泳池——讓血液好好循環一下。

墨菲： 事實上，公司還會補助員工加入健身中心的會費。

澤崎： 真的？也許我該研究一下這個可能。

Lesson 35 Stressed Out (4)

Words and Phrases

choir [kwaɪr]	唱詩班; 合唱團	strangle	將…絞死; 悶死
meditate	沈思; 冥想	workout class	運動或體操教室
sense *v.*	感覺; 察覺	pump	上下移動; 跳動
mount	（數量、程度、費用）增加	look into	研究; 探討

Vocabulary Building

- **fire**　解雇
  cf. Barry was fired up about his new position as sales manager.
  （貝瑞新近被任命為業務經理，他對這個新職務感覺雀躍不已。）

- **traumatic**　創傷的; 屬於精神上衝擊的
  Mary has never recovered from the traumatic experience of losing both her parents in a traffic accident.
  （瑪麗一直無法從車禍中失去雙親的創痛經驗裡恢復過來。）

- **settle the dust**　使塵土沈澱
  A rainfall will settle the dust.
  （一場雨會使塵土不再飛揚。）

- **perspective**　觀點; 看法
  The seminar gave me a new perspective on my career goals.
  （這場研討會使我對未來的生涯目標有了新的看法。）

▶ **Exercises**   在下列例句中，每句各有四個劃線部分，   (解答見263頁)
其中一個的文法有誤，請將之選出。

1. Never <u>let</u> alcohol <u>anywhere</u> <u>near</u> Thomas because he drinks like <u>a fish</u>.
       A   B   C   D

2. Since I took the <u>opposite side</u> <u>on</u> this issue, our <u>relationship</u> is <u>on the rock</u>.
                       A   B   C   D

3. When we <u>reached to</u> Los Angeles, we had to look <u>for</u> an <u>apartment</u> <u>in</u>
            A   B   C   D

the newspaper.

◆◆◆◆◆◆◆◆◆◆◆◆◆ 簡短對話 ◆◆◆◆◆◆◆◆◆◆◆◆◆◆

Egler: Shoichi, you've been looking awfully tired the past few days. Are you feeling all right?
Sawasaki: To be honest, I've been having some trouble sleeping.
Egler: Too much to worry about?
Sawasaki: It's not so much worrying as not being able to relax.
Egler: You've taken on a tremendous amount of work in the few weeks you've been here. Maybe you should slow down a bit.
Sawasaki: But I hate to lose the chance to learn more about the business.
Egler: You now, sometimes I find I learn more if I give myself more time to enjoy what I'm learning.

---

to be honest 說老實話　　**have trouble ...ing** 有…的困擾　　**take on** 承攬
(工作)

Lesson 35

Stressed Out — 總結

澤崎的工作態度顯示出他是個 A 型行為的人 (Type A behavior, 與血型無關)。 A 型行為的特徵是說話快、行動快、吃飯快 (hurried speech, rapid movement and eating), 經常在趕時間 (chronic sense of time urgency)、同時思考並進行數件事情 (thinking and performing several things at once) 等。

這種型的人很容易會有壓力方面的問題。而且 A 型行為的人罹患冠狀動脈疾病 (心肌梗塞等) 的機率和死亡率似乎也較大。

促使壓力產生的外在要素與刺激, 以及個人為要因應外在環境的變遷, 而產生的自我敦促, 統稱為 stressor。澤崎目前面臨著各式各樣的 stressor, 但其中最嚴重的大概是 work stressor。這是由於他在這個新的工作環境中從早到晚都要經歷到形形色色的緊張與壓力。他要插手旅館訂房的問題, 也要掛心 focus group discussion 若延至下週是否會太遲等等。諸如此類的 decision stressor 重重地壓在他身上。

澤崎來到陌生的芝加哥, 萬事皆新所帶來的 change stressors, 以及「我必須不負所望」(I have to deliver the goods) 的 emotional stressors 都使他心生壓力。或許澤崎肩上還有其他諸如 commuting stressors (通勤)、 environmental stressors (新工作環境 plus 新居住環境)、 physical stressors (生理)、以及 family stressors (家庭) 等的擔子。

至於莎莉所說的「壓力事件測定尺度」(scale for rating stressful events) 則與「壓力值」(stress value) 有關。所謂壓力值就是用數據來表示某一 life event 之 stressful 的程度為何。

如喪偶為 100, 分居為 65, 入獄或親密家屬的死亡為 63, 自己受重傷或生重病為 53, 結婚為 49, 遭解雇為 47 等。計算方式是將過去一年內該 event 的發生次數乘上其壓力值, 再全部加總, 即可診斷出整體的「受壓」程度。

據說壓力還會導致習慣性曠職、生產力低落, 以及龐大的醫藥費支出, 美國企業每年因此蒙受的虧損約有一千五百億美元。

Managing Change

（掌控時代的變遷）

◆ Lesson 36 的內容 ◆

　　任何人在本能上都會對新的或未知的事物感到不安。但不管
所採取的態度為何，變化依舊會臨到。所以才會有人說變化是唯
一不變的東西。今天的商業界可說是日新月異、變化激烈，「現
在」尚未結束，「未來」便已開始。而亞力士‧迪馬哥則認為，要
想存活下去，就得學習不受外界環境支配，自己要取得掌控權。
這也正是他的經營理念之一。

And the team will be
looking at methods
to help us deal
with rapid change.

Managing Change (1)（掌控時代的變遷）

●預習 — *Sentences*

- Let me take this chance to convey the message.
- He says these changes will be felt in several areas.
- Isn't this just another plea to work harder?
- Change is the only constant in this world.
- And nowadays the changes are happening so fast.

●*Vignette*

Parker: Since this is our first staff meeting since I got back from the annual management get-together in Tampa, let me take this chance to convey the message Alex gave us there. His theme for the session was "Change."

Winchell: Surprise, surprise.

Parker: He says Nelson ABC Foods will see change in the future that will make the '80s look like a picnic and that these changes will be felt in several areas. For instance, the distinction between our domestic and international markets will become almost irrelevant. Mergers and acquisitions will be driven by competitive pressures in the marketplace rather than simply being a matter of what's available. We're going to see technological advances that we can't even imagine yet. And on top of everything else, we're going to have to take a lead role in protecting the environment.

Swarbrick: I must say that sounds pretty impressive, Gil, but isn't this just another plea to work harder?

Parker: No, Peter, Alex really feels that that's the the only way to survive the present— or the future. He believes that change is the only constant in this world. And nowadays the changes are happening so fast that we've hardly begun to adjust to one set of them before a new one sets upon us. We'll also be reshaping the company. Alex has brought in a team of consultants who will work on managing change. The team is being led by Dr. James Lawrence, a college professor on sabbatical.

　　亞力士・迪馬哥今年的訊息重點是「變化」。他說未來將會有一些改變發生，這會使他們覺得 80 年代所經歷的簡直就像野餐一般輕鬆。我們也會聽到史瓦布利克略帶挖苦的評論。

帕克： 由於這是我在坦帕參加完年度管理會議回來後第一次召開的員工會議，所以容我藉此機會傳達一下亞力士在坦帕所給我們的訊息。他這次議程的主題是「變化」。

溫謝爾： 真令人驚訝啊!

帕克： 他說尼爾森 ABC 食品公司未來將面臨一些改變，這會使得我們在 80 年代所經歷的看來像是野餐一般輕鬆，而這些改變將顯現在好幾個方面。舉例來說，國內市場和國際市場的區別將不再合宜。事業兼併也不再只是有甚麼就併甚麼，它將受市場上競爭壓力的主導。我們也會見到一些自己甚至還無法想像的科技進展。還有最重要的是，我們將在業界帶頭做環保。

史瓦布利克： 吉爾，我得說這聽起來相當感人，不過，這是否又是另一個要鞭策我們努力的口實？

帕克： 不，彼得，亞力士真的覺得這是在今天 ── 或者說是在未來 ── 唯一能存活下去的方式。他相信，世界上唯一不變的就是「變革」。而現在變動的步調又這麼快，我們都還來不及適應其中的一部分，新的改變卻又接踵而至。我們也將重新塑造這個公司。亞力士引進了一個諮詢小組，專職變遷的掌控。這個小組是由一位正在休假中的詹姆士・勞倫斯教授所主導的。

Lesson 36　Managing Change (1)

Words and Phrases

get-together	會議〈非正式用語〉	technological advances	科技進步
convey	傳遞訊息	on top of	在⋯之上
distinction	界線; 區隔	take a lead role	居領導地位
irrelevant	不相關的; 不適切的	environment	環境
mergers and acquisitions　M&A		plea	要求
企業購併		survive	生存
marketplace	市場	reshape	重塑

Vocabulary Building

- **Surprise, surprise.**　真令人驚訝!〈這是個反語, 說話者其實是要表示, 這根本不是甚麼新聞, 更沒甚麼好驚訝的〉
  cf. That's a pleasant surprise.
  (那真是個驚喜。)

- **be driven by**　受⋯驅使
  Ted's driven by the desire to surpass his father.
  (在背後驅動著泰德的, 就是那股想勝過他父親的慾望。)

- **competitive pressures**　競爭壓力
  Competitive pressures are forcing us to cut costs across the board.
  (競爭壓力迫使我們全面刪減經費。)

- **on sabbatical**　在有薪休假中
  cf. Professor McDonald spent his sabbatical traveling around the world.
  (麥克唐納教授利用他七年一次的休假年來環遊世界。)

(解答見 263 頁)

▶**Exercises**　在下列例句中，每句各有四個劃線部分，
其中一個的文法有誤，請將之選出。

1. My <u>supervisor</u> said I <u>deserve</u> a <u>rise</u>, but I just wanted a pat on the <u>back</u>.
　　　Ａ　　　　　　　Ｂ　　　Ｃ　　　　　　　　　　　　　　　Ｄ

2. The port city <u>suffered</u> a <u>major</u> earthquake <u>in</u> <u>the</u> early 1995.
　　　　　　　　Ａ　　　　Ｂ　　　　　　　Ｃ　　Ｄ

3. The group <u>think</u> <u>putting</u> in <u>long</u> hours at work will <u>enable</u> them to com-
　　　　　　　Ａ　　　Ｂ　　　Ｃ　　　　　　　　　　　Ｄ

plete the assignment on time.

◆◆◆◆◆◆◆◆◆◆◆◆◆◆ 簡短對話 ◆◆◆◆◆◆◆◆◆◆◆◆◆◆◆◆

Swarbrick: Was change all you talked about in Tampa?
Parker: No, we covered other topics too, of course.
Swarbrick: Such as . . . ?
Parker: Plans for the year ahead were on the agenda, and we also reviewed
progress in integrating the Nelson and ABC organizations.
Swarbrick: Any more acquisitions in the works?
Parker: Well, Alex is the only one who could answer that for you. Even if
you asked him, though, he'd probably give a noncommittal answer.

Such as . . . ? 像是…?　　　**on the agenda** 在討論議程中　　　**review** 評
估　　**integrate** 整合　　**acquisition** 收購　　**in the works** 進行中
noncommittal 曖昧的; 態度不明朗的

Managing Change (2) （掌控時代的變遷）

●預習 — *Sentences*

- Dr. Lawrence made an impressive speech at the meeting.
- A company is also a collection of individuals.
- I can't quarrel with any of that, but what does it mean for us?
- Alex has hand-picked a high-level committee of managers.
- We've started a series of workshops.

●*Vignette*

Parker: And the team will be looking at methods to help us deal with rapid change.

Egler: It seems to me that DeMarco has been creating most of his own changes.

Parker: No, actually, what the company has been through— the downsizing, delayering, restructuring and so forth— has been a response to outside changes. Dr. Lawrence made an impressive speech at the meeting, in which he said that a company as an organic system must respond to external inputs, such as tougher competition and new technologies. But he emphasized that a company is also a collection of individuals, whose skills and enthusiasm are important to its success. We should all work to create an atmosphere in which change is encouraged and welcomed by everybody.

Sawasaki: I can't quarrel with any of that, but what does it mean for us?

Parker: Alex has hand-picked a high-level committee of managers, including myself, which is already in place. We've started a series of workshops on the best ways to interpret change and communicate it to the staff. Also, the committee will research and identify the most efficient ways of doing things across the company.

Egler: I guess the idea is that we can— and should— manage change instead of letting it manage us.

Parker: Exactly.

　　迪馬哥為了要能掌控這些變化，於是引進了一個諮詢顧問小組，專門研究急劇變遷的應對方式。但艾格勒卻說，幾乎所有的變化都是迪馬哥一手造成的。

帕克：　這個小組將找出方法協助我們處理快速的變遷。

艾格勒：　在我看來，幾乎所有的變化都是迪馬哥一手造成的。

帕克：　不是這樣，事實上，公司所經歷的 ── 包括縮編、簡化層級、重組等 ── 都是針對外在的變局而有的動作。勞倫斯博士在會議中有場精彩的演講，他說，公司就是個有機體系，它對於外來的刺激，像是競爭的加劇和新科技等的，都必須有所反應。但他強調，公司也是由一個個的人所組成的，每個人員的技術和熱誠都是公司成功的關鍵所在。我們應當合力創造出一種氣氛，使得事物的改變在其間能得到助長，也讓大家都能樂見改變的發生。

澤崎：　對這點我是無可爭辯，但這對我們有甚麼意義？

帕克：　亞力士親自挑選了一些主管組成高層委員會，我也是其中一員，現在都已就定位了。我們開始了一系列的討論會，要找出能解讀變遷並將之溝通給員工的最佳方式。還有，委員會也會做些研究調查，確認出當公司要展開全面行動時，甚麼才是最有效率的方式。

艾格勒：　我猜這意思就是我們可以 ── 而且也應該要 ── 掌控變化，而非被牽著鼻子走。

帕克：　正是如此。

Lesson 36 Managing Change (2)

Words and Phrases

deal with	處理；應付	response	反應
downsizing	企業規模縮小	organic	有機的
delayering	簡化層級	external inputs	外部資訊的輸入
restructuring	企業重組	workshop	討論會；研習會
and so forth	…等等	Exactly.	正是如此。

Vocabulary Building

- **I can't quarrel with that.**　　對那點我無可爭辯。
  cf. You've made your point.
  (你的意思已經很清楚了。)

- **hand-pick**　　親自挑選
  The president hand-picked a small group of managers to serve as the crisis management team.
  (董事長親自挑選了幾位經理，組成一個危機處理小組。)

- **be in place**　　在適當的位置
  All the necessary facilities are now in place.
  (所有必要的設備現在都已經擺在適當的位置了。)

- **(the) idea is that**　　意思就是…
  Alex's idea is that costs can be cut by cleaning out the deadwood.
  (亞力士認為只要裁汰冗員便能縮減支出。)

1. You should <u>look around</u> before you <u>check out</u> a hotel room. I once
            A   B

  <u>forgot</u> my <u>expensive</u> watch in a hotel in Paris.
    C   D

2. Ralph <u>gave</u> many <u>historical lectures</u> this year <u>at</u> the <u>university</u>.
       A   B   C   D

3. You should take <u>better</u> care <u>of</u> your <u>finances,</u> or you'll never be able to
               A   B   C

  afford <u>retiring.</u>
      D

◆◆◆◆◆◆◆◆◆◆◆◆◆◆ 簡短對話 ◆◆◆◆◆◆◆◆◆◆◆◆◆◆

Sawasaki: This high-sounding talk is all very well and good, but don't you think that the people in this organization could use a little less change for a while? That way we could catch our breath and adjust to the upheavals we've been through recently.

Parker: I know what you mean, but I fear that is not to be.

Sawasaki: No?

Parker: No, because unfortunately, even though we all might like to take a breather, the rest of the world isn't about to oblige us by standing still in the meantime.

Sawasaki: You mean that if we take time out, it'll make it even harder to catch up later.

Parker: Exactly.

---

high-sounding 立論崇高的　　**use** 利用；使用　　**catch one's breath** 喘一口氣　　**upheaval** 劇變　　**take a breather** 休息一下　　**stand still** 靜止不動　　**in the meantime** 同時　　**take time out** 停歇　　**catch up** 趕上

Managing Change (3) (掌控時代的變遷)

●預習 — *Sentences*

· Everybody instinctively fears the new and unknown.
· Our competitors are sure to beat us to the punch.
· Alex has never seen his role as chief decision maker.
· Lawrence calls Alex a "transformational leader."
· I really think things are changing in this organization.

●*Vignette*

Parker: Everybody instinctively fears the new and unknown, but change must be embraced, since it's what brings progress. Change will allow us to seek opportunities to do new things in business. If we don't think like that, our competitors are sure to beat us to the punch.

Winchell: I have a question. What is Alex's role in this? It doesn't seem like him to turn anything over to a committee or whatever.

Parker: Alex has never seen his role as chief decision maker. Lawrence calls Alex a "transformational leader." You see, in order for a company to change successfully, it's got to have forceful, vital leadership at the top. A good, transformational chief executive generates a sense of urgency and acts as a catalyst for change.

Winchell: I can also think of plenty of dynamic leaders who drove their companies right into the ground.

Parker: Don't be too cynical, Brad. I really think things are changing in this organization. I've never seen the top brass so excited. Everyone at Nelson ABC Foods has to be an "owner of the process," according to Lawrence. In other words, we've all got to stop reacting to change as a series of sudden surprises and start looking at it as a continuum. That's the only way we can keep abreast of it.

Swarbrick: So what does Alex see as the responsibilities of managers?

Parker: To guide, energize and excite other people rather than just supervise them.

　　迪馬哥的想法是要能掌控時代的變遷，而不是被牽著鼻子走。帕克也說：「由於變化能帶來進步，所以你必須敞開胸襟來接受它。」

帕克：　每個人在本能上都會懼怕新的和未知的事物，但我們必得要接受變革，因為進步就是由此而來。而變革也能使我們發現事業的新機。假如我們沒有這種觀念的話，我們的競爭對手一定會先發制人。

溫謝爾：　我有個疑問。亞力士在這裡所扮演的角色是甚麼？把事情都交由委員會或甚麼的來處理，這看來不像是亞力士的作風。

帕克：　亞力士從來沒有把自己定位為最高決策者。勞倫斯稱他為「轉型式領導者」。你看，為了要使公司能成功地轉變，上面就必須要有強勢且充滿生氣的領導風格。一位好的轉型式最高主管可以激使員工感受變革的迫切性，並且能為變革催生。

溫謝爾：　但我也可以想到有好些充滿幹勁的領導者把公司搞得一敗塗地。

帕克：　布雷，不要太過嘲諷了。我真的認為公司正在經歷一場變革。我從來沒有看過那些高層主管這麼興奮。勞倫斯認為，尼爾森ABC食品公司的每一位員工都應該「有分於這個過程」。換句話說，我們都不應該再把變革視作一連串突如其來的驟變，反該將之視為一個連續體，是本來就要有的東西。而這是我們能跟上時代的唯一辦法。

史瓦布利克：　那麼，亞力士認為經理人的職責為何？

帕克：　經理人要能指導、激勵和振奮員工，而非僅是盡監督之責而已。

Lesson 36 Managing Change (3)

Words and Phrases

instinctively 本能地	drive something into the ground
embrace 擁抱	把某事弄得一敗塗地
turn over 移交	cynical 冷嘲熱諷的
or whatever 或是任何其他的 (事	top brass 高級主管 (官員)
物)	in other words 換句話說
decision maker 決策者	react 反應
transformational 轉型的	continuum [kən'tɪnjʊəm] 連續
forceful 強勢的	(體)
urgency 迫切	

Vocabulary Building

- **beat someone to the punch**　先發制人；搶先
  We hoped to be the first to market frozen yogurt, but XYZ Foods beat us to the punch.
  (我們希望能成為首次推出冷凍優格的廠商, 但卻被 XYZ 食品公司捷足先登了。)

- **catalyst**　觸媒；催化劑
  The town officials hoped that the new resort would act as a catalyst for local development.
  (鎮上官員希望這個新的休閒度假勝地能刺激地方上的發展。)

- **keep abreast of**　與⋯並駕齊驅
  It's hard to keep abreast of all the new developments in my field.
  (在我的工作領域中, 要想跟上所有最新發展是相當困難的。)

- **energize**　鼓舞；激勵
  He's trying to energize the organization by revamping the compensation system.
  (他重新修訂薪資系統, 以提振公司士氣。)

1. You just can't <u>wait for</u> Lady Luck to <u>come</u>; you should go out <u>and</u> find
          A   B   C

   <u>it</u>.
   D

2. In the <u>old day</u>, my father <u>had a</u> <u>short fuse</u> when I didn't <u>complete</u> my
          A   B   C   D

   work.

3. My family <u>will</u> lose <u>their faces</u> if I <u>don't</u> <u>get accepted</u> by Yale.
            A   B   C   D

◆◆◆◆◆◆◆◆◆◆◆◆◆ 簡短對話 ◆◆◆◆◆◆◆◆◆◆◆◆◆◆

Winchell: The top brass may be excited, but personally I find it hard to share
   the enthusiasm. I feel more like crawling into a hole and hibernating for
   a while.

Parker: Brad, I realize that the merger and move to Chicago have placed a
   lot of pressures on you, but try not to be too negative about things.

Winchell: Well, I suppose you're right. But recently I've come to feel like
   a pawn in some game that Alex is playing. I don't have any sense of
   controlling my own destiny.

---

top brass　(政府、軍隊、企業的) 高層主管　　**crawl into a hole**　鑽進洞裡
hibernate　冬眠　　**pawn**　(棋的) 卒子　　**destiny**　命運

Lesson 36

Managing Change (4) (掌控時代的變遷)

● 預習 — *Sentences*

- We'll have to delegate more and trust more.
- He's giving people at every level a chance to win.
- What did you think of Gil's speech to the troops?
- Do you understand what's happening here?
- Middle management has been hacked to pieces.

● *Vignette*

Parker: Alex knows that if we're going to get the speed we need to respond to competition, we'll have to delegate more and trust more. He also feels that he has removed the layers of management that slowed things down, and he's giving people at every level a chance to win—or lose. At the top levels throughout the company, we have to undo the 19th-century idea of management and convince our managers that their role is not to stay "on top" of things but rather to foster self-confidence in the ranks.

*   *   *

Winchell: Well, what did you think of Gil's speech to the troops, Shoichi? Do you understand what's happening here?

Sawasaki: I think the idea of managing change is an interesting one. But I'm not sure the people in senior management are really ready to give up their control and trust the staff to do things properly.

Swarbrick: I'm with you on that. Some of those old guys will never loosen their grip on the reins.

Egler: Well, there aren't too many old guys left. Most have taken early retirement as part of the downsizing of the company. And we haven't been left with too many young guys either— middle management has been hacked to pieces.

Winchell: We baby boomers are moving into middle age at exactly the wrong time. On an individual level, managing change may be a matter of packing your own parachute and thinking of yourself as a free agent.

迪馬哥認為，經理人的職責不單只是管理下屬而已，更該要指導他們、激勵他們和振奮他們。他也相當重視對部屬的權限委任和對他們的信任。

帕克： 亞力士知道，如果我們要能來得及在面對競爭時採取任何動作，則我們對下屬的權限委任和信任度都要增加。他也覺得自己已經將會令事情進展緩慢的管理階層拿掉了，這使得每一層級的員工都有機會成功 —— 或是失敗。至於整個公司的高層主管則都應摒棄十九世紀的管理觀念，我們也當讓經理人瞭解，他們的角色並非「居高臨下」，而是要培養員工的自信心。

＊　　＊　　＊

溫謝爾： 嗯，昭一，你對吉爾所說的那番話有甚麼看法？你可知道這裡發生了甚麼事？

澤崎： 我認為掌控時代變遷是個蠻有意思的觀念。只是我不敢確定那些高層主管是否真的準備要鬆手，放心讓部屬去做了。

史瓦布利克： 這點我同意你的看法。有些大老把權限都抓得死緊，絕不願鬆手的。

艾格勒： 嗯，現在所剩的大老不多了。有很多人在公司縮編的時候就提早退休了。而年輕的也不太多，因為公司的中層管理階級都被打散了。

溫謝爾： 我們這群戰後嬰兒潮也真是倒楣，偏偏在這種錯誤的時機邁入中年。就個人層面而言，掌控時代變遷可能就是把你的降落傘打包好，準備跳機當自由人了。

Lesson 36 Managing Change (4)

Words and Phrases

layer of management	管理階層	loosen one's grip on the reins	
undo	摒棄；取消		放鬆控制權
convince	使人信服	early retirement	提前退休
stay "on top" of things	掌握狀況	middle management	中層管理階級
foster	培養	be hacked to pieces	砍成碎片
troops	一般職員；士兵 (常用複數)	free agent	不受契約限制的職員
give up	放棄		〈棒球的「自由契約選手」〉

Vocabulary Building

- **delegate**　授權；派代表
  cf. The art of delegation is one of the most difficult skills to learn and use.
  (授權是最難以學習運用的技巧之一。)

- **(the) ranks**　一般職員；具有共通特性的一群人
  Having worked 32 years for the same company, Bob has joined the ranks of the unemployed.
  (鮑伯已經在同一家公司工作了三十二年，但最後還是失業了。)

- **I'm with you.**　我同意你的看法。
  "The food is terrible in this restaurant."— "I'm with you. We should never come back here again."
  (「這家餐廳的食物糟透了。」「我有同感，我們下次絕對不要再來。」)

- **parachute**　降落傘
  Paul's golden parachute made the loss of his job a lot less painful.
  (保羅的黃金降落傘〈離職金或遣散費〉減輕了他失業的痛苦。)

在下列例句中，每句各有四個劃線部分，
其中一個的文法有誤，請將之選出。　　(解答見264頁)

1. Because of you are poor preparation, you failed the test.
　　　A　　　　B　　　　　　　　C　　D

2. From now on, we advise that you try study harder or you may flunk out
　　　　　A　　　　　　　　　　　B　　　　　　　C
of school.
D

3. I'm afraid I'll have to take a rain check for your dinner invitation.
　　　A　　B　　　　C　　　　　　　　D

◆◆◆◆◆◆◆◆◆◆◆◆◆ 簡短對話 ◆◆◆◆◆◆◆◆◆◆◆◆◆◆

Sawasaki: I like Gil's point about our freedom to shape our own jobs.
That's something I think we tend to lose sight of.

Winchell: Sure, we may be able to make some decisions about our own
work, but what good does that do if somebody on high suddenly decides
to liquidate our division?

Sawasaki: Granted, that risk is there. But what's the point in worrying
about something that you have no control over? If you're really feeling
concerned, try just taking it one day at a time for a while, until you get
over it.

Winchell: If I ever do.

---

shape 塑造　　**lose sight of** 忽略　　**somebody on high** 某個位階高的人
liquidate 廢止；清算　　**granted** 是這樣沒錯　　**What's the point in . . . ?**
…有甚麼用?　　**get over it** 克服；撐過去

Lesson 36

Managing Change — 總結

希臘哲學家赫拉克賴脫 (Heraclitus) 說，「變化是唯一不會變的東西」。 (There is nothing permanent except change.) 這也就是說，自然界唯一的現實就是「變化」。

至於商業界，更是瞬息萬變。能一直固守創業時的經營項目而獲致成功的大企業可說是寥寥無幾。大家為要求生存，總得順應時勢作些改變。所以，若有電器商來經營塑膠業或金融業，石油公司參與教育事業，或是電話公司手下有花店和廣告代理，大家也見怪不怪了。

90年代商業的關鍵字之一是「變化」。當然了，從古希臘至今，這個世界一直在變。變化是個連續體 (continuum)。只是現代這個發生變化的「時間框框」 (time frame) 正在受到極端的壓縮。由於科技及通訊，特別是電視的發達，以往要歷時數年的變化，現在只要在「一夕之間」便可發生了。近來東歐急劇的民主化情勢便是一個極佳的例子。唯一可以斷言的是，今後變化的速度只會增加不會減少。

此後商務人員所必須具備的也不再僅是過去實務經驗的累積，他還得要有 innovation 與 adaptability (革新性與適應性)。而最最需要的就是能夠敏銳洞察變化，預測未來，並具備分析事物脈絡 (implications) 的能力。

大家都必須帶頭採行對公司有正面影響的變革。而且要養成一個思考的習慣，去發現怎麼做事才能比平時更有效率、更有效果。若我們對變化的生成一味抱持負面 (negative) 的態度，那不僅沒有好處，也是相當不智。

本課的內容用一句話來說，就是 "We can— and should— manage change instead of letting it manage us." (我們不但能，而且也應該要掌控變化，而非受變化控制。) 我們都該學著掌握自己的命運，而不要被命運中一連串的變局牽著鼻子走。

Code of Conduct

（行為規範）

◆ **Lesson 37 的內容** ◆

　　數年前，尼爾森曾經發生過一件有外國政要涉案的賄賂事件，成了大眾傳播界的焦點。所以此後公司對類似事情都一直保持高度的關切。但若在某個視賄賂為商業習慣的國家，則外商也很難判定是否要斷然拒絕行賄，或是將之當作「事業成本」來處理。不管怎樣，他們每年還是會做個全公司的問卷調查，要求大家告訴公司有否耳聞任何弊案，不要知情不報。

In Japan businesses are pretty lavish in their entertainment and gift-giving practices.

Lesson 37

Code of Conduct (1)（行為規範）

●預習 —Sentences

- It must be in my mail basket.
- Here's an ethical question for you.
- Do you make the bribes or make tracks?
- The company actually has an answer to that.
- How would the company code view that?

●Vignette

Winchell: Shoichi, have you seen that questionnaire on the code of ethics yet? It asks us to tell the company if we've seen any evidence of unethical conduct.

Sawasaki: It must be in my mail basket. Yeah, here it is. I see it comes complete with a bulky policy book on the conduct of business.

Winchell: Most of it has to do with making illegal contributions to political parties or foreign officials, but there are also sections dealing with conflict of interest, equal employment opportunity, and general business conduct.

Sawasaki: Here's an ethical question for you: What do you do when bribery is an accepted business practice in a foreign country where we buy a lot of their goods? Do you make the bribes or make tracks?

Winchell: The company actually has an answer to that. If a small "tip" or facilitating payment is expected before a local official will be prompted to do his duty, the purchasing officer is expected to pay it and log it like any business expense. But major bribes to local politicos are out.

Sawasaki: Another question: In Japan businesses are pretty lavish in their entertainment and gift-giving practices. How would the company code view that?

Winchell: The key words are "gifts of nominal value" and "modest entertainment." Those are acceptable.

澤崎也拿到了一份道德規範的問卷調查。這份問卷的用意是要大家據實填報自己所知悉的不道德行跡。另外，公司還附了一本關於商業行為的公司政策，其中大部分是關於對政黨和外國政府官員的非法捐贈。

溫謝爾： 昭一，你有沒有看到那個關於道德規範的問卷調查？它要求我們告訴公司，是否看見過任何不道德的行跡。

澤崎： 這東西一定是在我的信件籃裡。有了，在這兒。我看到除了問卷以外，還附帶一大本關於商業行為的公司政策。

溫謝爾： 那本書裡面大部分都是在講對於政黨和外國政府人員的非法獻金，不過，裡頭也有些是談到利益衝突、就業機會均等、以及一般的商業行為。

澤崎： 這兒有一個道德問題要考考你：如果有這麼一個我們跟他大量買辦貨品的國家，收受賄賂是他們做生意上公認的商業習慣，那你怎麼辦？入境隨俗嗎？還是馬上撤退？

溫謝爾： 事實上，公司對於這個問題是有解答的。如果當地官員期望我們先給點「小費」或是付點業務促進費，之後，他們才會願意去做他們份內該做的事，那麼，公司會希望負責採購的人就照付這筆錢，並將之視同業務費用來登錄。可是，公司不允許用大筆金錢來賄賂當地政客。

澤崎： 另外一個問題：在日本商業界，招待和送禮的習慣通常會花掉很多錢。公司的規章如何看待這件事？

溫謝爾： 關鍵字就是：「小額的饋贈」和「適度的招待」。這些是公司可以接受的。

Lesson 37　Code of Conduct (1)

Words and Phrases

code of conduct　行為規範
questionnaire　問卷調查
ethics　道德
evidence　跡象
unethical　不道德的
mail basket　信件籃
bulky　厚重的
illegal　非法的
bribery　賄賂
accepted business practice　得到認
　可的商業慣例；公認的商業習慣

facilitating　有促進之效的；能以助
　長的
prompt someone to　促使某人…
purchasing officer　負責採購的
　人；採購官員
business expense　業務費用
politico　政客
lavish　浪費的；奢侈的
entertainment　招待
nominal　微少的

Vocabulary Building

● **conflict of interest**　利害衝突
One of the board members abstained from the vote because of a potential conflict of interest.
(由於潛在的利害衝突，委員會中有一名委員放棄了他的投票權。)

● **equal employment opportunity**　就業機會均等
I'm all for equal employment opportunity, but I have a problem with the idea of employment quota.
(我完全贊同就業機會均等的做法，只是，對於雇用限額的構想，我覺得有問題。)

● **make tracks**　(快速)離去
We'd better make tracks if we want to beat the rush-hour traffic.
(為趕在交通顛峰時間之前，我們最好快點走。)

● **log**　記錄
Be sure to log all your expenses before you forget them.
(趁你還記得，一定要把你所有的開支都記錄下來。)

▶ *Exercises*

在下列例句中，每句各有四個劃線部分，
其中一個的文法有誤，請將之選出。

（解答見264頁）

1. Kim should not be <u>chain smoking</u> <u>during</u> her <u>pregnant</u>, but she just can't
   $\qquad\quad$ A $\qquad\qquad$ B $\qquad\quad$ C

   seem to <u>kick</u> the habit.
   $\qquad$ D

2. It is not <u>advisable</u> to say <u>nothing</u> in the staff meeting <u>that</u> you <u>don't</u>
   $\qquad\quad$ A $\qquad\qquad$ B $\qquad\qquad\qquad$ C $\qquad$ D

   want the entire company to know about.

3. The key to success, <u>I think</u>, is <u>have</u> not only modern equipment, <u>but also</u>
   $\qquad\qquad\qquad$ A $\qquad\quad$ B $\qquad\qquad\qquad\qquad$ C

   capable <u>staff</u>.
   $\qquad$ D

◆◆◆◆◆◆◆◆◆◆◆◆◆ 簡短對話 ◆◆◆◆◆◆◆◆◆◆◆◆◆

Sawasaki: The issue of ethics is tough in a multinational organization like this, because we have to deal with so many different sets of practices and assumptions.

Winchell: You mean, what's accepted as ethical here may not be in a country like Japan, or vice versa?

Sawasaki: Right. For example, the casual approach that U.S. companies take in letting employees go is something that definitely doesn't go over well in Japan. I think it does involve differing views of right and wrong.

---

tough 艱難的；嚴苛的　　**multinational organization** 多國企業　　**assumption** 前提；假設　　**vice versa** 反之亦同　　**let go** 解雇　　**go over well** 受好評

Lesson 37

Code of Conduct (2) （行為規範）

預習 — *Sentences*

· Here I see a question that's a real mouthful.
· What would happen if I blew the whistle?
· My career here would be over.
· The charge would do nothing but damage.
· The company just wants these on file.

Vignette

Sawasaki: But the question is, what's "modest" when the sales people complain that they can't properly entertain their important customers against competition for less than a couple of hundred dollars a person in a Tokyo night spot?

Winchell: Wow! That much.

Sawasaki: Here I see a question that's a real mouthful: "Do you have knowledge of any false or artificial entries that have been made in the books and records of the company, such as the payment of any suppliers, consultants, agents, or any other parties for products or services not supplied?"

Winchell: That's quite a problem. Even if I knew for certain of a case like that, can you imagine what would happen if I blew the whistle on a fellow employee? Even if he or she were dismissed for unethical conduct, my career here would be over. No one would trust me. And if the person denied it? The charge would do nothing but damage, especially to me.

Sawasaki: Do you really think so? I'm not so sure.

Winchell: I hate to be cynical, but I think these questionnaires will all be turned in marked, "no, no, no"—like the three Japanese monkeys:"Hear no evil, speak no evil, see no evil." I think the company just wants these on file in case of legal trouble. That way they can say, "But your honor, we specifically asked . . . "

Sawasaki: Why don't we go talk to Peter Swarbrick for some more background on this?

*　　*　　*

溫謝爾說，他覺得大家會效法那三隻分別象徵「非禮勿聽，非禮勿言，非禮勿視」的日本猴子，在問卷上填入「沒有、沒有、沒有」，然後繳回。

澤崎： 可是問題在於，如果業務人員抱怨說，他們無法在東京帶客戶到那種消費額少於一人兩百美元的夜總會，因為那樣的招待太寒酸，敵不過其他的競爭者。在這種時候，甚麼叫做「適度」？

溫謝爾： 哇，要那麼多錢！

澤崎： 這裡我看到一個非常冗長又拗口的問題：「你知道在公司帳簿中，有任何不實或人為的帳目嗎？像是一些虛付給上游廠商、諮詢顧問、代理商、或是其他相關單位的費用，而公司實際上並沒有得到任何貨品或是服務。」

溫謝爾： 這真的是個問題。就算我真知道有這樣的事情，你可以想像如果我告發同事，會有甚麼後果嗎？即便這位同事因其不道德的行為遭到解雇，但我在這兒的工作也完了，因為沒人會信任我。而且，假如這個被告發的同事否認有這樣的事情，那這個指控只會造成損害，特別是對我自己。

澤崎： 你真的這麼認為嗎？我不是很確定。

溫謝爾： 我並不喜歡嘲諷，可是，我覺得大家只會全數填上「沒有，沒有，沒有」，然後把問卷繳回 —— 就像那三隻日本猴子：「非禮勿聽，非禮勿言，非禮勿視」。我想公司這麼做只是要把這些東西存檔，以防萬一有法律上的麻煩。因為如此一來，他們就可以說，「可是法官大人，我們曾明確地問過…」

澤崎： 我們何不去找彼得・史瓦布利克，跟他談談這件事，多知道一點幕後情形。

* * *

Lesson 37   Code of Conduct (2)

Words and Phrases

night spot	夜總會	dismiss	解雇
have knowledge of	知道有某事	cynical	憤世嫉俗的
false	虛偽的	"hear no evil, speak no evil, see no evil"	「非禮勿聽，非禮勿言，非禮勿視」
artificial	人為的		
supplier	上游廠商		
agent	代理商	on file	存檔
party	當事人	your honor	法官大人 (稱呼用語)
know for certain	確實知道		

Vocabulary Building

- **mouthful**　長而難唸的字
  Some Slavic names are a real mouthful.
  (有些斯拉夫語的名字真的是又長又難唸。)

- **entry**　記載事項
  Phil wrote no entry in his diary on the day he got fired.
  (菲爾遭解雇的那天沒寫日記。)

- **(the) books**　帳簿
  We've just closed the books for the fiscal year.
  (我們才剛結清這個會計年度的帳簿。)

- **blow the whistle**　密告；內部告發
  cf. The whistle-blower ended up losing his job.
  (那個密告者到最後也搞丟了工作。)

1. I'm sick and tired <u>for</u> beating <u>around</u> the <u>bush</u> with <u>her</u>.
               A   B   C   D

2. John is <u>buttering up</u> customers in <u>hope</u> of selling more products <u>than</u>
             A   B   C
his colleagues <u>do</u>.
              D

3. TV news, <u>showing</u> almost <u>hourly</u>, <u>keeps</u> viewers up-to-date <u>on</u> world
             A   B   C   D
events.

◆◆◆◆◆◆◆◆◆◆◆◆◆ 簡短對話 ◆◆◆◆◆◆◆◆◆◆◆◆◆◆

Sawasaki: But if everybody were to take your attitude about blowing the whistle, how could unethical behavior ever be uncovered?

Winchell: That's not my problem.

Sawasaki: You're sounding awfully cynical again.

Winchell: I know, Shoichi, but look, if the company expects me to be a watchdog, it's up to them to convince me that it's not going to cost me my job. After all, I've got a wife and kids to support.

Sawasaki: You have a point. But as I'm sure you know, there's something you need to protect more carefully than your job.

Winchell: Yeah? What's that?

Sawasaki: Your self-respect.

---

be uncovered 暴露；發現　　**watchdog** 看門狗；看守者　　　**up to** 由…來決定
cost *v.* 使受損失　　**You have a point.** 這倒是個理由。　　　**self-respect** 自
尊心

Lesson 37

Code of Conduct (3) (行為規範)

●預習 — *Sentences*

· These questionnaires are completely confidential.
· Basically it's a way of securing employee involvement.
· Employees are encouraged to ask for clarification.
· The section we added came out of that process.
· They're also less likely to sue if they're dismissed.

●*Vignette*

Swarbrick: As I was saying earlier, these questionnaires are completely confidential, and you don't have to worry about attribution if you report knowledge of any instances of misconduct.

Sawasaki: But we were curious why the company distributes the questionnaire. Is it done every year?

Swarbrick: Yeah, we started the practice of having each employee fill one in annually after we had a messy bribery case involving several government officials of a certain foreign country a few years ago. But basically it's a way of securing employee involvement to keep the codes from just gathering dust on the shelf. Each year, we also hold compliance review meetings and employees at all levels are encouraged to ask for clarification of any workplace rules, whether written or unwritten, that they find fuzzy. The section we added a few years ago on freedom from sexual harassment actually came out of that process.

Winchell: I see. Psychologists say that people who have a voice in setting rules of behavior are less likely to violate them.

Swarbrick: Exactly. And what's even more important in this litigious age, they're also less likely to sue if they're dismissed when they violate them.

　　史瓦布利克說，公司之所以要作問卷調查，是因為數年前曾發生過有國外政府官員涉案的賄賂事件。此外，在公司每年召開的檢討會議中，各階層的員工只要覺得公司的規定有模稜兩可的情形，不管是成文或不成文規定，都可以要求公司澄清。

史瓦布利克： 就像我稍早所說的一樣，這些問卷是完全保密的。而且，如果你向上級報備了所知悉的任何不法情事，你也不用擔心其歸屬問題。

澤崎： 可是我們很好奇，公司為甚麼要發這些問卷，每年都會做嗎？

史瓦布利克： 是啊，幾年前，公司曾爆發過一椿複雜的弊案，涉案的是某國的幾位政府官員。自從那次以後，我們每年都會要員工填問卷。不過，這基本上是一個可讓員工都參與其中，而不使那些公司規章徒然在架上蒙灰的方式。每年，我們也會召開紀律遵守情況的檢討會議，各階層員工若對任何工作守則有疑問，不管是成文或不成文的，只要他們覺得有模稜兩可的情形，我們都鼓勵他們把問題提出來，讓公司來澄清。事實上，我們幾年前在規章中加入了一個叫做員工有免於性騷擾的自由的條文，就是透過這種程序產生。

溫謝爾： 我瞭解了。心理學家說，在訂定行為規範的事上，人們如果能有發言權，那他們比較不可能以身試法。

史瓦布利克： 一點沒錯。而且更重要的是，在這個人人都愛循法律途徑解決的世代，萬一有員工因違規而遭解雇，他也比較不可能到法院去告我們。

Lesson 37 Code of Conduct (3)

Words and Phrases

confidential	機密的	workplace rules	工作場所的規則
attribution	歸屬	written or unwritten	成文或不成
messy	複雜的	文的 (規則)	
bribery case	賄賂事件	sexual harassment	性騷擾
government official	政府官員	psychologist	心理學家
employee involvement	員工的參與	have a voice in	在…上有發言權
compliance review meeting	檢討	violate	違反
員工遵守紀律情況的會議		sue	控告
clarification	澄清; 說明		

Vocabulary Building

- **misconduct**　違法行為
  Robert was dismissed on the ground of serious misconduct.
  (羅伯特因為犯下嚴重的違法行為, 所以被解雇了。)

- **gather dust on the shelf**　在架上蒙灰; 被束之高閣
  I bought some German-language textbooks, but they're just gathering dust on the shelf.
  (我買了一些德文教科書, 可是他們現在正在書架上生灰塵。)

- **fuzzy**　不明確的; 模稜兩可的; 乏晰
  Some Japanese researchers are working hard on applications of fuzzy logic.
  (一些日本研究人員正在努力發展乏晰邏輯的應用技術。)

- **litigious** [lɪ'tɪdʒɪəs]　好訴訟的
  cf. People in this country are too ready to resort to litigation.
  (這個國家的人動不動就要去法院拉鈴上訴。)

110

▶ *Exercises*

在下列例句中，每句各有四個劃線部分，
其中一個的文法有誤，請將之選出。　　　　(解答見 264 頁)

1. If Anita <u>read</u> the <u>instructions</u> <u>before starting</u> the machine, she wouldn't
      　　　A　　　　　B　　　　　　C
   have <u>encountered</u> so many problems.
          D

2. Our president <u>made up his mind</u> to <u>postpone</u> <u>to release</u> the <u>results</u> of
                        A　　　　　　　B　　　　C　　　　　D
   the climate survey.

3. Tommy used to work for a <u>trading house</u>, but he <u>was let go</u> after criticiz-
                                 A　　　　　　　　　　B
   ing <u>it's</u> lack <u>of</u> leadership.
       C　　　　D

◆◆◆◆◆◆◆◆◆◆◆◆◆ 簡短對話 ◆◆◆◆◆◆◆◆◆◆◆◆◆

Winchell: Peter, do you believe that we can take the company's assurances at face value?

Swarbrick: You know, I really do, even though I can't offer you any concrete evidence to back that up.

Winchell: So why do you think so?

Swarbrick: It's because of the general tone that Alex and the rest of the management team sets. They've managed to make it clear that their own moral standards are high, and so I'm confident that they'll keep any promises they make.

---

take something at face value 以其表面價值來看待某事　　**assurance** 保證
back up 支持　　　**tone** 調子　　**make something clear** 使某事清楚明白
moral standards 道德標準

Lesson 37

Code of Conduct (4) （行為規範）

●預習 —*Sentences*

- We designated a group of employees to set rules.
- They came up with a code that was more restrictive.
- Buy our cereal and you won't get cancer.
- Food companies have gone overboard in selling health.
- That's a good point.

●*Vignette*

Swarbrick: I'll give you an example. Last year we designated a group of employees—composed of smokers and nonsmokers, men and women, executives and secretaries, old-timers and newcomers—to set rules about smoking in the workplace. They came up with a code that was more restrictive than the smokers wanted but that stopped short of the total ban that many nonsmokers had been pushing for.

Sawasaki: I guess that also shows the rules are more acceptable if the people who have to observe them can take part in drawing them up. Right?

Swarbrick: Right.

Winchell: Some of us have an ethical problem with our current cereal advertising, which in essence says, "Buy our cereal and you won't get cancer." I think food companies have gone overboard in selling health. Nowadays the supermarket food aisles look like a modern medicine show, with all sorts of inflated claims for products' power against all sorts of medical complaints.

Swarbrick: That's a good point. In fact, it's bound to come up at the next review session.

■狀況

　　澤崎理解到，假如法規本身的執行對象也能參與其草擬過
程，則這些規定會更能令人接受。而溫謝爾則指出了「買我們的
麥片，你就不會得癌症」這個廣告詞在道德上的問題。

史瓦布利克：我舉個例子給你們聽。去年，我們指派了一組員工 —— 包括吸
　　菸者和非吸菸者，男性跟女性，主管與祕書，資深員工與新進人員 —— 來
　　訂定工作場所中關於吸菸的規定。結果他們訂出來的規章比吸菸者所希望
　　的還要嚴苛，不過它也不是以前那些非吸菸者所極力要求的全面禁止。

澤崎：我猜這也顯示，假如法規本身的執行對象也能參與其草擬過程，那這
　　些規定會更能令人接受。

史瓦布利克：沒錯。

溫謝爾：我們有些人對公司最近的麥片廣告有個道德上的疑問。那個廣告本
　　質上是說，「買我們的麥片，你就不會得癌症。」我覺得，如果食品公司
　　也在販賣健康，那實在是撈過界了。今天超級市場中的食品區過道，活像
　　是個現代醫藥展，滿了各種誇稱可勝過各種病痛的產品。

史瓦布利克：這個意見不錯。實際上，在我們下次的檢討會中，這一定會被
　　提出來討論的。

Lesson 37   Code of Conduct (4)

Words and Phrases

designate	指派	cereals	麥片
be composed of	由…所組成	go overboard	逸出常軌
restrictive	限制多的	food aisle [aɪl]	食品區的通道
total ban	全面禁止	medical complaint	病痛
observe	遵守	be bound to	一定會…
draw up	草擬		

Vocabulary Building

● **workplace**　　工作地方

The medical equipment manufacturer banned smoking in order to improve the workplace environment.

(為了改善工作環境，那個醫療設備製造商於是禁止吸菸。)

● **stop short of**　　沒有達到…

I reprimanded Rick severely, but stopped short of firing him.

(我很嚴厲地叱責了瑞克，但並沒有開除他。)

● **in essence**　　在本質上；重點上

In essence Kennedy's offer to give the company more capital was an attempt to take it over.

(甘迺迪願提供這家公司更多的資金，但其本意就是企圖取得該公司。)

● **inflated**　　誇大不實的

Peter made some inflated claims about his abilities on his résumé.

(彼得在他的履歷表上，膨脹了自己的能力。)

1. The <u>refugees</u> were <u>troubled</u> by the <u>hardship</u> of war <u>which</u> lasted more
      A   B   C   D

   than two years.

2. To hear Bette <u>says</u>, she's the <u>best</u> French <u>speaker</u> in her entire <u>class</u>.
            A   B   C   D

3. The researcher's <u>discoveries</u> in <u>genetics</u> brought him <u>a success</u> <u>in</u> the
               A   B   C   D

   academic community.

◆◆◆◆◆◆◆◆◆◆◆◆◆ 簡短對話 ◆◆◆◆◆◆◆◆◆◆◆◆◆

Winchell: In some countries, paying a little baksheesh is about like leaving a tip.

Swarbrick: Then how is baksheesh different from tipping?

Winchell: Let's see. You tip after a service is performed, and it's voluntary. But if the service won't even be performed unless you pay up front, it's baksheesh. You may have to pay it to get a package mailed, or to border officials to get out of a country. In those cases, it's never more than $10 or so.

Swarbrick: It's still dangerous. What is necessary in one country might land you in jail in another.

---

baksheesh [ˋbækʃiʃ] 賞錢　　**voluntary** 自願的　　**up front** *adv.* 在⋯之前　　**land in jail** 使入獄

Code of Conduct —— 總結

法律和道德的基準，會因國情和社會而有所不同。一般的美國企業對於賄賂 (bribes) 和回扣 (kickbacks) 等不正當的支付 (questionable or improper payments) 都採取嚴格的立場。至於在臺灣和日本等中秋、春節已成為習慣的節期性贈禮，則要由總公司查核，看其是否「企圖影響商業上的判斷」(intended to influence a business judgement)。

但是，更麻煩的是「奠儀」。在客戶或廠商方面有幹部死亡時，有時會需要包上數萬元的奠儀。可是美國人並沒有在葬禮上送錢的習慣，所以他們很難認可這筆開支。而且贈送奠儀可能不會有收據，所以也會有員工謊報金額的可能。

在 1970 年代中期，大多數的美國企業對於國外常有的 payoffs (賄賂)情形，產生了很大的道德質疑。此類支出在美國被清楚界定為賄賂，可是在當地卻認為是一種習慣而為一般所認可。

問題在於，到底要依照哪裡的道德標準來做生意呢？在賄賂與正當的 sales commission 之間，要如何來劃清界線呢？美國企業若把自己的道德基準「輸出」，那麼，在碰到與當地業界競爭的情況下，豈不是自縛手足嗎？

特別的是，若依照 Foreign Corrupt Practices Act 中的規定，則「為了獲取或保持生意上的往來而給與外國政府官員或政黨的金錢」(payment of any money or anything of value to a foreign official or foreign political party for purposes of obtaining or retaining business) 也是受到禁止的。

不過，在尼爾森 ABC 食品公司，若需要付小額的「小費」或是業務促進費 (a small "tip" or facilitating payment)，只要把這些當成業務費用登錄，那麼公司也默許了。

Plant Closing

（關閉工廠）

◆ Lesson 38 的內容 ◆

　　公司突然要關閉堪薩斯工廠 —— 這個早在二次大戰之前就有的老舊工廠。由於其廠齡的關係，公司認為，要把其中的設備全部汰舊換新，會花上一大筆錢，而且投資報酬率可能也會很差。所以基於利潤的考量，公司決定關廠。雖然新近的大幅裁員才告一段落，但還會再有三百名左右的勞工失業。當然，公司會付給遣散費，並會盡可能地幫他們找到新工作，不過，因為中西部的就業市場實在也不怎麼景氣，所以一般預料，這將會是一次怨聲載道的關廠行動。

A lot of the
blue-collar
employees
probably will
be out on
the street.

Plant Closing (1) （關閉工廠）

●預習 — *Sentences*

- They're closing the Kansas City plant.
- What are they doing with the operations?
- The Kansas City plant is considered too old for retooling.
- But most of the people are nonmanagerial types.
- A lot of the blue-collar employees will be out on the street.

●*Vignette*

Winchell: Oh, Shoichi. Have you heard about DeMarco wielding the ax again?

Sawasaki: No, what do you mean?

Winchell: They're closing the Kansas City plant. I haven't heard any official reasons yet, but KC was one of the oldest plants in ABC Foods. I suppose we should be surprised Alex hung on to it as long as he did.

Sawasaki: What are they doing with the operations?

Winchell: From what I heard this morning, they'll turn the canning and packaging operations over to the Tennessee and New Jersey plants. They both already have computer integrated manufacturing, and you know Alex wants all of our plants to be state-of-the-art CIM by 1998. I guess the Kansas City plant is considered too old for retooling.

Murphy: Oh, hi, Brad. Well, Shoichi, I gather you've already heard about Kansas City. You both have a meeting with Gil in 25 minutes.

Sawasaki: I imagine some of the workers there can be transferred if they want to move.

Murphy: Yeah, if they're willing to relocate. But most of the people are nonmanagerial types. Some have been with ABC Foods so long they've forgotten what it's like to do anything else.

Sawasaki: A lot of the blue-collar employees probably will be out on the street.

118

溫謝爾聽到消息說，堪薩斯城的工廠要關閉了。而它原來的罐頭和包裝作業則將移轉到田納西和紐澤西的工廠。

溫謝爾：噢，昭一。你聽到迪馬哥又在動斧了嗎？

澤崎：沒有啊，你指的是甚麼？

溫謝爾：他們將要關閉堪薩斯城的工廠。我還沒聽到甚麼正式理由。不過，堪薩斯工廠是 ABC 食品公司最老舊的工廠之一。我認為，如果亞力士還要繼續保留這間工廠，那我們才真該驚訝。

澤崎：那這工廠原來的運作要怎麼辦？

溫謝爾：據我今早所聽到的，他們要把罐頭和包裝作業轉移到田納西和紐澤西的工廠。這兩個工廠目前都已經有電腦一貫生產的作業流程了。你也知道的，亞力士要在 1998 年之前把我們所有的廠房都改成最新的 CIM 作業。我猜他們可能是認為堪薩斯城的工廠太過老舊，無法重新改裝吧！

墨菲：哦，嗨，布雷。嗯，昭一，我看你已經知道堪薩斯城的事了。二十五分鐘後，你們兩位與吉爾有個會要開。

澤崎：我猜想，如果那兒的員工願意搬家的話，應該可以調任吧！

墨菲：是啊，如果他們願意重新安家的話。不過大部分的人都不是管理級的職員。有些人跟著 ABC 食品公司都好久了，以至他們早已忘記做其他事情是甚麼樣子了。

澤崎：不少藍領階級的作業員可能會面臨失業一途。

Lesson 38 Plant Closing (1)

Words and Phrases

KC   Kansas City 的簡稱
operations   運作; 作業
canning   罐頭
packaging   包裝
computer integrated manufacturing, CIM   電腦一貫作業
retooling   重新整裝

gather   推測; 考慮
relocate   遷徙他地
nonmanagerial type   非主管階級的人
blue-collar employee   藍領階級的勞動者

Vocabulary Building

- **wield the ax**   揮動斧頭; 砍別人的頭
  Few executives are so cold-blooded as to enjoy wielding the ax.
  (很少有主管會冷血到以裁人為樂。)

- **hang on to**   固守; 堅守
  If you hang on to everything with sentimental value, you'll end up buried in your belongings.
  (如果你太重感情, 每一件東西都捨不得丟, 終有一天, 你會被埋在你所有的東西底下。)

- **transfer**   調任
  cf. Some employees refuse to be transferred abroad for family reasons.
  (有些員工因為家庭的緣故, 拒絕調到國外。)

- **be out on the street**   失業
  I found myself out on the street just as the holiday season was approaching.
  (正當新年假期來到之際, 我卻得知自己失業了。)

120

1. Professor Smith <u>goes over</u> his <u>student's</u> papers <u>with</u> a fine-tooth <u>comb</u>.
                       A   B   C   D

2. <u>As long as</u> I am concerned, <u>normal</u> <u>body</u> temperature is 36 degrees
      A   B   C
   <u>centigrade</u>.
      D

3. Mr. Burns <u>attributes</u> his company's <u>success</u> <u>to</u> working <u>diligent</u>.
            A   B C   D

◆◆◆◆◆◆◆◆◆◆◆◆◆ 簡短對話 ◆◆◆◆◆◆◆◆◆◆◆◆◆◆◆

Sawasaki: Have you ever been to the plant?

Winchell: Yeah, I stopped by just last month.

Sawasaki: Oh, yes, you were checking out the new production line for those Krispie Krunchies.

Winchell: Yeah. What a mess! They were due to go on the market in a month, but there were still so many glitches in the manufacturing system that I could've cried.

Sawasaki: And I remember you told me that labor-management relations weren't too good either.

Winchell: They were the pits. It was practically open warfare.

---

stop by 途中經過訪問　　**check out** 調查　　**production line** 生產線
mess 混亂　　**due to** 預定要　　**go on the market** 上市發售　　**glitch**
(機器的)毛病；故障　　**labor-management relations** 勞資關係　　**pits** 最低
處；地獄　　**open warfare** 野戰

Plant Closing (2) （關閉工廠）

●預習 — *Sentences*

- How many people are there at the Kansas City plant?
- I heard there are almost 300, if you count the hourly workers.
- Even 300 jobless is a lot for any Midwestern city to absorb.
- They might try making a good product for a fair price.
- There's a real need for a careful handling of this closure.

●*Vignette*

Sawasaki: The company will give them a financial handshake and try to help them find new jobs. How many people are there at the Kansas City plant?

Winchell: I heard there are almost 300, if you count the hourly workers.

Sawasaki: That's not so many.

Murphy: The number of people thrown out of work may not be large by comparison with the huge job massacres that have been carried out in places like Detroit or Silicon Valley, but even 300 jobless is a lot for any Midwestern city to absorb these days.

Winchell: It's amazing that they still think downsizing the company is the answer to something. If you ask me, they don't know what's wrong and they can't think of anything else to do.

Murphy: They might try making a good product for a fair price.

Sawasaki: I've got to go back to my office and pick up my note pads. See you later in Gil's office, Brad.

Winchell: OK. See you, Shoichi.

*   *   *

Parker: There's a real need for a careful handling of this closure. We don't want people to think the company is doing this casually or out of desperation. We have many sensitive points to consider. We have to avoid lawsuits, for one thing. Every time a plant closes, that's a risk.

　　聽說堪薩斯城工廠的員工，包括時薪制的雇員在內，有將近三百位左右。若跟底特律或矽谷等地的大幅裁員相比，這樣的數字可能不太多，但由於這次裁員是發生在中西部的堪薩斯，所以情況也不能同日而語。

澤崎：　公司會付給他們一筆遣散費，一次給付，並設法幫他們找新工作。堪薩斯城工廠的員工有多少？

溫謝爾：　我聽說有將近三百位，假如連按時計酬的雇員也算進去的話。

澤崎：　那不太多嘛！

墨菲：　如果要跟底特律或矽谷的大幅裁員相比，這樣的數目可能不太多。不過，在這個時候，以一個中西部城市而言，要吸收這三百名失業人口也太多了。

溫謝爾：　令人震驚的是，他們還是認為公司能藉裁員來解決某些問題。如果你問我的話，我會告訴你，他們根本不知道問題在哪裡，也不知道除了裁員之外還能做甚麼。

墨菲：　他們或許可以嘗試生產一種價格合理的優良產品。

澤崎：　我得回辦公室去拿拍紙簿了。布雷，一會兒再跟你在吉爾的辦公室碰頭。

溫謝爾：　好的。昭一，待會兒見。

＊　　　＊　　　＊

帕克：　關於這次的關廠，真的是需要小心處理。我們不希望大家以為公司在草率處理此事，或只是走投無路才這麼做。我們得考慮很多敏感的問題，其中一個就是，我們得避免有訴訟事件發生。每次有工廠關閉，就會有這種危險。

Lesson 38　Plant Closing (2)

Words and Phrases

hourly worker	按時支薪的雇員	downsizing	企業規模縮小; 裁員
out of work	失業中	note pads	拍紙簿
by comparison with	與…相比	handling	處理
job massacre	大量裁員	casually	馬虎地; 隨便地
jobless	失業者	desperation	絕望; 走投無路
these days	近來	lawsuit	訴訟案件
amazing	令人驚異的	risk	危險; 風險

Vocabulary Building

- **financial handshake**　一次領完的退休金或獎金

  The financial handshake that the laid-off employees got should tide them over for a few months.

  (遭解雇的員工可以領到一筆遣散費, 一次領清, 這筆錢可維持他們度過幾個月。)

- **absorb**　吸收

  I see you absorbed in thought. What's on your mind?

  (我看得出來你在深思之中。你在想些甚麼?)

- **closure**　封閉

  The plant closure dealt a major blow to the city's economy.

  (關廠事件對於這個城市的經濟是一大打擊。)

- **for one thing**　其一

  I'm not satisfied with your performance on the job. For one thing, you've been coming in late much too often.

  (我對你在工作上的表現並不滿意。其中一點是, 你太常遲到了。)

(解答見 265 頁)

▶ **Exercises** 在下列例句中，每句各有四個劃線部分，其中一個的文法有誤，請將之選出。

1. When Kathy <u>saw</u> that the audience was enthralled <u>by</u> her superb perform-
   A   B
   ance, she <u>felt</u> <u>dazzling</u> by her success.
             C   D

2. I was <u>so</u> shocked to <u>hear</u> the news of my company's bankruptcy that I
           A   B
   <u>didn't feel like</u> <u>to go</u> out.
       C   D

3. People <u>have</u> largely refused <u>listening</u> <u>to</u> the government's request <u>for</u>
         A   B   C   D
   water conservation.

◆◆◆◆◆◆◆◆◆◆◆◆◆ 簡短對話 ◆◆◆◆◆◆◆◆◆◆◆◆◆◆

Sawasaki: I suppose a plant closing like that can really do a job on the local economy.

Winchell: Can it ever! It's not just the people losing their paychecks who are affected. Sometimes it can put the whole local retail sector on the skids.

Sawasaki: Also, I'd imagine that it must depress property values if a lot of people try to relocate and put their homes on the market.

Winchell: That's right. A lot of people may find it hard to unload their houses at any price.

---

do a job on 使垮臺; 搞得一團亂　　**paycheck** (以支票形式給付的) 薪資
affect 影響　　**retail sector** 零售業　　**on the skids** 走下坡; 即將失敗
depress 降低; 使不景氣　　**property value** 不動產價格　　**relocate** 遷徙他
地　　**unload** 出售

Lesson 38

Plant Closing (3) (關閉工廠)

●預習 — *Sentences*

· What would be the grounds for a suit?
· There are labor laws, like the rules against union-busting.
· The tax implications are also rather complex.
· We'll be doing everything possible to help them.
· Actually, the closure will be a fairly slow process.

●*Vignette*

Sawasaki: What would be the grounds for a suit?

Parker: Oh, there are a number of different laws against just packing up a plant and moving it. Then there are labor laws, like the rules against union-busting. The tax implications are also rather complex. Anyway, if we do this the right way, paying proper attention to the legal aspects, it'll mean that both the company and the employees are well taken care of. We've got to make it clear that we're not "firing people." We're eliminating positions.

Winchell: I'm sure that distinction will be a great comfort to a 15-year veteran of the cannery.

Parker: It's true that it's hard on some people, Brad, but we'll be doing everything possible to help them. Now, let's get back on the track and look at the plant closing checklist.

*   *   *

Murphy: Clarence? Got a minute?

Williams: Sure, Patti, what's up?

Murphy: I was just thinking about some friends of mine in the Kansas City plant and I was wondering how long they'll have a job.

Williams: Actually, the closure will be a fairly slow process. They won't just lock the doors some morning. I imagine it'll take several months to move some of the operations. And a lot of people will be kept on for some time after the plant's technically closed 'cause they'll be needed to help with the "winding down" process— paperwork and so forth.

126

　　要關閉工廠可不是說關就關。光是把實際作業移轉到其他工廠就要花上數個月之久。而工廠在其運作停擺之後，也還要有些工作人員來處理善後事宜。

澤崎： 訴訟的根據會是甚麼？

帕克： 噢，有許多不同的法規禁止公司就這樣子把工廠打包好搬家。還有，勞工法上也有禁止破壞工會的條例。而稅金上的牽扯也相當複雜。不管怎樣，只要我們用正確的方式來做，好好注意法律方面的問題，那麼，公司和員工雙方都會得到妥善的處理。而且我們必須讓他人明白，公司並不是在「裁員」。我們只是在減少一些職位。

溫謝爾： 我確定那樣的區別對於一個在罐頭工廠工作了十五年的老手而言，會是個很大的安慰。

帕克： 布雷，對某些人來說，這件事的確讓人很不好過，可是，我們會盡一切的可能來幫助他們。現在，讓我們回到正題，看一下關廠清單。

　　　　　　　　＊　　　＊　　　＊

墨菲： 克雷倫斯？你有沒有一點時間？

威廉斯： 當然，派蒂，是甚麼事？

墨菲： 我剛剛在想我在堪薩斯城工廠工作的一些朋友，不知道他們還能做多久？

威廉斯： 實際上，關廠這件事會進行得相當緩慢。他們不會在某個早晨就突然把門關了。我推測，廠裡一些作業的轉移可能會花上幾個月的時間。而且，工廠在運作停擺之後，公司還是得留下不少人，因為他們還得幫忙處理後續的關門事宜 —— 一些文件處理等的。

Lesson 38 Plant Closing (3)

Words and Phrases

suit 訴訟

pack up 收拾打包

labor laws 勞工法

union-busting 破壞工會的

tax implications 稅金的牽連

eliminate a position 削減職位

distinction 區別

comfort 安慰

cannery 罐頭工廠

Got a minute? 你有空嗎?

What's up? 甚麼事; 發生甚麼事了?

lock the doors 關門大吉

'cause (<because) 因為

wind down 慢慢地停下來

paperwork 文件處理

and so forth 等等

Vocabulary Building

- **grounds** 根據; 理由
  Incompatibility is sufficient grounds for divorce in some states.
  (在某些州, 單是個性不合就足以構成離婚的理由了。)

- **veteran** 老手; 有經驗的人; 老資格
  The pharmaceutical company named a 15-year veteran of marketing operations to head the new public relations department.
  (這家藥廠任命一位有十五年經驗的行銷界老手來掌理新成立的公關部門。)

- **be hard on** 對…而言很辛苦
  The move to Chicago was hard on my kids.
  (搬到芝加哥對我的孩子們而言不是件容易的事。)

- **get back on the track** 言歸正傳
  It's time for us to leave that thought aside and get back on the track.
  (我們先把這種想法擱到一邊, 該回到正題上來了。)

▶ **Exercises**　在下列例句中，每句各有四個劃線部分，
其中一個的文法有誤，請將之選出。　（解答見 265 頁）

1. McIntyre Enterprise just completed a big deal to an Indian semiconduc-
<u>　　　　　　　　　A　　　　B　　　　　　　　C　D</u>

   tor company.

2. Robert's taste in clothing has never suited with Tim.
<u>　　　　　　　A　　B　　　　　C　　　D</u>

3. When you start working, you should join the corporate pension plan for
<u>　　　　　　A　　　　　　　　　B</u>

   the financial security it provides during your retirement.
<u>　　　　　　　　　　　　C　　　　　D</u>

◆◆◆◆◆◆◆◆◆◆◆◆◆◆ 簡短對話 ◆◆◆◆◆◆◆◆◆◆◆◆◆◆

Parker: Brad, I don't want you to think that management cares nothing about the fate of the employees being laid off.

Winchell: If management cares so much, why not retool the Kansas City plant instead of closing down?

Parker: That option was considered, but it turned out to be impractical in cost terms.

Winchell: In other words, the almighty bottom line is more important to the company than people's livelihoods.

Parker: Brad, but we're not running a charity. Our prime responsibility as a corporation is to make a profit for our shareholders.

---

retool 更新工廠的機械設備　　**option** 選擇　　**impractical** 不實際的
almighty 全能的　　**bottom line** 純益；利潤　　**livelihood** 生計　　**run a charity** 經營慈善事業　　**prime** 最重要的；第一的

Lesson 38

Plant Closing (4) （關閉工廠）

●預習 — *Sentences*

- We'll try to accommodate everybody who wants to relocate.
- Morale is zero, as you can imagine.
- That's one of the dangers of downsizing in any way.
- The survivors get nervous and lose faith in their employer.
- That takes a bit of the load off my mind.

●*Vignette*

Williams: Also don't forget that we'll try to accommodate everybody who wants to relocate. That probably won't be many, but the option is always there.

Murphy: They must be feeling terrible right now.

Williams: Oh, sure, morale is zero, as you can imagine. Even here at headquarters morale drops when something like this happens. That's one of the dangers of downsizing in any way. The survivors get nervous and lose faith in their employer. I hope this is the last time the company does anything this drastic.

Murphy: So what's the company doing for the people who are losing their jobs?

Williams: As you can imagine, we've had a lot of outplacement experience lately. There are several things we do for the people who are leaving, ranging from self-esteem counseling to training in interview and salary negotiations.

Murphy: Are we talking about factory workers?

Williams: Sure, if they want it, we'll help them prepare letters and résumé and try to find them suitable jobs in the area. The most important thing, as far as I'm concerned, is the health benefits package. The company picks up the bill for 90 days, and after that employees can keep their health benefits for up to 18 months as long as they pay the premiums. Many people do.

Murphy: That takes a bit of the load off my mind. I'm still sad the plant is closing, but it's good to know that the company isn't simply abandoning everybody.

　　堪薩斯工廠的員工士氣是零。這件事對總公司和其他工廠也開始產生影響。而公司對於這些即將離職的員工，也還有許多安排新工作的相關事宜要處理。

威廉斯：　而且不要忘記，對於想要搬遷的人，我們都會盡量給他們工作。想搬的人可能不會很多，但他們總是有這個選擇在。

墨菲：　　他們現在一定覺得糟透了。

威廉斯：　噢，當然，就如妳所能想像的，員工士氣是零。就算是在總公司這裡，如果有這種事發生，士氣也會大為低落。不管怎麼說，這都是裁員的危險之一。繼續留下的人會變得神經兮兮，不信任他們的老闆。我希望，這是公司最後一次做這麼激烈的事。

墨菲：　　對於丟掉飯碗的人，公司怎麼辦？

威廉斯：　就像妳所知道的，我們最近有不少在裁員之前為其安排新工作的經驗。對於將離開的人，我們會做幾件事，包括從提高自尊心的諮商，到如何面試以及如何跟人談薪水的訓練。

墨菲：　　我們是在講工廠作業員嗎？

威廉斯：　當然囉，如果他們要的話，我們還會協助他們準備信件和履歷表，並設法替他們在當地找到合適的工作。就我個人而言，最重要的事就是健康保險給付方案。公司在員工離職後的 90 天內，都還會負擔他們的醫療費用，在這以後，員工只要繳保費，那他們的健康保險就可以再持續一年半。很多人都是這樣。

墨菲：　　那我就稍微放心了。對於工廠要關的事，我還是很難過；不過，我也蠻高興知道，公司並不是僅僅把人遣走就算了。

Words and Phrases

accommodate	收容; 容納	interview	面試
morale [moˈræl]	士氣; 工作意願	factory worker	工廠作業員
survivor	倖存的人	résumé	履歷表
drastic	激烈的; 徹底的	health benefits package	健康保險給付方案
outplacement	在解雇人之前為其安排新工作	take the load off someone's mind	減輕某人心中的擔子
self-esteem counseling	為提高個人自尊心所作的諮商	abandon	拋棄

Vocabulary Building

- **relocate**　移居他處

  I wanted to relocate, but my wife said the move would interfere with her career.

  (我想搬到別的地方去, 可是我太太說, 搬家對她的事業會有所阻礙。)

- **option**　選擇; 選擇權

  If you seriously disapprove of your employer's actions, you always have the option of quitting.

  (假使你真的很不贊同你雇主的行為, 你總是可以選擇辭職他去一途。)

- **pick up the bill**　付帳

  Who's going to pick up the bill for cleaning up after the massive oil spill?

  (石油大量外洩後的清理費用要由誰來支付呢?)

- **premium**　保險金; 保費

  You will receive no benefits under this insurance policy unless your premiums are paid up in full.

  (按這保險條例, 除非你都能按時繳交保費, 否則將得不到任何給付。)

1. On Guam, <u>when</u> enjoying <u>its</u> wonderful climate, we should <u>take care</u> to
　　　　　　A　　　　　　　　B　　　　　　　　　　　　　C
   avoid <u>overexposure</u> to the sun.
　　　　　　D

2. <u>For</u> estimate how much it will <u>cost</u> to <u>visit</u> Chile, <u>add</u> the total cost of
   A　　　　　　　　　　　　　　B　　　　C　　　　　D
   air fare, hotels, meals, and ground transportation.

3. This old cabin, <u>that</u> I have been using every summer <u>since</u> I <u>was</u> in
　　　　　　　　　A　　　　　　　　　　　　　　　　　　　B　　　C
   kindergarten, was originally <u>built</u> by my uncle.
　　　　　　　　　　　　　　　　D

◆◆◆◆◆◆◆◆◆◆◆◆◆ 簡短對話 ◆◆◆◆◆◆◆◆◆◆◆◆◆

Williams: I didn't realize that you knew people at the plant.

Murphy: Actually, I used to live in the KC area for a while myself. And a few
years ago, when I heard that the company was hiring there, I referred a
few of my friends to the plant, and they've been working there ever since.
That's why this closure comes as something of a personal blow to me.

Williams: I can certainly relate to that. News like this is especially hard to
take when your own friends are involved.

Murphy: It's like I directed them into a dead end.

Williams: Don't be too hard on yourself. You had no way of knowing this
was going to happen.

---

refer 介紹　　　**closure** 關閉　　　**something of** 幾分；稍有　　　**blow** 打擊
direct 指示方向　　　**dead end** 死路

Lesson 38

Plant Closing — 總結

■　■　　■

　　美國在 80 年代後期, 颳起了一陣工廠關閉和大幅裁員的旋風。這跟 70 年代至 82 年間景氣衰退期的人員裁減不同, 這個現象乃是由於對長期性世界經濟的前途感到不安而產生的。

　　至於美國企業界的沈重擔子, 則來自跟以日本為首的外國企業間的激烈競爭, 以及為求具競爭力而導致的削減成本 (尤其是間接費用) 的壓力。

　　企業兼併的風潮會產生很多冗員 (redundancy)。但就算沒有兼併事件, 大部分的企業也都會有一至二成的多餘人員 (float)。而經營者大都想要把這些多餘的贅肉除去, 使公司變得 lean and agile (無肉一身輕)。80 年代後半, 美國的頂尖企業 (全美前五百家大公司) 中, 合計有三百五十萬員工遭到解雇的命運。

　　表示「解雇」之意的最普遍用語是 dismiss 和 discharge, 但由於遭到解雇有點像被人「以斧 (ax) 斬首」的感覺, 所以有時也會用 get the ax (被解雇) 和 give the ax (要人走路)。本課一開頭所用的 wielding the ax (動斧) 就是由此而來。

　　所謂 downsizing (縮小編制) 乃是具有人員裁減 (staff cutback) 意味的代表性詞彙。這是一種較委婉的說法, 原本使用於汽車的小型化之意, 現在更有所謂的 right-sizing, 這是取其正確適中, 不過大也不過小之意。其他還有 retrenchment、demassing、realignment、reduction in force (RIF) 等委婉的詞彙, 其意義都是一樣的。

　　隨著這種傾向的發展, 就產生了所謂 outplacement service 這種新式的服務。也就是對被解聘的員工進行諮商, 教導他們如何寫履歷表, 來幫助他們找到新東家。

　　Outplacement 的目的, 是希望讓這些被裁撤的員工能在較短的時間內找到合適的工作, 而提供給他們一些就業指導, 並給與當事人精神上的支持, 同時也助其順利地適應新工作。

Lesson 39

Self-Esteem

（自尊心）

◆ Lesson 39 的內容 ◆

　　史瓦布利克斷然表示：「這是自尊心的問題。」因為他都已經向上司開口要求職務上的擢升了，但卻得不到甚麼承諾，所以，為了自尊心，他不得不辭職。其實，他早就厭倦了他目前的職務 —— 一個高級跑腿員；他希望能有一點自己的決策空間。同時，他自己也很清楚，就算下一份工作還沒著落，他也要儘速辭職離去，擺脫目前的環境，回復自己的心理健康，這才是首要之務。而他這樣的心情，令澤崎頗有所感。

Lesson 39

Self-Esteem (1)（自尊心）

●預習 —*Sentences*

- I still can't believe you've decided to leave, Peter.
- What in the world made you decide to quit?
- I'm afraid he doesn't think much of my opinion.
- I was tired of just being a messenger for Gil.
- You're underestimating your role in the company.

●*Vignette*

Waitress: So that's two drafts, a white wine, onion rings and a cheese plate.

Winchell: Yes, thank you.

Sawasaki: I still can't believe you've decided to leave, Peter. What in the world made you decide to quit? I know that Gil is high on you.

Swarbrick: Maybe so, but I'm afraid he doesn't think much of my opinion. When I asked for a bigger share of the action, he turned me down, and so I pretty much had to go. It's a matter of self-esteem.

Winchell: What do you mean?

Swarbrick: I was tired of just being a messenger for Gil. I get along with him all right, but he has his own ideas about the media and public relations, and that doesn't leave me any decisions to make. I just run errands. It's not that he's wrong. It's just that he's no more right than I am.

Sawasaki: I think you're underestimating your role in the company, Peter. You're very good at what you do, and you've contributed a great deal to Nelson ABC Foods.

Swarbrick: Well, I really like this company, but I was unhappy with my responsibilities, and I really didn't know what to do. Finally I decided to go to a career counselor.

史瓦布利克突然決定要辭職。這令大家都覺得相當意外。面對澤崎的詢問，他的回答是「這是自尊心的問題。」

女服務生： 所以你們要的是兩杯生啤酒、一杯白酒、洋蔥圈，還有一個起士盤。

溫謝爾： 就是這樣，謝謝。

澤崎： 彼得，我還是無法相信你居然決定要走。到底是甚麼原因令你想辭職？我知道吉爾很看重你。

史瓦布利克： 也許吧，不過他恐怕不怎麼看重我的意見。我向他要求能多擔負一些責任，但他回絕了我，所以我是非走不可了。這是自尊心的問題。

溫謝爾： 怎麼說？

史瓦布利克： 我厭倦了只是作吉爾的信差。我跟他之間的相處沒有問題，可是對於媒體和公關，他有他自己的想法，這使得我沒有任何下決斷的空間。我只是個跑腿的。並不是說他有錯，只是他沒有我來得正確。

澤崎： 彼得，我覺得你低估了你在這公司裡所扮演的角色。你所做的都很好，而且你對尼爾森 ABC 食品公司貢獻良多。

史瓦布利克： 嗯，我是很喜歡這家公司，可是我不喜歡自己的職責。我是真的不知道該怎麼辦，於是，我就決定去找個事業諮詢顧問。

Words and Phrases

draft	生啤酒	get along with	與…相處
quit	辭職	media	媒體
turn down	拒絕	no more right than	不比…來得
matter of	…的問題		正確
self-esteem	自尊心	underestimate	低估; 小看
messenger	使者; 信差	career counselor	生涯諮詢顧問

Vocabulary Building

● **what in the world**　到底是甚麼

What in the world can have possessed you to insult the CEO's wife?

(你到底是著了甚麼魔, 居然會去侮辱總裁夫人?)

● **be high on**　非常喜愛; 對…極感興趣; 重視

I'm high on the prospects for growth in the car navigation equipment market.

(我非常重視汽車駕駛配備市場的成長遠景。)

● **share of the action**　責任的擔當

Jack's boss persuaded him to stay on by offering him a bigger share of the action.

(傑克的老闆讓傑克擔當更大的責任, 以說服他待下來。)

● **run errands**　跑腿; 辦差事

You don't have to go to the post office by yourself to get stamps. In this company we have messenger boys to run errands like that.

(你不必自己跑到郵局去買郵票。 在這家公司, 我們有專門的送信小弟跑腿辦這些事。)

1. I'm still <u>in the middle of</u> talking to my father on the phone, but <u>I'll be</u>
   　　　　　A　　　　　　　　　　　　　　　　　　　　　　　　　B

   <u>ready</u> to go <u>ten minutes later</u>.
   　C　　　　　　D

2. Mr. Adams has been <u>surveying</u> the travel business <u>during</u> the past half-
   　　　　　　　　　　　　A　　　　　　　　　　　　　　B

   year and <u>has</u> concluded that it <u>has a great future</u>.
   　　　　　C　　　　　　　　　　D

3. Chuck is very <u>knowledgeable</u> about <u>vital</u> political and <u>economical</u> issues
   　　　　　　　　　A　　　　　　　B　　　　　　　　　C

   the nation <u>now faces</u>.
   　　　　　D

◆◆◆◆◆◆◆◆◆◆◆◆◆ 簡短對話 ◆◆◆◆◆◆◆◆◆◆◆◆◆◆◆

Winchell: How long have you been feeling this way?

Swarbrick: For about a year, I'd say. But during the past couple of months it's reached the point where I can barely force myself to get out of bed and go to the office in the morning.

Winchell: That's nothing. My wife has to kick me out of bed, push me out of the house, and bolt the door behind me. Otherwise you'd never see me at work— not before about 3 in the afternoon, anyway.

Swarbrick: But you're not thinking about switching jobs?

Winchell: Constantly. Believe me, if something better came up, I'd jump at it.

---

reach the point where　到達某個⋯的階段　　　**force oneself to**　逼自己⋯
bolt　把門閂住　　　**switch**　轉換

Lesson 39

Self-Esteem (2)（自尊心）

●預習 — *Sentences*

- Her first piece of advice to me was not to jump ship.
- I said I didn't care what my title was.
- I had to be closer to the chief corporate spokesperson.
- I must say that he was pretty gentle about it.
- I'll be around for two more months, though.

●*Vignette*

Sawasaki: What did he say?

Swarbrick: Actually, it was a she. Her first piece of advice to me was not to jump ship without trying to improve my situation. She suggested that I ask my boss for a position that would be a major improvement, so that if he said yes, I'd have a real option to stay.

Winchell: So you asked for a promotion?

Swarbrick: Not a promotion so much as a restructuring of the operation. I told him that as manager of public relations, I should report directly to Alex. I said I didn't care what my title was, and I wasn't looking for more money, but I had to be closer to the chief corporate spokesperson to do my job well.

Winchell: And he turned you down?

Swarbrick: He turned me down. I must say that he was pretty gentle about it, and he did offer me a raise, but it was my last hurrah. I'll be around for two more months, though. I have a lot of irons in the fire, and I don't want to just walk away.

Sawasaki: Well, I must say you're behaving in a very responsible manner. But you know, I was intrigued by what you said a moment ago about self-esteem.

Swarbrick: What happened was that I realized I was losing faith in myself. The longer I stayed at Nelson ABC Foods, the more I doubted myself.

140

　　對史瓦布利克而言，他所在意的並不是頭銜或加薪。他要的是身為一個公關部門經理所該有的權限。所以他要求能直接向公司總裁負責。

澤崎：　他怎麼說？

史瓦布利克：　事實上，她是個女的。她給我的第一個建議是，在沒有試圖改善我目前的處境之前，不要辭職。她勸我向上司要求一個能大大改善現狀的職位。而如果他同意了，那我就很有理由待下來了。

溫謝爾：　所以你提出了升遷的要求？

史瓦布利克：　我要求的升遷並不至於大到要令整個組織運作改組。我告訴他，身為公關部門的經理，我應該直接向亞力士負責。我說我不在乎頭銜是甚麼，我也不要求加薪；可是，為了把工作做好，我必須跟公司首席發言人保持密切接觸。

溫謝爾：　而他拒絕了？

史瓦布利克：　他拒絕了我的要求。我得說，他是相當溫和地拒絕我，他還要給我加薪，可是我感覺這事就只有到此為止了。不過，我還會再待兩個月。因為我手上的事情太多了，我不願意說走就走。

澤崎：　嗯，我得說你做事的方式很有責任感，可是你知道嗎，你剛剛在說自尊心的時候，我覺得很好奇。

史瓦布利克：　我的情況是這樣的，我瞭解到自己正在失去自信。在尼爾森ABC公司食品公司待得愈久，我就愈加懷疑自己。

Lesson 39 Self-Esteem (2)

Words and Phrases

option	選擇	raise	加薪
restructuring	企業重組	walk away	離去
look for	尋求	be intrigued by	對…很有興趣
corporate spokesperson	公司發言人	lose faith in	對…失去了信心

Vocabulary Building

- **jump ship** 逃離; 辭職
  Our new researcher jumped ship after only three months on the job.
  (我們新任的調查員只做了三個月就辭職不幹了。)

- **report to** 部屬 (向上司) 呈報; 向…負責; 隸屬於…
  The number of people who report to you is not necessarily an accurate indication of your status.
  (你手下人員的數目並不見得就能代表你真正的地位。)

- **be around** 在旁邊
  cf. See you around.
  (待會兒見。)

- **irons in the fire** 攬事太多
  Jill's problem is she's got too many irons in the fire. And none of them ever seems to work out.
  (吉兒的問題在於, 她手邊同時在處理的事情太多, 可是卻沒有半件有順利進行的跡象。)

（解答見 266 頁）

▶ **Exercises**　在下列例句中，每句各有四個劃線部分，
其中一個的文法有誤，請將之選出。

1. It is <u>said</u> that <u>space</u> is the last <u>frontier</u> for <u>the man</u> to explore.
       A   B   C   D

2. Mike tried to <u>avoid</u> <u>to take</u> the final exam <u>with the excuse of</u> a death
             A   B   C

 <u>in the family</u>.
   D

3. This chart <u>gives</u> us a dramatic representation of the rapid <u>rise</u> in <u>drug use</u>
        A   B   C

 <u>between</u> teenagers.
   D

◆◆◆◆◆◆◆◆◆◆◆◆◆ 簡短對話 ◆◆◆◆◆◆◆◆◆◆◆◆◆

Winchell: I can't believe that you'd ask to report directly to Alex.

Swarbrick: You think it was too presumptuous of me? I felt that way a bit myself too, but I decided to go for it anyway.

Winchell: I mean, sure, if you want something, there's no reason to be shy about trying to get it. It's just that I think Gil is a much easier person to work for than Alex could ever be.

Swarbrick: I don't doubt that. I might have found Alex too much to cope with. But I seriously felt the nature of my job demanded that I deal directly with him rather than going through intermediaries all the time.

---

report directly to 向⋯直接負責；直隸於⋯　　**presumptuous** 僭越的；無顧忌的　　**go for it** 努力求得；爭取　　**be shy about** 對於⋯覺得不好意思　　**nature** 性質　　**deal with** 相處；打交道　　**intermediary** 中間人

Self-Esteem (3) （自尊心）

●預習 — *Sentences*

· Both you and your company end up as losers.
· Self-esteem is a hot topic all over the country.
· Children think they can do anything they want to.
· Peter, you don't seem to fear being unemployed.
· I had no idea you were so unhappy.

●*Vignette*

Swarbrick: I know from my own experience that you have to believe in yourself to accomplish anything.

Winchell: I know what you mean. If you don't think your ideas are important, you gradually stop coming up with new ones.

Swarbrick: Or at least you stop expressing them. Both you and your company end up as losers. If you don't think much of yourself, you probably aren't going to think much of anybody else, either.

Winchell: Self-esteem is a hot topic all over the country. In inner-city schools, for instance, a lot of children are almost hopeless by the time they hit grade school. They have to overcome poverty, crime, drugs, absent parents, child abuse, and sometimes racial discrimination. Children like that aren't going to build up the sense of self-worth they need to succeed without some support.

Sawasaki: It's hard to imagine having to teach self-esteem to children. Children think they can do anything they want to. Incidentally, Peter, you don't seem to fear being unemployed. Do you have any idea what you're going to do when you leave Nelson ABC Foods?

Swarbrick: Well, technically, as I'm sure you're aware, I shouldn't have resigned from the company till I had another job lined up, but I decided it was more important to my mental health to be out of this situation than to be employed.

Sawasaki: I had no idea you were so unhappy.

　　自尊心是個全美熱門的話題；那些面對貧窮、犯罪、毒品、父母不在身邊和孩童虐待這些問題的孩子們，若缺乏某些鼓舞，將無法建立起賴以成功的自我價值感。

史瓦布利克： 我從自身的經驗得知，一個人若要完成某事，一定要對自己有信心才行。

溫謝爾： 我知道你的意思。如果你認為自己的意見不重要，那麼慢慢地，你也不會再想出新東西來了。

史瓦布利克： 或是說，你至少不會再將之表達出來。結果呢，你和你的公司都會是輸家。如果你都不看重自己，那你可能也不會看重別人。

溫謝爾： 自尊心是個全國熱門的話題。舉例來說，在位於人口稠密的市中心學校中，很多小孩到他們要上小學的年齡時，就幾乎已經無可救藥了。他們必須克服貧窮、犯罪、毒品、父母不在身邊、以及孩童虐待的問題，有時還會有種族歧視。像那樣的小孩若缺乏某些鼓舞，將無法建立起賴以成功的自我價值感。

澤崎： 這真的是很難想像，居然還得教小孩自尊心這種東西。在小孩子的想法裡，他們可以做任何自己想做的事。彼得，我順道問一下，你看來好像不擔心失業的問題。你有沒有想好在離開尼爾森 ABC 食品公司之後要做甚麼？

史瓦布利克： 這個嘛，我想你也知道的，就現實面來看，在下一個工作還沒有著落之前，我不該就這樣辭職。可是，我決定還是我的心理健康比較重要，所以我寧可脫離這種處境，也不繼續受雇。

澤崎： 我以前居然不知道你這麼不快樂。

Lesson 39 Self-Esteem (3)

Words and Phrases

accomplish　達成	absent parents　不在家的父母親
end up　結局是…	child abuse　兒童虐待
loser　輸家	sense of self-worth　自我價值感
inner-city　市中心 (的)	line up　安排；預備
poverty　貧窮	

Vocabulary Building

● **think much of**　看重…

cf. No one thinks a great deal of Bruce's new assistant, who just seems to be coasting on the job.

(布魯斯的新任助理做起事來漫不經心，沒有人看重他。)

● **hot**　熱門的；搶手的

Hawaii used to be a hot honeymoon destination, but Australia has now become more popular with the honeymooners.

(夏威夷以前一直是個熱門的蜜月勝地，不過，近來澳洲也愈來愈受度蜜月者的青睞了。)

● **technically**　就現實面而言；規則上

Technically, you're not supposed to ask a job applicant his or her age.

(規定上，你不應該去問求職者的年齡。)

● **mental health**　心理健康

Having a spouse who nags you all the time is not very good for your mental health.

(就心理健康而言，有個老愛在你耳邊嘮嘮叨叨的配偶可不是件好事。)

1. <u>After</u> <u>speaking with</u> the human resources manager, Sara <u>was not longer</u>
    A   B   C
  fascinated <u>with</u> job prospects in the company.
              D

2. Patricia will <u>have a difficult time</u> telling <u>which</u> of these two used cars <u>are</u>
                        A   B   C
  in <u>better</u> condition as both look brand new.
        D

3. Should there <u>is</u> a <u>need</u> to make <u>changes</u> in our plan for tomorrow, please
             A   B   C
  call me <u>as soon as possible.</u>
            D

◆◆◆◆◆◆◆◆◆◆◆◆◆◆ 簡短對話 ◆◆◆◆◆◆◆◆◆◆◆◆◆◆

Winchell: California once funded a study about self-esteem. They're really into far-out ideas and movements out there.

Swarbrick: I don't see what's so "far out" about studying self-esteem.

Winchell: There's nothing far out about self-esteem itself, I grant you. But I do question the need to spend people's tax dollars to research a topic like that. My only point was that California tends to be more open to things that would be laughed at in the rest of the country.

---

fund *v.* 供給資金   **far-out** 嶄新的；前衛的   **I grant you** 你說得不錯；
我同意你的說法   **tax dollars** 稅金

Lesson 39

Self-Esteem (4) (自尊心)

● 預習 — *Sentences*

- I decided to take my troubles to a career counselor.
- And did she help with new job ideas?
- I won't have any trouble paying the rent for a few months.
- If you're serious, there's someone you ought to meet.
- I'll give her a call first thing in the morning.

● *Vignette*

Swarbrick: Well, it's not very professional to run around complaining about your bosses. You're cutting your own throat as far as advancement is concerned, and you're not pleasant to be around. So I decided to take my troubles to a career counselor.

Winchell: And did she help with new job ideas?

Swarbrick: I've had a few interviews, but nothing really exciting has come up yet. Still, I won't have any trouble paying the rent for a few months, and by then I'm sure I'll have something. One idea that's very attractive to me is to join a small company of some sort that's completely different from what I've been doing. My counselor has arranged some meetings with computer firms. Also I've been reading about micro marketing lately, and I think I'd enjoy matching wits with consumers on a smaller playing field.

Sawasaki: Really? If you're serious, there's someone you ought to meet.

Winchell: You mean Maria?

Sawasaki: Yeah, Brad and I have a friend here in Chicago who recently started a micro marketing firm with her husband. Would you like to meet her?

Swarbrick: Sure. I'd love to.

Sawasaki: I'll give her a call first thing in the morning. In the meantime, how about another beer?

若是對小眾市場行銷有興趣的話，就得見見瑪莉亞‧古岱茲。她過去待過 ABC 食品公司，最近在芝加哥和她先生倆人開了家小眾市場行銷公司。

史瓦布利克：　嗯，跑來跑去地跟別人抱怨自己的上司，這並不像是件專家會做的事。以升遷的考量來看，這是在自斷前途，而且人家看到你在旁邊也會覺得很討厭。所以，我就決定要把我的問題帶去問生涯諮詢顧問。

溫謝爾：　她有沒有指點你甚麼新工作的點子？

史瓦布利克：　我面試過幾家，可是還沒有真正令我很感興趣的。而且，再付上幾個月的房租，對我還不成問題，不過，我相信在那之前我應該就找到事了。有一個主意倒是很吸引我，就是加入某種小公司，做些跟現在完全不同的事情。我的諮詢顧問給我安排了一些電腦公司的面談。而我最近也在看一些小眾市場行銷的書，我覺得我會喜歡在較小的活動範圍中跟消費者鬥智。

澤崎：　真的嗎？如果你真有此意，那麼有一個人你該見見。

溫謝爾：　你是說瑪莉亞嗎？

澤崎：　對，布雷和我在芝加哥有個朋友，她最近跟她先生開了家小眾市場行銷公司。你想見她嗎？

史瓦布利克：　當然。我很願意。

澤崎：　我明天一早就給她撥個電話。另外，再來杯啤酒如何？

Lesson 39   Self-Esteem (4)

Words and Phrases

run around　　到處跑	擊破的行銷手法〉
advancement　　升遷	playing field　　(活動的)舞臺
micro marketing　　小眾市場行銷	first thing in the morning　　早上
〈將商品所針對的消費者加以區隔,	第一件事
瞄準單一的消費者族群, 而予以各個	in the meantime　　同時

Vocabulary Building

● **cut one's own throat**　　自殺; 自斷生路
If you turn down this promotion, you'll be cutting your own throat.
(如果你回絕了這個升遷機會, 那你無異是在自斷生路。)

● **as far as something (or someone) is concerned**　　對…而言
As far as I'm concerned, I can find a way to make my living. So don't worry about me.
(就我個人而言, 謀生是沒問題的。所以別為我擔心。)

● **have trouble**　　有問題
Jeremy has trouble remembering people's names.
(傑若米不擅長記人名。)

● **match wits with**　　與…鬥智
Taking this job offers you the chance to match wits with some of the best minds in securities.
(接受這個工作會使你有機會與一些證券業的佼佼者鬥智。)

在下列例句中，每句各有四個劃線部分，
其中一個的文法有誤，請將之選出。 　　　　(解答見 266 頁)

1. Top corporate management usually interprets workforce needs by asking
   <u>A</u>   <u>B</u>   <u>C</u>
   about it on the shop floor.
   D

2. Because of the economy recession, at least five companies have gone
   A   B   C
   bankrupt.
   D

3. We have been busy discussing about cost-cutting measures for the last
                A   B   C
   month or two.
   D

◆◆◆◆◆◆◆◆◆◆◆◆◆ 簡短對話 ◆◆◆◆◆◆◆◆◆◆◆◆◆◆

Winchell: You know, Peter, that sounds really attractive—the idea of working for a smaller outfit. There wouldn't be all these layers of management and bureaucratic rules to cope with.

Swarbrick: If you feel that way, then maybe you should think about moving to a smaller organization yourself.

Winchell: Oh, I could never do that.

Swarbrick: Why not?

Winchell: Look, I depend on having a lot of capable types like you and Shoichi around to keep the organization I'm working for afloat. If I went to some small outfit, I'd probably end up sinking it in no time.

---

outfit 公司　　**layer of management** 管理層級　　**bureaucratic rules** 官僚式的規章　　**cope with** 應付　　**keep afloat** 不使下沈; 使免於經濟困難　　**in no time** 立刻

Lesson 39

Self-Esteem —— 總結

∎ ∎ ∎

"Man shall not live by bread alone." (人活著不是單靠食物) 是聖經馬太福音中著名的一節, 而彼得‧史瓦布利克卻能把麵包 (加薪) 撇在一邊, 寧願保有他的自尊心。

所謂自尊心 (self-esteem) 便是「自尊的感覺」和「對自己的信賴感」, 換句話說, 就是「自豪」。這也和自我形象 (self-image) 或自信 (self-confidence) 大有關聯。

自尊心來自對自我的認可, 或他人對自己的認同。不過, 對許多商業人士而言, 自尊心有更多是源自於工作。一方面, 工作生產力若高, 則自尊心跟著提高。另一方面, 當生產力低下的時候, 自尊心也一落千丈, 而且還會有惡性循環之虞。

一般來說, 擁有健全自尊心的人有以下特點:

- 擁有自我價值觀和原則(values and principles)
- 犯錯也不會想不開, 不會為明天憂慮
- 縱使經歷挫折失敗, 依舊信賴自己處理問題的能力(ability to deal with problems)
- 不輕看他人
- 親切, 尋找別人的優點(look for the best in others)

而自尊心低下的人有以下特徵:

- 懶得跟別人接觸 (make contact with other people)
- 優柔寡斷, 而且常無法將決心付諸實行
- 常感覺周圍的人對自己懷有敵意(hostility)
- 常擔憂他人如何看待自己

不過, 就算是自尊心健全的人, 也不是無懈可擊的完人。他仍會犯錯, 仍會被他人拒絕, 只是, 他看待事情的態度會相當地正面而積極。

Micro Marketing

（小眾市場行銷）

◆ Lesson 40 的內容 ◆

　　史瓦布利克為了要探詢新工作的發展可能，特地拜會了在芝加哥經營小眾市場行銷諮詢公司的古岱茲。他並不是十分清楚小眾市場行銷的真實意義。古岱茲的說法是，現在美國已沒有「大眾市場」了，而為要接近那些「真正的消費者」，行銷活動應該要對準目標來進行。

Well, advertising, for instance, can be anywhere— or everywhere.

Micro Marketing (1) (小眾市場行銷)

預習 ── *Sentences*

- I'm excited about discussing your company's work.
- I don't have experience in micro marketing.
- It's a brand new field for practically all of us.
- Is it basically a matter of local advertising campaigns?
- That's the American dream, from an advertiser's point of view.

Vignette

Swarbrick: Thank you for seeing me so soon, Ms. Cortez. I'm excited about discussing your company's work, but I hope you realize that I don't have experience in micro marketing.

Cortez: Oh, don't worry about that. Very few people do anyway. It's a brand new field for practically all of us. Shoichi spoke highly of your abilities, and I see from your résumé that you have plenty of experience with marketing communications, so I don't think you should be too concerned about your background. And please, call me Maria.

Swarbrick: Thank you, I will. And my name's Peter. But I must say, Maria, I'm a bit confused about what exactly is meant by micro marketing. Is it basically a matter of local advertising campaigns?

Cortez: Well, yes and no. The whole concept of micro marketing is based on the idea that the famous America "mass market" no longer exists. You know the picture: the family sits down to watch TV together and then Mother goes out the next day to do the shopping—and buys the products that were advertised on the tube the night before.

Swarbrick: Sure, that's the American dream, from an advertiser's point of view. But we've known for some time that the "typical family" doesn't exist anymore. Maybe it never did.

Cortez: You're right.

　　史瓦布利克一開始便率直地表示，他並不清楚小眾市場行銷和一般的產品行銷有甚麼不同。「這是否就是地區性的廣告活動呢？」

史瓦布利克： 古岱茲女士，謝謝妳這麼快就能見我。能跟妳談談你們公司在做的事，我覺得很興奮，不過，我希望妳能瞭解，我對於小眾市場行銷並沒有甚麼經驗。

古岱茲： 噢，這你不用擔心。其實也沒多少人有經驗。這對我們每一位而言幾乎都是個全新的領域。昭一對於你的能力評價相當高，而我從你的履歷表上也看到你有不少行銷溝通的經驗，所以我想你也不用太在意你的背景。還有，請叫我瑪莉亞。

史瓦布利克： 謝謝，我會的。我叫彼得。可是瑪莉亞，我得說一下，我有點搞不清小眾市場行銷的確實意義。這在基本上，是否就是地區性的廣告活動呢？

古岱茲： 這個嘛，可以說是，但也可以說不是。小眾市場行銷概念的形成是基於著名的美國「大眾市場」已不復存在的這種想法。你應該知道那種情形的：一家人坐下來一起看電視，然後媽媽隔天去購物 —— 她所買的就是前晚電視廣告上的產品。

史瓦布利克： 我知道，以廣告商的角度來看，這就是美國夢。不過，我們也早就知道，這種「典型家庭」不再存在。也或許它根本就不曾存在過。

古岱茲： 你說的沒錯。

Lesson 40 Micro Marketing (1)

Words and Phrases

be excited about	對…覺得興奮	advertising campaign	廣告活動
brand new	嶄新的	concept	概念
practically	幾乎	mass market	量販市場；大量市
be concerned about	關切		場；大眾市場
be confused about	對…不清楚		

Vocabulary Building

- **micro marketing**　小眾市場行銷

  Maria and her fiancé decided to start a business in the new field of micro marketing.

  (瑪莉亞和她的未婚夫決定在小眾市場行銷這個新興的領域中開始他們的事業。)

- **speak highly of**　對…評價甚高

  Frank was careful not to speak too highly of his secretary in front of his jealous wife.

  (法蘭克小心翼翼地避免在他那善妒的老婆面前太過誇獎他的祕書。)

- **know the picture**　知道那個狀況

  cf. I'm not sure I get the picture. Just what do you expect this team of consultants to do for us?

  (我不確定自己有沒有搞清楚狀況，你到底是期望這個諮詢小組為我們做些甚麼？)

- **tube**　電視

  Anything good on the tube tonight?

  (今晚電視上有甚麼好節目嗎？)

(解答見 266頁)

▶ **Exercises**

在下列例句中，每句各有四個劃線部分，
其中一個的文法有誤，請將之選出。

1. Charles <u>agreed with</u> my suggestion to <u>relocate</u> his <u>corporate headquarters</u>
           A   B   C

   <u>to</u> Osaka.
   D

2. If there's <u>anything</u> Pat <u>doesn't need</u>, it's <u>more</u> unwanted <u>advise</u>.
            A   B   C   D

3. Sports trainers <u>agree</u> that <u>concentrating</u> is the <u>key</u> to building strength,
                  A   B   C

   <u>not</u> long hours of exercise.
   D

◆◆◆◆◆◆◆◆◆◆◆◆◆◆ 簡 短 對 話 ◆◆◆◆◆◆◆◆◆◆◆◆◆◆◆◆

Swarbrick: I suppose Shoichi has told you that I want out of Nelson ABC Foods so badly that I've already submitted my resignation?

Cortez: No, he didn't say anything like that. He just indicated that you wanted to check out what options might be available to you.

Swarbrick: That was discreet of him. He probably thought it would weaken my position in your eyes if you knew I was about to be out of a job.

Cortez: Well, I can't read Shoichi's mind, but I can tell you that what you say doesn't make the least bit of difference as far as I'm concerned.

---

submit one's resignation 提出辭呈　　**check out** 調查　　**option** 選擇
discreet 慎重的　　**in someone's eyes** 在某人的眼中　　**out of a job** 失業
read someone's mind 讀出某人的心裡在想甚麼

Lesson 40

Micro Marketing (2) （小眾市場行銷）

●預習 — *Sentences*

- A lot of advertising money went down the drain.
- Many of those same women are working outside the home.
- Or maybe the husband does it on Sunday mornings.
- How can you begin to suggest remedies to your clients?
- A lot of executives are obsessed with the quick fix.

●*Vignette*

Cortez: A lot of advertising money went down the drain, because it wasn't reaching the real consumers, and today that's more true than ever. Take dishwashing products, for instance. At one time, marketing people could assume that a fairly large percentage of the nation's housewives were tuned in to a certain soap opera, so that's where they sank their advertising budget. But today we know that many of those same women are working outside the home during the day.

Swarbrick: Or getting a master's degree, or something.

Cortez: Yes. The person shopping for the family might be the 15-year-old son on his way home from school. Or maybe the husband does it on Sunday mornings. Marketers have to aim their products at old people, Hispanics, young men, working women— all sorts of people.

Swarbrick: I can see the basic problem, but as a consultant, how can you begin to suggest remedies to your clients?

Cortez: I think our main job is to convince manufacturers or their marketing people that they would be foolish to keep investing huge amounts of money in the hope of producing one boffo TV ad that will quickly boost sales.

Swarbrick: Looking for instant results.

Cortez: Right. A lot of executives are obsessed with the quick fix, because their jobs are structured to depend on it, but we've got to make them realize that they're not going to get it from television— at least not network television.

　　古岱茲表示，現代的行銷人員必須以老年人、美籍拉丁裔人、年輕男性、職業婦女等各階層的人為目標。但是，身為一個諮詢顧問，要如何向客戶提出因應方案呢？

古岱茲： 由於廣告無法把訊息傳達給真正需要該商品的消費者，所以花在廣告上的大把鈔票也都付諸東流。今天事實更是如此。就拿清洗碗碟用的產品來說好了，曾經，行銷人員可以假定說，全國大半的家庭主婦都會收看某齣電視連續劇，所以他們會把經費拿來買那個節目的廣告時段。可是今天我們卻知道，同樣的那群婦女有很多現在白天都在外頭工作。

史瓦布利克： 或是在唸碩士或甚麼的。

古岱茲： 沒錯。而家裡要用的東西可能是由他們十五歲的兒子在放學回家途中買回來，或是由先生在星期天早上出門購物。所以市場行銷人員必須將他們的產品對準了老年人、美籍拉丁人、年輕男性、職業婦女 —— 要以各階層的人為目標。

史瓦布利克： 我看得出問題的重點所在，但身為諮詢顧問，你要怎麼樣向你的客戶提出因應方案呢？

古岱茲： 我認為我們主要的工作就是說服製造商或他們的行銷人員，如果他們繼續把大筆金錢投資下去，期望能產生出甚麼爆笑的廣告節目，而使銷售額因之快速躍升，那他們也太愚蠢了。

史瓦布利克： 想要立即見效啊！

古岱茲： 就是這樣。有好多主管終日所想的都是要事情能立竿見影，因為他們工作本身的結構就是有賴於此，但我們得讓他們明白，投資在電視上不會有他們想要的成效 —— 至少電視廣播網不會。

Lesson 40 Micro Marketing (2)

Words and Phrases

dishwashing product　清洗碗碟用的產品

tune in to　收看

soap opera　連續劇

sink　投資；投入

budget　預算

master's degree　碩士學位

on one's way home　回家途中

aim　對準

Hispanic　（美國境內講西班牙語的）拉丁裔美國人

remedy　治療法；解決之道；因應之道

convince　說服

boffo *adj.*　〔美俗〕爆笑節目

boost　提高；增進

instant results　立即效果

network television　電視廣播網〈像是 ABC, NBC, CBS 等大型廣播電視公司〉

Vocabulary Building

- **go down the drain**　付諸東流；浪費
  All our efforts to cultivate contacts in the government went down the drain when there was a coup d'état.
  （我們在政府培植熟人的努力，於一場政變後全數化為烏有。）

- **in the hope of**　期望…
  Jane attends seminars and conventions in the hope of finding an interesting new opening.
  （珍之所以會參加研討會和會議，其目的是希望能找到個有趣的新工作。）

- **be obsessed with**　心中縈繞著…（想法）
  Our new CEO is obsessed with cutting costs, even if it means giving up our hold on some major markets.
  （我們新任的總裁老想著要減低開支,即使這意味著要放棄一些主要市場也無所謂。）

- **quick fix**　特效藥；能立即見效的解決之道
  I want a solution that gets to the root of the problem, not just a quick fix to tide us over for a few months.
  （我要的是能使問題解決的根本之道，而不是那種可以使我們撐幾個月的特效藥。）

(解答見 266 頁)

▶ **Exercises**   在下列例句中，每句各有四個劃線部分，
其中一個的文法有誤，請將之選出。

1. Let's <u>don't</u> <u>go out</u> tonight. It <u>looks like</u> a snowstorm is <u>on its way</u>.
        A   B   C   D

2. The <u>datas</u> in this newsletter are usually <u>trustworthy</u>, but there were
       A   B
  <u>a lot of</u> errors in the last <u>issue</u>.
     C   D

3. Sally <u>looks like</u> <u>a bit</u> cold, but <u>actually</u> she is a <u>warm-hearted</u> person.
       A   B   C   D

◆◆◆◆◆◆◆◆◆◆◆◆◆ 簡短對話 ◆◆◆◆◆◆◆◆◆◆◆◆◆◆◆

Swarbrick: Shoichi told me that you used to work for ABC Foods. What made you decide to go into micro marketing, if you don't mind my asking?

Cortez: Not at all. It was a field that I had been interested in for some time, but what really made up my mind was the merger with Nelson. No offense, Peter, but I just couldn't see myself working at a place owned by a cigarette company.

Swarbrick: Oh, I understand your feelings. But even so, it must have taken a lot of courage to start up your own business.

Cortez: Well, yes, but my fiancé and I had this dream of working together, and setting up our own company seemed like the best way of doing it.

---

if you don't mind my asking 如果你不介意我問的話   **no offense** 沒有惡意
fiancé 未婚夫

Lesson 40

Micro Marketing (3) (小眾市場行銷)

●預習 — *Sentences*

- Isn't that still the best bet for a big audience?
- The networks' share of the audience has dropped.
- It's about $185,000 now.
- A lot of them are focused on much smaller audiences.
- They specialize in fine arts performances.

●*Vignette*

Swarbrick: Isn't that still the best bet for a big audience, though? Prime time TV?

Cortez: Actually, the figures on prime time constitute one of our best arguments for putting the advertising dollars someplace else. Even during prime time, the networks' share of the audience has dropped by more than 25 percent in the last ten years, but the price of a choice 30-second prime-time spot has shot up 85 percent. It's about $185,000 now.

Swarbrick: Well, you've certainly sold *me*, but what do you suggest to people after you've talked them out of mass marketing?

Cortez: That's where micro marketing stops being a science and becomes an art. Each product has to find its consumers, wherever they might be. One of the best answers is still television, of course, but it's a type of television that the old ad men wouldn't recognize.

Swarbrick: You mean cable TV?

Cortez: Sure. There are thousands of cable channels and even networks springing up, each with its own audience. Some of them are not much different from network TV in terms of the broadness of their target audiences, but a lot of them are focused on much smaller audiences. There are channels that consist entirely of Chinese-language programming, for example. Others are dedicated entirely to old movies, or maybe they specialize in fine arts performances.

近十年來，美國三大電視廣播網在黃金時段的收視率降了超過 25 個百分點。可是 30 秒的廣告費用倒漲了 85%，大概要十八萬五千美元左右。所以現在有線電視正逐漸受到重視。

史瓦布利克：可是，那不也仍是最有可能掌握收視群的地方嗎？黃金時段的電視節目？

古岱茲：事實上，黃金時段的收視數據，正好成了我們最有理由要人把廣告費轉投他處的論點之一。就算是在黃金時段，電視網的觀眾群在近十年來也降了超過 25 個百分點，可是，若要在收視最佳的黃金檔買個 30 秒的廣告，費用倒漲了 85%。現在大概要十八萬五千美元吧！

史瓦布利克：嗯，妳真的說服我了，不過，在說服了他人不再走大眾行銷的路線之後，妳要建議他們怎麼做？

古岱茲：那時，小眾市場行銷就要搖身一變，不再只是一種科學，而要成為一種技術。每一項產品都得去找到自己的消費群，不管那些人是在哪裡。當然了，最好的答案之一還是電視，不過，這是一種舊時廣告人所無法認可的電視。

史瓦布利克：妳是指有線電視？

古岱茲：沒錯。數以千計的有線電視頻道，甚或有線電視網，正如雨後春筍般地出現，每個都有它自己的觀眾群。其中有些也跟電視廣播網沒啥不同，都是針對廣大群眾，但大部分有線電視的對象都是較小的觀眾群。舉例來說，有些頻道全都是中文節目，有些則專門都在播放老片子，或者有的只專門播映一些藝術公演節目。

Lesson 40　Micro Marketing (3)

Words and Phrases

constitute	構成	wherever they might be	不管他們有可能在哪裡
argument	論點		
advertising dollar	廣告費	ad (<advertising) man	廣告人
someplace else	別的地方	spring up	長出; 萌芽
audience	觀眾; 聽眾	consist of	由…組成
choice *adj.*	上選的; 最好的	be dedicated to	專注於…
prime-time spot	黃金時段的廣告	specialize in	專門做…
shoot up	快速上升	fine arts performance	藝術公演
sell	說服		

Vocabulary Building

● **prime time**　黃金時段

The computer company decided to pour its advertising dollars into splashy commercials aired during prime time.

(那家電腦公司決定把廣告費全數投入黃金檔時段，播出一些誇大誘人的商業廣告。)

● **talk someone out of**　勸某人不要做…

I tried to talk Peter out of quitting, but his mind was made up.

(我試著勸彼得不要辭職，可是他已決意如此了。)

● **target audience**　收視對象; 針對的觀(聽)眾

The target audience for this program consists largely of high school students.

(這個節目所針對的收視者多半都是中學生。)

● **focus on**　集中於…

Today's meeting will focus on plans for the April-June quarter.

(今天會議的重點是四到六月這一季的計畫。)

1. Thomas <u>has</u> <u>had</u> time to <u>get</u> in contact with us from Geneva, <u>has he</u>?
　　　　　A　　B　　　　　C　　　　　　　　　　　　　　　　D

2. We hope the new <u>equipments</u> <u>on order from</u> your company <u>will be</u> sent
　　　　　　　　　　　A　　　　　　B　　　　　　　　　　　C
to us <u>without delay</u>.
　　　　　D

3. <u>By</u> this time next year, we will <u>not only</u> have <u>moved to a new city</u>, but
　A　　　　　　　　　　　　　　B　　　　　C
<u>will build</u> our house.
　D

◆◆◆◆◆◆◆◆◆◆◆◆◆ 簡短對話 ◆◆◆◆◆◆◆◆◆◆◆◆◆

Swarbrick: I bet you could do a lot of other good advertising with that kind of money.

Cortez: Right. And there's a big question in my mind just how effective the networks are as an advertising medium.

Swarbrick: Because of the drop in viewership?

Cortez: Yes, and on top of that, there's the fact that they're always juggling their program schedules. It's not like the old days, when a sponsor could back a popular series and expect it to stay on the air for years and years.

---

advertising medium 廣告媒體　　**viewership** 收視率　　**on top of that** 尤有甚者　　**juggle** 動手腳　　**on the air** 播放　　**for years and years** 無終止地

Lesson 40

Micro Marketing (4) （小眾市場行銷）

●預習 — *Sentences*

- I don't really watch much TV.
- That's a perfect example of micro marketing.
- Haven't you noticed the advertising on rental video cassettes?
- The ads are just for other movies from the same company.
- I'm working with a narrowcasting company here in Chicago.

●*Vignette*

Swarbrick: I had no idea that things had changed so much. I don't really watch much TV. About the only time I switch the set on is when I pop a video into the VCR.

Cortez: Actually, that's a perfect example of micro marketing. Haven't you noticed the advertising on rental video cassettes lately? It only started a few years ago, but now it's pretty standard, even if the ads are just for other movies from the same company.

Swarbrick: What about non-video marketing?

Cortez: Well, advertising, for instance, can by anywhere—or every-where. One big manufacturer recently developed at least six different toothpaste campaigns aimed at different groups including kids, older people, blacks, and Hispanics. They're trying in-store exhibits, coupons, billboards, ethnic newspapers, all sorts of things. One avenue that I've been exploring lately is radio spots in supermarkets.

Swarbrick: In supermarkets?

Cortez: Yes. You know how most supermarkets play background music through ceiling speakers? I'm working with a narrowcasting company here in Chicago that puts together packages of music and very low-key advertising. It reaches people while they're right there in the store.

史瓦布利克： 我竟不知道事情有了這麼大的轉變。我自己是不太看電視的，只有在要看錄影帶的時候才會開機。

古岱茲： 實際上，這正是小眾市場行銷的絕佳範例。你注意到近來出租錄影帶上的廣告了嗎？這是幾年前才開始的一種作法，可是現在幾乎每卷錄影帶上都會有，就算是只給同公司出品的其他片子打打廣告都好。

史瓦布利克： 那關於非螢幕類的行銷呢？

古岱茲： 嗯，廣告，舉例來說，可以無所不在 —— 或者說，到處都有。有一家大製造廠新近開發了至少六種的牙膏，它的宣傳活動針對了不同的族群，包括小孩、老人、黑人和美籍拉丁人。他們正在嘗試透過店內展示、折價券、告示板、和種族性報紙來做宣傳，方式可說無所不有。我最近在開發的一種方式是超級市場裡的無線電插播廣告。

史瓦布利克： 在超市裡？

古岱茲： 是啊。你知道大部分的超市是怎樣經由天花板上的擴音器來播放背景音樂的嗎？我正在跟芝加哥本地的一家窄播公司聯手策劃一些案子，要把音樂和非常不顯眼的廣告結合在一起。只要人們一進到超市，他們就在廣告的觸角範圍內了。

Lesson 40   Micro Marketing (4)

Words and Phrases

have no idea　全然不知	billboard　告示板；看板
VCR (video cassette recorder)　錄影機	ethnic newspaper　以某種族的語言製作的報紙
standard　標準的；普遍的	avenue　道路；方式
anywhere or everywhere　在所有的地方	explore　開發；探索
toothpaste　牙膏	radio spot　無線電的插播廣告
kid　小孩	ceiling　天花板
black　黑人	put together　擺在一起
	low-key　低調的；不顯眼的

Vocabulary Building

- **switch on**　打開 (電器等的開關)
  When Joanna switched on the radio, sparks came flying out of it.
  (喬安娜一打開收音機, 就有火花冒出來。)

- **pop into**　放進去
  I'll just pop this casserole into the microwave, and it'll be ready to eat in a couple of minutes.
  (我只要把這鍋食物放進微波爐裡, 幾分鐘就可以吃了。)

- **in-store exhibit**　店內展示
  We arranged for an in-store exhibit of our popcorn popper.
  (我們安排了一個爆米花機的店內展示。)

- **narrowcasting**　窄播 〈與傳統的 broadcasting (廣播) 相對, 是以限定地區內的特定族群為其視聽對象〉
  Narrowcasting can offer a cost-effective way of reaching a small specific audience.
  (窄播可以提供一種相當符合成本效益的方式, 以觸及到少數的特定觀眾群。)

168

1. I <u>told</u> Jack that he had to <u>finish</u> the unfinished job <u>completely</u> <u>until</u> he
     A   B   C   D

   went home.

2. <u>How</u> many journalists <u>do you know</u> is not so important <u>as</u> how <u>you are</u>
    A   B   C   D

   <u>known</u> to them.

3. Today's newspaper <u>carried</u> many <u>news</u> about the <u>impending</u> airline strike.
     A   B   C   D

◆◆◆◆◆◆◆◆◆◆◆◆◆◆ 簡短對話 ◆◆◆◆◆◆◆◆◆◆◆◆◆◆◆

Swarbrick: I've seen some of those ads on rental videos, but frankly I don't see the point. I'd just fast-forward over them, and I would imagine that most other people do the same thing.

Cortez: I haven't seen any sort of statistics on that, but my own guess would be that about half the viewers sit patiently watching the ads.

Swarbrick: Maybe you're right, but it's certainly not the same sort of captive audience that you have for the commercials on a TV program.

---

fast-forward　快速往前卷帶　　**captive audience**　被迫非看 (聽) 不可的觀 (聽) 眾

Lesson 40

Micro Marketing —— 總結

■ ■ ■

美國的「商業周刊」雜誌每年都會將政治、經濟、企業經營、金融、以及社會上的「流行與過時」(what's in and what's out) 集結為一頁加以刊載。

在1990年當中，屬於企業經營領域的「流行」動向有 micro marketing、simplicity (單純)、early retirement (提前退休)、和 team effort (團隊努力)。而相對應的「過時」則有 bells and whistles (不具實際用的附贈品或小東西)、corporate loyalty (對企業的忠誠)、direct order (直接訂購)及 mass marketing。

此外，在社會動向上，volunteerism (志願服務精神) 和 customer service (客戶服務)為 "in"，而 narcissism (自我崇拜)和 rudeness (無禮)則為 "out"。

所謂小眾市場行銷，是基於「一般大眾」(general public) 這個概念已不復存在的想法，而將顧客層詳加分析，並透過各種行銷手法來使「真正的」消費者接收到產品信息的做法。

從 mass marketing 到 micro marketing 的改變，也可說是從原本「槍法不準多打幾發也會中」的 shotgun approach (霰彈槍手法) 轉移到 rifle approach (來福槍手法)。此外，小眾市場行銷的特徵如下：

- 分析顧客　運用高級技術手法，使顧客的輪廓明確化，並經常調整 (fine-tune) 行銷方式。
- 運用新媒體　從有線電視到學校 lunch room 的公布欄，以及錄影帶和血壓計，這些都成了新興的媒體。
- 不使用媒體的市場行銷　藉著贊助體育性活動、音樂會、或是民族節慶來滲透該地的市場。
- 對商店內消費者的市場行銷　由於消費者通常是在商店裡才決定好要買些甚麼，所以就可利用店內廣播和購物指南等來傳達商品資訊。

Lesson 41

New Consumers

（新消費者）

◆ **Lesson 41 的內容** ◆

　　小眾市場行銷並非只是在傳統的廣告上做一些變動而已。它還要對超市附近的區域做人口調查，並配合當地居民的喜好，重新調整架上的商品。而且依據不同的情況，有時會不經由媒體，而以贊助體育活動、音樂會、或民俗慶典等活動的方式，間接進行商品促銷。小眾市場行銷更要使用到電腦，來分析消費者的購買動向。史瓦布利克想要參與的興趣愈來愈大了。

Yeah. I was amazed at the information that stores and advertisers are getting from those electronic checkout scanners.

Lesson 40

New Consumers (1)（新消費者）

●預習 — *Sentences*

- We also do demographic studies of the neighborhood.
- There'd be an impossible number of markets to deal with.
- Some of them are obvious.
- Brand names mean nothing to the new under-30 crowd.
- Sales of some imports are way down.

●*Vignette*

Swarbrick: What you say about reaching people in supermarkets is certainly <u>something</u>. Still, aren't most of the things you're doing basically just variations on traditional advertising?

Cortez: Yes, to some extent. But we also do <u>demographic</u> studies of the neighborhood where a supermarket is located and rearrange shelf displays to appeal to local ethnic tastes. You see, micro marketing isn't just a matter of targeting advertising more effectively. We also suggest that some companies consider non-media marketing, like sponsoring sports events, concerts, or ethnic festivals to reach local markets.

Swarbrick: I'd think there'd be an impossible number of markets to deal with.

Cortez: Not really. Some of them are obvious. For instance, the young professionals with a little money to spare— the ones who would have been called "yuppies" a few years ago. Many manufacturers are still trying to sell products to this age group through <u>snob appeal</u>. With these companies, our job is to convince them that the new generation is very <u>noncommittal</u>. Brand names mean nothing to the new under-30 crowd—they're even mocked. No product is safe. Auto importers, for example, are now marketing to a generation too young to remember the Detroit clunkers of the early '70s. Sales of some imports are way down.

　　古岱茲解釋道，對現今三十歲以下的新人類而言，穿名牌不但不具任何意義，還會被視為笨蛋。而且，要推銷東西給雅痞的話，那種訴諸虛榮心的作法也已經落伍了。

史瓦布利克：你說要在超市內對顧客打廣告，這是個蠻不錯的點子。可是，基本上，你所做的事當中，大半都只是在傳統廣告手法上作一些改變而已，不是嗎？

古岱茲：在某種程度上，是這樣沒錯。但我們也會在超市所在地附近做人口統計學研究，並以當地種族的口味為訴求，重新安排架上貨品的陳列。你瞧，小眾市場行銷還不只是如何更有效地對正目標打廣告而已。我們也會建議一些公司考慮非媒體的市場行銷，像是贊助體育活動、音樂會、或是民俗節慶，藉以打進當地市場。

史瓦布利克：我會認為說，有很多市場是你難以攻破的。

古岱茲：不盡然。有些是很顯而易見的。比方說，像是那些有點閒錢的專業人士 ── 就是幾年前被稱作「雅痞」的那班人。有不少製造商仍舊在嘗試要以虛榮心為訴求，來把產品推銷給這個年齡層的人。跟這些廠商做事，我們的工作就是要說服他們，現在這個新世代是很難掌握的，你摸不清他們到底要甚麼。對於這些不到三十歲的新人類而言，名牌沒甚麼意義，他們甚至會嘲笑名牌商品。沒有甚麼商品有絕對的市場保證。舉例來說，汽車進口商現在就在把車推銷給一個年輕的世代，這個世代年紀輕到他們甚至不記得有70年代初期的美國製爛車。而有些進口車的銷售額一路下滑。

Lesson 41 New Consumers (1)

Words and Phrases

variation 變化	sponsor 贊助; 支持; 發起
traditional 傳統的	obvious 清楚的; 明白的
to some extent 在某種程度上	yuppie (young urban professional)
rearrange 重新安排	雅痞
shelf display 商品架上的陳列	convince 說服
appeal to 訴求於…	under-30 crowd 三十歲以下的人士
ethnic 種族的; 民族的	mock 嘲笑
target 對象	auto importer 汽車進口商
non-media marketing 非媒體的	Detroit clunker 底特律生產的破
市場行銷	車; 美國製爛車

Vocabulary Building

● **something**   了不起的人或物

cf. Adam's new girlfriend is really something else. She's right out of fashion pages.

(亞當的新女朋友確實是與眾不同。她簡直就像是從流行雜誌裡跑出來的人物。)

● **demographic**   人口統計學的

The demographic profile of Japan is aging rapidly.

(以人口統計學的角度來看, 日本社會有急速高齡化的現象。)

● **snob appeal**   以消費者的虛榮心為訴求

The ad agency used snob appeal to market the imported car.

(這家廣告代理商以虛榮心為訴求來推廣該進口車。)

● **noncommittal**   不明確的; 模糊的

Phil's "maybe" boss always gave noncommittal response to the question Phil posed to him.

(菲爾的老闆對菲爾所提出來的問題總是一會兒「也許」, 一會兒「大概」的, 從沒明確過。)

(解答見 267 頁)

▶ **Exercises**　在下列例句中，每句各有四個劃線部分，其中一個的文法有誤，請將之選出。

1. If you <u>have time</u>, Tom, please <u>bring</u> this letter to the post office and
           A   B
<u>mail it</u> <u>for me</u>.
  C   D

2. Mary will go to a <u>four-years</u> college <u>after</u> she <u>graduates</u> <u>from</u> high school.
                    A   B   C   D

3. The <u>majority</u> of the residents <u>have moved</u> to other <u>places</u> <u>by</u> May of
      A   B   C   D
next year.

◆◆◆◆◆◆◆◆◆◆◆◆◆ 簡短對話 ◆◆◆◆◆◆◆◆◆◆◆◆◆◆

Swarbrick: I have never encountered a single individual who identified himself or herself as a yuppie.

Cortez: That doesn't mean that they didn't, or don't, exist. But since the term has negative connotations— materialistic, selfish, shallow— people shy away from putting that label on themselves.

Swarbrick: I see your point. Come to think of it, it was the same with the "hippies" a couple of decades ago. They were there all right, but they didn't generally run around calling themselves that.

Cortez: Exactly.

---

encounter 碰到　　**identify oneself as** 自認為是⋯　　**negative** 否定的
connotation 弦外之音　　**materialistic** 唯物主義 (者) 的　　**shallow** 膚淺
的　　**shy away from** 遠避⋯　　**put a label on** 給⋯掛上某標記　　**come
to think of it** 想想這件事

New Consumers (2) (新消費者)

●預習 —Sentences

- It's not just young people who are resisting hype and glitter.
- Americans in general are pinching pennies.
- I don't buy anything now unless I need it.
- Consumers are becoming more interested in long-term value.
- You may as well forget those top-of-the-line designer jeans.

●Vignette

Swarbrick: It sounds as though you have to keep your eye on general buying trends, not just possible marketing techniques.

Cortez: That's right. We may specialize in micro marketing advice, but as marketing consultants, we also have to watch the big picture. For instance, we seem to be in an era of "back to basics." It's not just young people who are resisting hype and glitter. Maybe it's the economic climate, but Americans in general are pinching pennies.

Swarbrick: I know I am. I don't buy anything now unless I need it, and when I do, I make sure it's going to last a while. I guess the feeling is that we baby boomers should be saving more for educating our children and retirement instead of spending our money on imported cars and other materialistic pleasures.

Cortez: You're not the only one, Peter. Part of our job is to convince companies to take advantage of the new mood that says well-made is more important than brand name. Consumers today are becoming more interested in long-term value than short-term fads. You can see the style on the street shifting from expensive polo shirts to comfortable T-shirts. And you may as well forget those top-of-the-line designer jeans. It's up to manufacturers and retailers to understand the changing mood of the buying public. People are looking for simpler pleasures.

* * *

　　身為行銷諮詢顧問，必須掌握所有相關的消費趨勢。特別是現在有不少人會抗拒大而華麗的宣傳攻勢。而且，今天的美國人都變得蠻節儉的。

史瓦布利克： 聽起來，你好像得要隨時注意整個的消費趨勢，而不只是些可能的行銷手法。

古岱茲： 沒錯。我們是專門給些小眾市場行銷的建議，但身為行銷諮詢顧問，我們也得要有全面的概觀。比方說，我們所身處的，似乎是個「回歸原點」的年代。現在可不是只有年輕人在抗拒宣傳廣告和外表閃亮的東西而已。也許，這是一種經濟現況，不過現在美國人一般都蠻節儉的。

史瓦布利克： 我自己就是這樣。現在除非必要，否則我不會買東西，而且一旦買了，我就要確定這東西可以用上一陣子。我想，這是因為我們嬰兒潮世代的人覺得，錢不該都花在進口車和物質享受上，倒該多存點，作為孩子的教育費，也為退休預作打算。

古岱茲： 彼得，你可不是唯一一個這麼想的人。很多人都有這種新的體認，覺得品質比品牌重要，而我們工作的一部分，就是說服這些廠家，要善加利用消費者這種心態上的轉變。今天的消費者是不一樣了。令他們更感興趣的，是東西的長程價值，而不是短期的流行。你可以在街上看到，今日的時尚已從昂貴的套頭襯衫，轉變成舒適的 T 恤。你不妨忘掉那些名家設計的高級牛仔褲。現在就看那些製造商和零售業者能否瞭解消費大眾在心態上的轉變了。人們都在尋求樸實一點的享受。

＊　　　＊　　　＊

Lesson 41 New Consumers (2)

Words and Phrases

keep one's eye on	釘住；監視	last	支持；耐久
resist	抵抗；抗拒	materialistic pleasure	物質享受
hype	宣傳；推廣	take advantage of	利用…
glitter	(外表)閃亮的東西	fad	流行
economic climate	經濟狀況	designer jeans	名家設計的牛仔褲
make sure	確定		

Vocabulary Building

- **watch the big picture**　縱觀全體
  I tend to get bogged down in details, so I have to keep reminding myself to watch the big picture.
  (我很容易就會陷在一些細節上出不來，所以我必須一直提醒自己，要就整體來看事情。)

- **back to basics**　回歸原點；回到起點
  In this era of "back to basics," we've got to convince consumers of the intrinsic value of our products.
  (在這個「回歸原點」的年代裡，我們必須讓消費者信服我們產品本身的價值。)

- **pinch pennies**　節儉的；小氣的
  cf. Preston's penny-pinching approach to management alienated many of the people working for him.
  (普瑞斯敦在經營管理上的小氣作風，使得很多人都不願在他手下工作。)

- **top-of-the-line**　最高級的
  The price of our top-of-the-line ice cream is a bit lower than our leading competitor's.
  (本公司所生產的最高級冰淇淋，其售價比我們最大的競爭對手所生產的要低一點。)

1. Henry <u>can't hardly</u> run <u>since</u> he <u>broke</u> his leg <u>playing</u> baseball.
　　　　　A　　　　　　B　　　　C　　　　　　　D

2. All <u>students</u> must either write a term paper <u>and</u> present an <u>oral</u> report
　　　　A　　　　　　　　　　　　　　　　　B　　　　　　　C
to the <u>class</u>.
　　　　D

3. Yesterday I <u>asked to</u> Mr. Roberts which day he <u>sent</u> the postcard and
　　　　　　　　A　　　　　　　　　　　　　　　　　B
he said he <u>was</u> not sure that he <u>sent</u> it at all.
　　　　　　C　　　　　　　　　　D

◆◆◆◆◆◆◆◆◆◆◆◆◆ 簡短對話 ◆◆◆◆◆◆◆◆◆◆◆◆◆

Cortez: Another aspect of the popular mood now is the increased awareness
of environmental issues on the part of the average consumer. People are
thinking more about whether the products they buy are ecologically sound
or not.

Swarbrick: We were talking about that at Nelson ABC Foods a couple of
months ago. What triggered the discussion was the announcement that the
company was going to plant a million trees in the next decade.

Cortez: I read about that in the paper. That was quite a PR coup, I thought.

---

ecologically sound 無害生態環境的　　　**trigger** 引起　　　**PR coup** PR(公
關)的成功

New Consumers (3) (新消費者)

●預習 —*Sentences*

- Maria can teach me a great deal about marketing, too.
- Thanks so much for the introduction.
- I'm really pleased that you two got along so well.
- Someday *all* marketing might be micro marketing.
- The same thing applies to Nelson ABC Foods.

●*Vignette*

Sawasaki: Oh, hi, Peter. How did your talk with Maria go?

Swarbrick: It was really great. It went so well, in fact, that we've arranged to talk again. I think micro marketing may be the way for me to go. You were right, Shoichi. Maria is very nice, and she can teach me a great deal about marketing too. Thanks so much for the introduction.

Sawasaki: I'm really pleased that you two got along so well. You know, I've been doing some reading about micro marketing myself. It looks like someday *all* marketing might be micro marketing. Did you talk about the things that are happening in point-of-sale marketing?

Swarbrick: Yes, including radio ads coming from the ceiling. I never realized before just how many decisions I was making at the supermarket based on packaging or presentation—why I was buying a particular brand of soap, for instance. Maria told me about the quote by the tycoon who said, "Half of the money I spend on advertising is wasted, and the trouble is, I don't know which half."

Sawasaki: The same thing applies to Nelson ABC Foods. But as you probably realize after your talk with Maria, that's beginning to change. We're beginning to learn which half is wasted, you might say. It's another field that couldn't really exist without computers.

聽了古岱茲的話，史瓦布利克覺得：「或許小眾市場行銷會是我將來的出路。」他衷心地感謝澤崎的引薦。

澤崎： 噢，嗨，彼得。你跟瑪莉亞談得如何？

史瓦布利克： 棒極了。事實上，事情順利到我們已經在安排第二次的談話了。我想，小眾市場行銷會是我要走的路。昭一，你說得沒錯，瑪莉亞人很好，而且她還可以教我很多行銷上的事。非常謝謝你替我引薦。

澤崎： 我真的很高興你們處得這麼好。你知道嗎，我自己也正在看關於小眾市場行銷的書。看來，似乎所有的行銷有一天都會走上小眾市場行銷的路。你們有談到店頭行銷嗎？

史瓦布利克： 有啊，還包括了從天花板放送的無線電廣告。我以前一點都不知道，我在超市會買哪些東西，都是根據他們的包裝或展示 —— 像是我為何要買某種特定的香皂等的。瑪莉亞還告訴我關於某個商業鉅子所說過的話，他說，「我花在廣告上的錢有一半都浪費掉了，麻煩的是，我根本不知道是哪一半。」

澤崎： 同樣的情形也適用於尼爾森 ABC 食品公司。不過，在你跟瑪莉亞談過之後，你可能也會瞭解，這種情形要開始改觀了。或者你也可以說，我們就要開始知道，是哪一半給浪費掉了。這是另一個沒有電腦就無法存在的領域。

Words and Phrases

quote *n.*	引用句	apply	適用

Vocabulary Building

- **introduction**   介紹

  Several years ago Sandra gave me introduction to the president of a major oil company, and now they're one of my biggest customers.

  (幾年前，珊卓給我引見了一位大石油公司的總裁，現在這家公司是我最大的客戶之一。)

- **get along**   (與人)相處

  I don't mean to boast, but I can get along with just about any type of person.

  (我不是有意吹噓，但我幾乎跟每一種人都能處得來。)

- **point-of-sale marketing**   店頭行銷

  For supermarkets, successful point-of-sale marketing can turn a break-even operation into a highly profitable one.

  (對於超級市場而言，成功的店頭行銷可以扭轉其不賺不賠的營運狀況，而使利潤大為提升。)

- **tycoon**   (實業界、政界的)鉅子；大亨

  James started his business on a shoestring. But after many years of hard work, he's become a tycoon of the retail trade.

  (詹姆士是以極小的資本起家的，但經過數年的努力，他已經成為零售業的鉅子了。)

▶**Exercises**　在下列例句中，每句各有四個劃線部分，
其中一個的文法有誤，請將之選出。　　(解答見 267頁)

1. The <u>exam results</u> stunned the <u>math teachers</u> because <u>any</u> of the students
　　　　A　　　　　　　　　　　　B　　　　　　　　C
　<u>could</u> answer the basic equations.
　　D

2. The <u>guest of honor</u>, sitting <u>with</u> his wife and three children, <u>were</u> intro-
　　　　A　　　　　　　　B　　　　　　　　　　　　　　　　C
　duced <u>at</u> the state dinner.
　　　D

3. If one does not sleep <u>soundly</u> at night, <u>you</u> cannot <u>expect</u> to work effec-
　　　　　　　　　　　　A　　　　　　　B　　　　C
　tively <u>the next day</u>.
　　　　　D

◆◆◆◆◆◆◆◆◆◆◆◆◆◆ 簡短對話 ◆◆◆◆◆◆◆◆◆◆◆◆◆◆

Sawasaki: So you think you may decide to work for Maria?

Swarbrick: Well, she didn't actually come out and offer me a job.

Sawasaki: But you're going to be getting together again, right?

Swarbrick: Yeah, a week from tomorrow.

Sawasaki: She wouldn't have set up another meeting if she weren't interested in you.

Swarbrick: That's what I thought too, though I didn't want to jump to any
conclusions.

---

offer a job　提供工作機會　　**a week from tomorrow**　明天起算一個禮拜後
jump to a conclusion　急著下結論

Lesson 40

New Consumers (4)（新消費者）

●預習 — *Sentences*

- We're working on that as a test case in California.
- We can get weekly information on how a brand is doing.
- I'm going to need your advice about a lot of things, Shoichi.
- I've been planning to ask *you* for help.
- Gil has asked me to take over some of your duties.

●*Vignette*

Swarbrick: Yeah. I was amazed at the information that stores and advertisers are getting from those electronic checkout scanners. I thought they were just foolproof cash registers, but Maria said that supermarkets are gathering an immense amount of marketing data that way, and sharing it with their suppliers.

Sawasaki: You know, sometimes the distributors are linked right into a store's computers. We're working on that as a test case in some of our California districts. The information is far more accurate than what you get from the old method of asking consumers about their preferences. We can get weekly information on how a brand is doing, including a breakdown by item and size, and we can see what happens if we try a regional coupon, for instance. I've heard that some distributors are planning campaigns down to the level of the individual store.

Swarbrick: It seems that marketing in general is becoming another information battleground. In the increasingly competitive market-place of the '90s, it'll really be important to stand out. You know, if I do jump into micro marketing as a field, I'm going to need your advice about a lot of things, Shoichi.

Sawasaki: It's funny you should say that. I've been planning to ask *you* for help. There's going to be a hiring freeze, and Gil has asked me to take over some of your duties, and so I'm going to need your advice.

Swarbrick: No problem. We'll have mutual education sessions.

　　市場行銷似乎正在成為另一個資訊戰場。在 90 年代這個競爭加劇的市場上，能夠出類拔萃是相當重要的。現在是小眾市場行銷登場的時候了。

史瓦布利克： 是啊。令我驚訝的是，店家和廣告人居然可以從電子結帳掃瞄器上獲得那樣的資料。我還以為那種機器只是簡單好用、又不容易出錯的收銀機罷了。可是瑪莉亞卻說，超市藉著這種收銀方式，得到了龐大的行銷數據，而且他們也會跟供應商分享。

澤崎： 你知道嗎，有時候經銷商會直接跟商店的電腦連線。我們公司此刻就在一些加州的銷售區作實例測試。比起以前用詢問來得知顧客喜好的老方法，現在我們所獲得的資料可要來得正確多了。我們每個禮拜都可以知道某個品牌賣的情形如何，甚至還包括賣出數量和商品尺寸的明細。而且我們也可以獲知，像是說，假使嘗試發行地區性折價券的話，會有甚麼樣的結果。我還聽到說有些經銷商正計畫要在一家一家的商店作推廣活動。

史瓦布利克： 就一般而言，看來市場行銷正在成為另一個資訊戰場。在 90 年代這個競爭加劇的市場上，能夠出類拔萃是相當重要的。你知道嗎，昭一，如果我真的進入小眾市場行銷界，有很多事我會需要你的建議。

澤崎： 你這樣說有點好笑。我才正打算要向你求援呢！因為公司即將會有人事凍結，而吉爾要我接一些你的工作，所以我會需要你的建議。

史瓦布利克： 沒問題。我們將會有相互的教育聚會。

Lesson 41　New Consumers (4)

---**Words and Phrases**---

cash register　收銀機
immense　龐大的
electronic checkout scanner　電子結帳掃瞄器〈使用於較大賣場的一種新式收銀機，它採用光學原理，讀取商品上的條碼，使商品的所有資料全數載入電腦，而令結帳速度加快，且不易出錯〉
distributor　經銷商
accurate　正確的
down to　往下到⋯
information battleground　資訊戰場
jump into　躍入

Vocabulary Building

- **foolproof**　極簡單的；愚人也會的；相當安全的
Josh developed a foolproof mix for perfect brownies.
（賈西開發出了一種作法相當簡易的速食配料，可製作出極佳的花生巧克力糖。）

- **preference**　喜好；嗜好；偏好
We have no dress code in this office. What people wear is totally a matter of personal preference.
（我們這個辦公室沒有穿著上的規定。大家愛穿甚麼就穿甚麼。）

- **breakdown**　分析；明細
The Department of Labor demanded a breakdown of our workforce by age, gender, race, and job category.
（勞工部要求公司交出一份員工分析表，裡頭要有員工的年齡、性別、種族、和工作類別。）

- **hiring freeze**　人事凍結
As a result of the hiring freeze and attrition, the number of our employees has dropped 20 percent.
（由於人事凍結加上人員自然減少的結果，我們的員工數目減少了百分之二十。）

1. Millions of people use computers, but most would not consider them-
   　A　　　　　　B　　　　　　　C

   selves as computer literate.
   　　　D

2. Compare the cost of housing in Japan to that of other countries to get
   　A　　　　　　　　　　　　　B　　C　　　　　　　　　　D

   a real sense of the value of money.

3. According to some researchers, the sea level appears to have raised
   　　A　　　　　　　　　　　　　　　　　　　　　　　　　B

   around the world throughout the last decade.
   　　　C　　　　　　　D

◆◆◆◆◆◆◆◆◆◆◆◆◆ 簡短對話 ◆◆◆◆◆◆◆◆◆◆◆◆◆

Sawasaki: I wasn't sure how well you'd take to the idea of interviewing with
a woman a couple of years younger than you.

Swarbrick: Oh, I have no problems with that at all. I'd much rather report
to an intelligent person like Maria, regardless of her gender or age, than
to an older male for whom I couldn't feel respect.

Sawasaki: I guess my concern may just be a residue of my Japanese preju-
dices.

Swarbrick: I wouldn't say that. Some American men still have trouble
accepting women as bosses. I'm not one of them, though.

---

take to the idea of 喜歡某種主意　　**regardless of** 不論…　　**gender** 性別
residue 殘餘　　**prejudice** 偏見

Lesson 41

New Consumers —— 總結

我們試著從 Yankelovich 公司所發行的Yankelovich Monitor 中, 以 what's in and what's out 的方式來展望 90 年代美國的消費動向。

- 在高級百貨公司購物為"out", 郵購 (mail order) 則為"in"。「便利」成為商品的最大特色。
- 用完即丟的瓶子為"out"。 recycling才是正確的觀念。
- 縱使價錢較貴, 消費者也不惜多花一點錢購買符合環境生態的 green product。
- 沙拉吧或酸乳酪為"in", 含脂肪的食物則為"out"。人們希望能「繼續保持年輕健康」 (remain young and fit)。
- 因此, 化妝品業也要趕搭這輛列車。
- yuppies 消失了, 戰後嬰兒潮成為社會的中堅。他們要為子女的教育及自己退休後的生活儲蓄, 所以, 高級進口車或物質享受皆為"out"。
- 在西元 2000 年之前, 美國的不吸菸人口將達八成, 啤酒或其他酒精類飲料的銷售額也會降低 (相反地, 非酒精或低酒精飲料的銷售則會上升)。
- 在嬰兒潮之後的出生率劇降期間, 由於出生率低至 1.2%以下。所以, 今後勞動力不足的現象會更加嚴重。
- 激烈的 ("burn it") 運動為"out"。高爾夫、壘球或是散步、庭院勞動等的適度運動則為"in"。
- 定期調薪為"out", 獎金則為"in"。由於現在仍屬前途不明的年代, 所以短期性的工作能力將益發受到重視。
- 女性的社會地位大增, 目前有不少女性本身的權利正逐漸受到立法保障。
- 退休年齡提前, 而老人獨居的情形將增多。
- 食品類中唯一銷售量增加的是微波食品, 消費者可以依照包裝上標示的營養成份來選購。
- 電腦將與人類的生活更加密不可分, home banking或home shopping 的方式亦將更為普遍。
- 在美國人眼中, 流行 (fad) 將成為不具實質意義的字眼。

Volunteerism

（自願活動）

◆ Lesson 42 的內容 ◆

在尼爾森 ABC 食品公司，自願活動占了社區公關工作的絕
大部分。比起企業直接出錢贊助，公司員工若也能盡上自己的一
分，那更能給社區留下良好的印象。企業之所以要藉自願活動來
維繫其與社區間的互動關係，雖有部分原因是要彌補其惡劣形
象，但其實一般美國人也常常會參加自願活動。即便是具有相當
地位的人，也常去帶童軍團、當足球教練、或是到托兒所照顧兒
童等的。撥不出時間來的人，則捐款贊助各種社會活動。

Other people volunteer
their time-to act as
Scout leaders or
football coaches, or
to help out at a day-
care center,
keeping an
eye on the
kids.

Lesson 42

Volunteerism (1)（自願活動）

●預習 — *Sentences*

- You said volunteerism was a big part of community relations.
- In a way, all community relations work is volunteerism.
- I'm impressed by the amount of time that the company spends.
- Volunteerism is a very important part of life.
- I think most of the nonprofit organizations would collapse.

●*Vignette*

Sawasaki: Oh, hello, Peter. Have a seat.

Swarbrick: How's it going, Shoichi, Sally? Got enough to do?

Egler: Oh, no, we're just sitting here trying to figure out what to do with all our spare time.

Sawasaki: Right. Seriously, though, Peter. I've been reading over your files, and I've realized you weren't kidding when you said volunteerism was a big part of community relations.

Swarbrick: In a way, all community relations work is volunteerism, but personal commitment by individual people is far more impressive to members of the community than simply seeing the company write a check.

Sawasaki: Either way, I'm impressed by the amount of time and effort that the company spends on things that don't seem to directly affect our business.

Swarbrick: Right. Volunteerism is a very important part of life in the United States— not just for businesses, but for individuals. Even people who don't even think of themselves as volunteers or "joiners" often write several checks a year to help support everything from public television to saving the whales.

Egler: I think most of the nonprofit organizations in this country would collapse if it weren't for people's willingness to respond to direct-mail solicitation.

史瓦布利克說：「就某方面來看，所有的社區公關工作都是自願活動。」但在澤崎的想法中，公司居然會把時間和人力投注在這些與公司業務無關的事物上，實在是不可思議。

澤崎：　噢，哈囉，彼得。請坐。

史瓦布利克：　昭一、莎莉，事情進行得如何？工作量夠不夠啊？

艾格勒：　不夠啊！我們正坐在這兒想辦法打發時間。

澤崎：　就是啊。不過，彼得，跟你說正經的，我正在看你整理的檔案，我這才瞭解，原來你說社區公共關係有大半都是自願活動並不是開玩笑呢。

史瓦布利克：　就某方面來看，所有的社區公關工作都是自願活動。可是，若公司個別的員工也能獻出自己的力量，那對於社區民眾而言，會比單紙的公司捐款要來得令人印象深刻。

澤崎：　不管是哪一種，我蠻敬佩公司把時間和精力花在那些看來不會直接影響公司業務的事情上。

史瓦布利克：　是啊，自願活動是美國生活中相當重要的一部分，這還不單是針對事業團體而已，對個人也是一樣。甚至那些不認為自己是自願者或「愛參加社團活動者」的人士，也常會一年開個幾張支票來協助支持各種活動，其對象從公共電視到反對捕鯨的運動都有。

艾格勒：　我覺得，要不是有人願意回應那些直接寄給他們的募款信函，那這個國家內大部分的非營利機構是無法經營下去的。

Lesson 42 Volunteerism (1)

Words and Phrases

figure out	解決；想出來	joiner	喜歡參加社團活動的人
spare time	空暇時間	public television	公共電視
kid *v.*	開玩笑	save the whales	反對捕鯨 (運動)
in a way	就某種意義而言；或多或少	collapse *v.*	崩潰
individual *adj.*	個人的	respond	反應
write a check	開支票	direct-mail solicitation	直接用信
affect	影響		函來做的募款或求援

Vocabulary Building

- **volunteerism**　自願活動
  Volunteerism is fine, but it alone can't solve all our social problems.
  (自願活動是不錯，但單靠它還不能解決我們所有的社會問題。)

- **community relations**　社區公共關係〈為促進與地方社會的關係而推行的活動〉
  We've tried to turn our community relations program into something more than a publicity campaign for company.
  (我們設法要讓我們的社區公共關係計畫不僅僅是一種公司的宣傳活動而已。)

- **nonprofit organization**　非營利團體
  This firm wasn't intended to be a nonprofit organization. It just turned out that way!
  (這家公司並非有意要成為一個非營利機構。它只是經營到後來賺不到錢罷了！)

- **if it weren't for**　要不是有…
  I never could have succeeded in turning the company around if it hadn't been for the support of the employees.
  (要不是有員工的支持，我是決計無法成功扭轉公司局面的。)

▶Exercises

在下列例句中，每句各有四個劃線部分，
其中一個的文法有誤，請將之選出。

(解答見 268頁)

1. This computer is <u>capable of</u> <u>storing</u> millions of <u>pieces of</u> <u>informations</u>.
                A   B   C   D

2. My uncle always <u>says</u> <u>lots of</u> jokes and funny stories <u>when</u> he <u>gets drunk</u>
                     A   B   C   D
  on wine.

3. I <u>have lain</u> your keys under the door mat <u>so that</u> you <u>won't</u> <u>miss</u> them.
    A   B   C   D

◆◆◆◆◆◆◆◆◆◆◆◆◆ 簡短對話 ◆◆◆◆◆◆◆◆◆◆◆◆◆◆

Sawasaki: I didn't realize that nonprofit organizations used direct mail to solicit contributions.

Swarbrick: Is that right? Most of us get hit for contributions through the mail so frequently it's hard to imagine that somebody could live here for any length of time without getting on at least one organization's mailing list.

Sawasaki: I suppose they'll get to me eventually. Anyway, I'd much rather deal with a request in the mail than a panhandler on the street.

---

solicit 募集   **contribution** 捐獻   **panhandler** 乞丐

Lesson 42

Volunteerism (2)（自願活動）

●預習 —Sentences

- Other people volunteer their time to act as Scout leaders.
- A successful business creates wealth, jobs, and stability.
- It's as if companies had Jekyll and Hyde personalities.
- Volunteerism is also good for the volunteers themselves.
- It makes them feel better about themselves, right?

●Vignette

Swarbrick: Other people volunteer their time— to act as Scout leaders or football coaches, or to help out at a day-care center, keeping an eye on the kids.

Sawasaki: This is all still kind of new to me. In Japan, the philosophy is that a profitable company benefits the community merely by existing. A successful business creates wealth, jobs, and stability to benefit the community. In America, it's as if companies had Jekyll and Hyde personalities. Competing mercilessly with other companies. Laying off workers by the thousands, if necessary. And yet finding ways to give millions of dollars worth of support to their communities.

Swarbrick: Well, historically, companies didn't let people go by the thousands. But in a way, you're right, Shoichi. One of the reasons community involvement is so important is because the image of business today is negative.

Egler: From your notes I get the impression that volunteerism is also good for the volunteers themselves. It makes them feel better about themselves, right?

Swarbrick: It certainly does. It also makes them feel more a part of their community, which is good for anybody.

Sawasaki: I now know something about the "adopt-a-school" program.

　　澤崎說，「在美國，企業似乎都有雙重人格。必要時可以一次裁員數千人，可是在另一方面，卻還要想辦法把價值數百萬美元的援助提供給他們的社區。」

史瓦布利克： 其他人貢獻他們的時間 —— 去帶領童軍團、做做足球教練、或是在日間托嬰中心幫忙看小孩。

澤崎： 這對我而言都還太新了點。在日本，我們的哲學是，一家賺錢的公司可裨益社區的方式是：別關門大吉就好了。因為一個成功的企業能給地方上帶來財富和工作機會，而且也有穩定社會的功效。但在美國，企業似乎都有雙重人格。一方面，他們無情地與同業展開競爭，而且必要的話，還會裁掉數以千計的員工。可是在另一方面，他們卻還要想辦法把價值數百萬的援助提供給他們的社區。

史瓦布利克： 嗯，就歷史上來看，公司並沒有讓上千的員工走路。不過，昭一，在某種意義上，你是對的。與社區連結之所以重要的原因之一是，今日的企業形象是負面的。

艾格勒： 從你所做的摘記，我有種感覺，就是自願活動對於自願者本身也頗有益處，可以幫助他們提升對自己的感覺看法，對嗎？

史瓦布利克： 這是當然，而且也能使他們對自己的社區更有歸屬感。這對任何人都是件好事。

澤崎： 我現在知道一點關於「認養學校」計畫的事了。

Lesson 42　Volunteerism (2)

Words and Phrases

Scout leader　童軍領隊	mercilessly　無情地
day-care center　日間托嬰中心	lay off　裁員
keep an eye on　留意; 照顧	if necessary　必要的話
kind of　〔口語〕有點	let someone go　解雇某人
benefit　裨益	note　摘記; 注釋
Jekyll and Hyde personalities	"adopt-a-school" program　「認
雙重人格〈出自 R. L. Stevenson 所	養學校」計畫〈藉著提供支援或資源
著的 *The Strange Case of Dr. Jekyll*	而與學校建立起新關係的一種計畫〉
and Mr. Hyde〉	

Vocabulary Building

- **philosophy**　哲學; 人生觀
  My philosophy is that you should only take on as much work as you can do properly without rushing.
  (我的人生哲學是, 不要一次肩負太多的工作, 總要以能不慌不忙地處理每件事為原則。)

- **by the thousands**　數以千計地
  Protest letters poured in by the thousands after the government official made a racial slur on an open debate program on TV.
  (自從那個政府官員在某電視公開辯論節目中作了個帶種族歧視的誣衊性評論之後, 數以千計的抗議信函湧了進來。)

- **negative**　否定的; 負面的; 消極的
  Jones will never get anywhere in this company unless he can get rid of his negative outlook on life.
  (除非瓊斯能拋掉他那種消極的人生觀, 否則他在這家公司是不會有所成就的。)

- **get the impression**　得到某種印象
  I get the impression from your presentation that your company has little experience in consumer promotion. Is that right?
  (我從你的簡報中得到一種印象, 就是你們公司在消費者提升上沒甚麼經驗。是這樣嗎?)

(解答見 268 頁)

▶ *Exercises*

在下列例句中，每句各有四個劃線部分，
其中一個的文法有誤，請將之選出。

1. The <u>cost of living</u> has <u>raised</u> <u>over</u> 15 percent in the <u>past</u> six years.
        A   B   C   D

2. David <u>asked</u> the caller to <u>repeat again</u> because he <u>did</u> not catch him
        A   B   C
<u>the first ime</u>.
     D

3. The <u>duty</u> of school teachers <u>are</u> to teach their subjects, to <u>grade</u> their
     A   B   C
<u>students, and to give them guidance</u>.
   D

◆◆◆◆◆◆◆◆◆◆◆◆◆ 簡短對話 ◆◆◆◆◆◆◆◆◆◆◆◆◆

Sawasaki: Did you have any other ideas about organizing the volunteer effort, Peter?

Swarbrick: My dream would be to have the centerpiece of the whole volunteer program follow the lead of some corporations and have what you might call a "social service corps."

Sawasaki: How would it function?

Swarbrick: This could be a few people from throughout the company who have some seniority and who'd like to take a leave of absence for a year or two to work on some vital nonprofit activity.

Sawasaki: I see the value of a program like that.

---

centerpiece 中心物　　**follow the lead of** 跟從…的帶領　　**function** *v.* 起作用　　**leave of absence** 留職停薪

Lesson 42

Volunteerism (3) (自願活動)

預習 — *Sentences*

- The school program just scratches the surface.
- Maybe you should do what I've been thinking about.
- The same person might not mind pushing a good cause.
- Different people have different skills.
- What about the people who can't contribute their time?

Vignette

Sawasaki: Coordinating volunteer tutors for that program will be a job in itself. And I can see from the information you've given us that the school program just scratches the surface.

Swarbrick: That's right. We have volunteers doing all sorts of things. Long before I took over the job, a major part of Nelson's public relations effort was directed toward finding donations or volunteers for this group or that— a children's symphony or aid for Africa— pretty much on an ad hoc basis. Maybe you should do what I've been thinking about, which is to break our volunteer effort down into certain areas, and try to match volunteers with programs.

Sawasaki: How would that work?

Swarbrick: For instance, maybe a person doesn't want to tutor because he or she isn't much of a teacher, but the same person might enjoy talking to people and not mind pushing a good cause. People like that could visit service clubs or alumni groups to enlist their help with things. Different people have different skills, and they would probably enjoy volunteering more if they could do something that felt comfortable.

Egler: What about the people who can't contribute their time? Some people have young families. Some are looking after elderly relatives. Some work overtime every day. How can they take part?

198

　　史瓦布利克建議，將來可以設法把自願活動細分成幾個不同的範疇，使自願者與企畫案相結合。由於每個人的所長各自不同，所以若能讓他們做些自己覺得能勝任的事，那是再好不過了。

澤崎：　要去協調計畫中的自願家庭教師，這本身就是件工作了。而且我可以從你給我們的資料上看出，這個學校計畫才剛有點眉目而已。

史瓦布利克：　是沒錯，我們有自願者在做各式各樣的事。早在我接這個工作之前，尼爾森公關部門的工作重點，都是著重於為這個組織或那個團體 —— 兒童交響樂團或非洲救濟活動 —— 募款或尋求自願者，經常都是倉促成軍，沒啥計畫可言，也許你們該做點我一直在想的事，就是把我們自願者的力量細分成幾個特定領域，並設法使自願者與企畫案相配合。

澤崎：　那將如何運作？

史瓦布利克：　比方說，也許某個人不怎麼想當家庭教師，因為這位男士或女士對於教書並不太在行，可是同樣這個人可能很愛跟人說話，並且也願意為了達到任何良好目的而努力。像這樣的人可以去拜訪服務性社團或校友會，以在各面尋得援助。不同的人有不同的技能，如果能令他們做些心理上舒服一點的事，也許他們會更喜歡這樣的自願工作。

艾格勒：　對於那些撥不出時間來的人怎麼辦？有些人家裡有小孩，有些必須照顧家中的老年人，有些則每天要加班。他們要如何參與其事？

Lesson 42　Volunteerism (3)

Words and Phrases

tutor	家庭教師	alumni [əˈlʌmnaɪ] group	校友會
direct toward	朝向…(而去)	enlist	募得
donation	捐款	skill	技巧
ad hoc	臨時的; 特別的	contribute	貢獻
match with	與…配合	look after	照顧

Vocabulary Building

- **scratch the surface**　只涉及事件的表面(皮毛)
  We've already found 20 areas where we can cut costs, and we've only scratched the surface.
  (我們已經找到了二十個可以削減開支的地方了，不過這還只是在事情的表面打轉而已。)

- **break something down into**　把某物分解或分散至…
  Rex was overwhelmed by the magnitude of the job, but he found it easier after he broke it down into more manageable pieces.
  (這項工作的規模之大，頗令雷克斯覺得承擔不起，不過，在他把工作細分成比較處理得了的單位之後，他發現事情容易多了。)

- **not much of**　不是甚麼了不起的…
  Fred's a great salesman, but he's not much of a manager.
  (弗瑞德是個了不起的推銷員，但他當起經理來就不怎麼樣了。)

- **push a cause**　為著某個理想或目標而努力
  People will work hard to push a cause they truly believe in.
  (人們對於自己所真實確信的標的，都會為之全力以赴。)

▶ **Exercises** 在下列例句中，每句各有四個劃線部分，
其中一個的文法有誤，請將之選出。 （解答見 268 頁）

1. Every man <u>and</u> woman 18 years of age <u>or older</u> <u>are</u> <u>eligible</u> to have a
          A   B   C   D
    driver's license.

2. I majored <u>in</u> statistics <u>in</u> college and am interested <u>in</u> <u>their</u> application
             A   B   C D
    to technology.

3. Many Japanese <u>are marveled</u> at the <u>cost</u> of Japanese <u>products</u> overseas
                      A   B   C
    because they are cheaper <u>than in Japan.</u>
                                 D

◆◆◆◆◆◆◆◆◆◆◆◆◆ 簡短對話 ◆◆◆◆◆◆◆◆◆◆◆◆◆

Sawasaki: Have you discussed the social service corps concept with any of the senior people here yet?

Swarbrick: Not really. I did run the idea by Gil a couple of months ago, though, and he wasn't really interested.

Sawasaki: If we handle it properly, something like that also has a lot of potential to generate good publicity for the company.

Swarbrick: I certainly think so. I'm only sorry I don't have the rails already laid for you on this one.

Sawasaki: Don't worry about it. But I'm really glad you shared the idea with me.

---

run something by 向…說明某事　　**potential** 可能性　　**lay the rails** 鋪設
軌道

Lesson 42

Volunteerism (4) （自願活動）

預習 — Sentences

- You know money is the gift that keeps on giving.
- We have a good matching grant program here at Nelson.
- The company will match it, up to a limit of $2,000.
- The company has been doing it for some time.
- You guys will have to pick up the ball.

Vignette

Swarbrick: Well, you know money is the gift that keeps on giving, Sally. We have a good matching grant program here at Nelson.

Egler: How does that work?

Swarbrick: I'm surprised they didn't tell you more about this when you came aboard. If you want to make a contribution to a nonprofit organization, the company will match it, up to a limit of $2,000.

Egler: That's extremely generous.

Swarbrick: The company has been doing it for some time. I guess I haven't done a good enough job of publicizing it. You guys will have to pick up the ball.

Sawasaki: I agree with Sally. This must cost the company a pretty penny. Why do they do it?

Swarbrick: It's a way of making sure that the company puts some of its community contributions in places that its own employees care about. And it makes the employees feel good too, because it allows them to make a major contribution to their favorite causes, and it lets them know that their company is backing them up on something they feel is important.

Egler: It sounds good, but I honestly don't see where we're going to find the time for all this.

Sawasaki: Cheer up, Sally. Between us we'll manage somehow.

撥不出時間參加自願活動的人可以出錢贊助。在尼爾森有一個同額補助捐款計畫，如果員工要捐錢給非營利機構，公司會補助同樣數額的錢，最高可以到 2000 美元。

史瓦布利克：嗯，莎莉，妳也知道，金錢是種可以一直給出去的禮物。在尼爾森有個相當好的同額補助捐款計畫。

艾格勒：那是怎麼個運作法？

史瓦布利克：我真驚訝！他們居然沒在你們進公司的時候多告訴你們一些這個計畫的事！它是這樣的，如果你們要捐錢給非營利機構，公司會補助同樣數額的錢，最高可以到 2000 美元。

艾格勒：那真的是非常慷慨。

史瓦布利克：公司這樣做已經有一段時間了。我想我沒有善盡宣傳之責。現在這個球可是傳到你們手上了。

澤崎：我同意莎莉的話。這得花掉公司一大筆錢，他們為甚麼要這麼做？

史瓦布利克：藉著這種方式，公司可以確定，其社會捐助款項中有某些部分是捐給自己的員工所關心的機構。而這也能體貼員工的心，因為員工可以捐贈大筆金錢給自己所關切的運動或機關團體。員工會因此明白，公司也在他們所重視的事上支持他們。

艾格勒：聽來不錯，可是我真的不知道我們甚麼時候才會有時間來做這樣的事。

澤崎：高興一點，莎莉。我們兩個會有辦法解決的。

Lesson 42　Volunteerism (4)

Words and Phrases

come aboard	進公司	put in place	放進
up to a limit of	到…的限度	cause	主義; 主張; 目標; 理想
generous	寬大的; 慷慨的	back up	支持
publicize	宣傳		

Vocabulary Building

- **matching grant program**　同額補助捐款計畫
  Taking advantage of your employer's matching grant program enables you to double the value of your contribution to your favorite cause.
  (你可以利用公司的同額補助捐款計畫, 那麼, 你所關切的機關團體就會得到兩倍於你原欲捐獻的款額。)

- **pick up the ball**　接手 (繼續進行某事)
  I've done my best to get the energy-saving program started. Now it's your turn to pick up the ball.
  (我已經盡我所能地來使這個節約能源計畫開始進行。現在輪到你們來接管這檔子事了。)

- **pretty penny**　一筆不小的費用
  Having his teeth fixed cost Paul a pretty penny.
  (保羅花了一大筆錢來整治他的牙齒。)

- **Cheer up.**　振奮起來。
  Cheer up. After all, things could be a lot worse.
  (快樂一點。畢竟, 事情有可能比現在糟得多的。)

▶ **Exercises**　在下列例句中，每句各有四個劃線部分，其中一個的文法有誤，請將之選出。　（解答見 268 頁）

1. <u>Neither</u> the United States nor the countries of Europe <u>requires</u> vaccina-
   A   B
   tion <u>against</u> any <u>kind</u> of illness.
        C   D

2. <u>Everyone</u> who <u>majors</u> in archaeology or anthropology <u>have to study</u> so-
   A   B   C
   ciology in order to understand <u>humanity</u>.
                                  D

3. There <u>have</u> been several objections <u>raised</u> <u>about</u> the new Supreme Court
         A   B   C
   judge concerning his <u>passed</u> personal scandals.
                        D

◆◆◆◆◆◆◆◆◆◆◆◆◆ 簡短對話 ◆◆◆◆◆◆◆◆◆◆◆◆◆◆◆

Sawasaki: This idea of matching grants is another new one to me. Did you think that up yourself, Peter?

Swarbrick: Lord, no. It's actually quite common at American companies. Has been for quite some time, I believe.

Sawasaki: I've never heard of anything like it in Japan. Of course, since people there aren't really in the habit of making charitable donations that much, there might not be many takers for a program like that.

Swarbrick: That seems too bad.

---

think something up 想出 (發明) 某件事　　**Lord, no.** 當然不是。　　**be in the habit of** 有習慣做…　　**charitable donation** 慈善捐款

Lesson 42

Volunteerism — 總結

■ ■ ■

在美國，自願活動並不僅限於企業，對個人而言，它也是生活中重要的一環。這或許是因為他們的先祖曾在極其嚴苛的環境下，靠著互助度過難關，而因此沿襲下來的傳統觀念，要不就是基督教精神使然吧！

當然，所謂自願活動，本來就是屬於個人自由意志的範疇，只是有不少美國企業也透過制度上的優惠來鼓勵員工參與自願活動。某大電腦商聽說就有以下的制度：

1. 若有員工希望能停職一段時間，到慈善機構去做義工，則在公司審查通過之後，不僅可以留職，還可以繼續支薪。

2. 對於員工、已退休者或員工配偶所服務的慈善團體，公司會從特別基金中撥款補助。

3. 若員工在退休後尚服務於某慈善機構，則公司仍會給付其在退休時薪資的一定比例的金錢，期限最長可達兩年。

自願活動包含了社會福利、環境維護、社區性活動、以及國際交流等領域，範圍非常廣泛。紐約的日本工商會議所就曾針對美國的日資企業，刊行過一本「自願活動手冊」*A Handbook for Better Corporate Citizenship in the United States* (1990年1月)，其中列舉了下述的 categories of volunteer involvement。

- 地區性的 Volunteer Center, Voluntary Action Center, Volunteer Bureau, 以及全國性的 ACTION, United Way of American, Red Cross 等全美的自願團體的活動
- Arts and Culture (藝文)
- Civic and Neighborhood Affairs (少數民族的公民權運動、反毒運動、犯罪防範、防火，以及對無家可歸者的濟助等)
- Education (教育)
- Environmental and Animal Welfare (環境與動物保護)
- Family Volunteer Opportunities, Healthcare (家庭與關懷健康行動)
- Helping People with Special Needs (對於老年人、肢障者和青少年的援助)
- Religious Charities (宗教慈善活動)

Office Politics

（辦公室內的政治活動）

◆ Lesson 43 的內容 ◆

　　不管是哪裡的企業都一樣，就算表面乍看平穩，底下卻是暗濤洶湧，常有權力鬥爭和扯後腿的事情發生。有些是拍上司馬屁，有些是附和上司不怎麼好笑的笑話，有些是穿跟上司一樣的衣服，有些則專門散布流言，作法不一而足。這看起來雖然像是時間和精力的浪費，但辦公室內的政治活動卻是真有其事，其目的則是為要獲得公司內有限的「人力」、「物力」和「財力」資源。在現今這個世界，光努力工作是不夠的。但人是否該為了要生存下去而學習這種辦公室內的政治哲學呢?

...in the hope of someday "accidentally" landing in a foursome with Alex, who just happens to belong to the same club.

Office Politics (1)（辦公室內的政治活動）

●預習 — *Sentences*

- I don't think we have a very political office, do you?
- I could tell you stories that would curl your hair.
- Your boss is in good with Alex, which always helps.
- But there's plenty of politicking going on here.
- Gossip is a form of office politics too, you know.

●*Vignette*

Williams: Good morning, Shoichi. Are we too early?

Sawasaki: Hi, Brad, Clarence. No, you're not too early. I was just pouring the coffee now. Come on in. Patti and I were just talking about office politics.

Winchell: Why? Is something going on I should know about?

Sawasaki: No, not here. It was something that happened to a friend of hers at another company. I don't really think we have a very political office, do you?

Williams: Oh, we definitely do have office politics here. I could tell you stories that would <u>curl your hair</u>.

Sawasaki: Really? I haven't noticed that sort of thing.

Williams: You're not vulnerable to other managers trying to grab territory. Also, your boss <u>is in good with</u> Alex, which always helps. But there's plenty of <u>politicking</u> going on here. Some of it is almost comical.

Winchell: Any juicy stories for us, Clarence?

Williams: Well, of course, I won't <u>name names</u>. Gossip is a form of office politics too, you know. But there's a line manager in the cereals division who joined a golf club he really can't afford in the hope of someday "accidentally" landing in a foursome with Alex, who just happens to belong to the same club.

Winchell: Poor guy. I hope he enjoys golf.

　　澤崎原先連想都沒有想過在尼爾森 ABC 食品公司裡的政治活動有那麼盛行；可是威廉斯卻說：「有些是能令你汗毛直豎的故事。」不過也有些是相當可笑的行為。

威廉斯： 早安，昭一。我們來得太早了嗎？

澤崎： 嗨，布雷、克雷倫斯。不會，不會太早。我正在倒咖啡。請進。派蒂和我才在談辦公室內政治活動的事。

溫謝爾： 為甚麼？發生了甚麼我該知道的事嗎？

澤崎： 沒有，不是在這兒。是件發生在派蒂朋友身上的事，她朋友在別家公司上班。我並不真的以為我們辦公室裡能有甚麼政治活動，你們看呢？

威廉斯： 噢，我們辦公室裡絕對有政治活動。我可以告訴你一些會令你汗毛直豎的故事。

澤崎： 真的嗎？我倒不曾注意到有這樣的事。

威廉斯： 這是因為在那些企圖擴張自己勢力範圍的經理們眼中，你並不是甚麼好欺負的對象。而且，你老闆跟亞力士關係不錯，這點總是有所助益。不過，這裡是有不少人在搞政治，而且有些幾乎到了可笑的地步。

溫謝爾： 克雷倫斯，可以讓我們聽些有趣的故事嗎？

威廉斯： 嗯，當然啦，我不會指名道姓。就像你們知道的，搬長弄短也是辦公室內政治活動的一種形式。話說有這麼一位麥片部門的生產線經理，他參加了一個自己實際上負擔不起的高爾夫球俱樂部，目的就是希望哪天能「碰巧」和亞力士排在同一個四人組中，因為亞力士正好也在那家俱樂部。

溫謝爾： 可憐的傢伙！我希望他會喜歡打高爾夫球。

Lesson 43 Office Politics (1)

Words and Phrases

office politics　公司內部的政治活動	gossip　閒言閒語
pour　注入	line manager　部門經理; 生產線經理
definitely　明確地; 確定地	cereals　麥片或穀物食品
vulnerable　易受攻擊的	in the hope of　期待著…
grab　攫取	accidentally　偶然地
territory　領土	land in　陷入…; 著落於…
comical　可笑的	foursome　四人組
juicy　有趣的	Poor guy.　可憐人!

Vocabulary Building

● **curl one's hair**　令人毛骨聳然

What Timothy told me about the backstabbing among the division heads curled my hair.

(提摩西告訴我一些關於部門主管相互陷害的事，聽得我心裡毛毛的。)

● **be in good with**　與…關係良好

Since Leo thought he was in good with the boss, he was really shocked to be fired.

(由於里奧覺得自己跟老闆的關係不錯，所以當他被解雇時，真是震驚不已。)

● **politicking**　搞政治

Try not to get caught up in politicking. It can seriously interfere with your work.

(你在公司裡搞政治活動的時候，儘量別被逮個正著。因為這會嚴重妨害到你的工作。)

● **name names**　指名道姓

Without naming names, Bill made it obvious who he was talking about.

(比爾並沒有指名道姓，但他使聽的人都清楚知道他說的是誰。)

▶Exercises 在下列例句中，每句各有四個劃線部分，其中一個的文法有誤，請將之選出。 （解答見 268 頁）

1. The Class of 1944 <u>was consisted of</u> <u>only</u> 98 students, but <u>no less than</u>
   　　　　　　　　　　　　A　　　　　　　B　　　　　　　　　　　C
   300 students <u>will</u> graduate this year.
   　　　　　　　　D

2. It may be difficult to <u>understand</u> the <u>true</u> Japanese spirit <u>unless</u> you have
   　　　　　　　　　　　　A　　　　　　B　　　　　　　　　C
   lived in <u>the Japanese society</u>.
   　　　　　　　D

3. It is an accepted <u>custom</u> in some cultures for <u>a man</u> to <u>let</u> women <u>go first</u>
   　　　　　　　　　　A　　　　　　　　　　　　　　B　　　　C　　　　　D
   into the elevator.

◆◆◆◆◆◆◆◆◆◆◆◆◆◆ 簡短對話 ◆◆◆◆◆◆◆◆◆◆◆◆◆◆◆

Sawasaki: You know, Brad, this talk about gossip reminds me of a conversation I had with Eric Turner. It was when I went to ask him about a rumor you had shared with me.

Winchell: Oh yeah, about our operation being disbanded, right?

Sawasaki: Right. Anyway, I got the feeling that Eric was just a bit too much "above it all." The problem was that he often seemed to be the last to know about what was going on in the office.

Winchell: Yeah, you can sometimes really miss out of if you don't keep up with what's going around on the grapevine.

---

disband 解散　　**above it all** （立場）超然的　　**miss out** 漏失　　**keep up with** 跟上…的腳步　　**on the grapevine** 謠傳中的

Lesson 43

Office Politics (2)（辦公室內的政治活動）

預習 — *Sentences*

- Take a look around and see how many men are dressed like Alex.
- Why would anyone waste time and energy on politics?
- No one has all of the budget or subordinates that they want.
- I guess I've always been lucky.
- My parents taught me that hard work was its own reward.

Vignette

Williams: Also, at the next management meeting, just take a look around and see how many men are dressed just like Alex. If you're looking for it, it's astounding. You know those Italian suits with the padded shoulders that he wears? He looks good in them, but most people don't. And they're not cheap either.

Sawasaki: That's ridiculous. Do they honestly think Alex would take any notice of something like that?

Winchell: Sure, Shoichi. In some companies, if you don't dress like the boss, you might as well wave a flag that says you don't think like the boss either.

Sawasaki: But why would anyone waste time and energy on politics around here?

Williams: It's resources, Shoichi. Politics are a fact of life. Money, material, and people are limited in every organization. Even in large prosperous companies, no one has all of the budget or subordinates that they want. And when you've been downsized half to death, like we have lately, there's a real battle for resources among the middle managers.

Sawasaki: I guess I've always been lucky. My parents taught me that hard work was its own reward, and that if I did a good job, I would always be promoted when my time came.

Winchell: With that attitude, Shoichi, you have been lucky. Especially here in the States.

　　有些經理會為了能和總裁迪馬哥「碰巧」在一起打球,而參加自己實際上負擔不起的高爾夫球俱樂部。他們為何要浪費這些時間和精力來搞政治呢? 威廉斯說:「是為了爭取經營資源。」

威廉斯: 還有,下次召開管理會議的時候,四面望一望,注意一下有多少人的穿著跟亞力士一樣。如果你仔細找的話,你會發現數目驚人。你們知道亞力士所穿的那種有墊肩的義大利西裝嗎? 穿在他身上是不錯,可是大多數的人都不適合。何況那種衣服也不便宜。

澤崎: 這太可笑了。他們真的以為亞力士會注意到這種事嗎?

溫謝爾: 當然了,昭一。在某些公司,假如你穿的跟老闆不一樣,那你倒不如揮個旗子,上頭寫著「我想的也跟老闆不一樣。」

澤崎: 可是在我們這裡,為甚麼也會有人把時間和精力浪費在這些政治手法上呢?

威廉斯: 為了經營資源啊,昭一。權力鬥爭是生活中的一種現實面。在每一個事業組織中,金錢、物資和人力都是有限的。就算是在蓬勃發展的大公司裡,也沒有人能隨心所欲地要支多少預算就支多少預算,要有多少下屬就有多少下屬。而且,就像我們前些日子所經歷到的,當公司縮減編制,搞得你都快半死不活的時候,在中級經理之間,就會有場很現實的資源爭奪戰。

澤崎: 我想我一直都很幸運。我父母教導我,勤奮工作本身就是一種報酬,而且,如果我把工作做好了,那麼時候一到,我自然會得到升遷。

溫謝爾: 昭一,能有這種態度,你是很幸運,特別是在美國這種地方。

Lesson 43   Office Politics (2)

Words and Phrases

padded shoulder	墊肩	budget	預算
ridiculous	可笑的	subordinate	下屬
waste time and energy　浪費時間 與精力		downsize　減少人員編制; 縮減企業 規模	
resources	(經營)資源	reward	報酬
prosperous	繁榮的	attitude	態度

Vocabulary Building

● **take a look around**　四周看一下
Before you quit, take a look around and see how many people are already
out on the street looking for jobs.
(在你辭職之前，先看看你的周遭，有多少失業的人正在找工作。)

● **wave a flag**　表明自己的意思
Jill practically waved a flag saying, "Don't you dare smoke."
(姬兒實際上就是擺明了說:「你敢給我吸菸就試試看。」)

● **fact of life**　現實
The world is not fair. That's one of the facts of life.
(世界是不公平的。而這正是生活的一個現實面。)

● **to death**　至死; 到極點
We've beaten that idea to death. Let's move on to discuss something else.
(這個構想我們討論得都要爛掉了，換個別的吧!)

▶ *Exercises*

在下列例句中，每句各有四個劃線部分，
其中一個的文法有誤，請將之選出。

(解答見 268 頁)

1. According to <u>news</u> some mammals are <u>no longer</u> <u>on</u> the <u>endangered</u>
              A   B   C   D

   species' list.

2. Each of the partners <u>need</u> to <u>draw</u> the same salary <u>regardless of</u> <u>his</u>
                             A   B   C   D

   experience.

3. <u>For the</u> <u>last couple years</u>, the hiring freeze <u>has been on</u> to <u>cut down on</u>
  A   B   C   D

   overhead costs.

◆◆◆◆◆◆◆◆◆◆◆◆◆ 簡短對話 ◆◆◆◆◆◆◆◆◆◆◆◆◆◆◆

Williams: You know what they say: "Imitation is the sincerest form of flattery."

Sawasaki: Sure, and I can understand trying to imitate your boss's good points. But wearing the same type of suits as the CEO—that strikes me as too silly for words.

Williams: Sure, you don't have to convince me. I'm not advocating it, after all. I'm just trying to describe some of the things that go on around here.

Sawasaki: Yes, I understand that, Clarence. Still, I'd like to think that I'd never fall that low myself—aping my boss's clothes, I mean.

Imitation is the sincerest form of flattery. 模仿是種最真心誠意的諂媚。　　**too silly for words** 蠢得無以言喻　　**advocate** 擁護　　**ape** *v.* 模仿

Lesson 43

Office Politics (3)（辦公室內的政治活動）

●預習 — *Sentences*

- Most people here learn that hard work is not enough.
- Everyone in the agency was fighting for clients.
- What are some of the things to watch out for?
- In the office environment, it's better to be skeptical.
- That goes for all kinds of situations.

●*Vignette*

Winchell: Most people here learn soon after they leave college that hard work is not enough. In my first real job, I realized after about one month that I had been thrown into competition with a bunch of real glory-seekers. Everyone in the agency was fighting for clients, so they never missed an opportunity to impress the partners in the company. They smiled like idiots at everything the partners said. They stayed late every night— or at least until the partners left. They would send copies of their memos to everyone, and they would only drink in bars where they might meet important people.

Sawasaki: That sounds boring.

Winchell: It *was* boring, but I found myself playing the same games. I felt that I had to in order to survive.

Williams: Nelson ABC Foods isn't that bad, but there are still basic points to be aware of just in case someone starts playing politics with you.

Winchell: What are some of the things to watch out for?

Williams: Well, one thing is very obvious. If someone flatters you, you have to be strong with yourself and ask what they really want from you. In the office environment, it's better to be skeptical.

Sawasaki: What can you do about a situation like that?

Williams: If you think someone's playing games with you, you have to confront them. You can do it gently, but you've got to do it. That goes for all kinds of situations.

　　為了不讓人跟你玩政治，就得多疑一點。若聽到有人拍你馬屁，要能不為所動，反要詰問對方的動機為何。

溫謝爾：　在美國，大部分的人在大學畢業，出到社會後不久，就會瞭解到一件事：光努力工作是不夠的。在我第一份正式工作中，上班約一個月後我就明白，我已投身於一場名利之戰中了，而參戰者是一群真正在追求名譽地位的人。代理行中的每個人都在搶客戶，誰也不願放過任何可以給公司合夥人留下好印象的機會。不管合夥人說了些甚麼話，大家都笑得跟白癡一樣，然後每天晚上都待到很晚 —— 或者至少要等到合夥人都走了才行。他們會把自己的備忘錄影印給每個人看，而且只到那些會碰到重要人物的酒吧裡喝酒。

澤崎：　聽起來很無趣。

溫謝爾：　是無趣沒錯，可是我卻發現自己在搞同樣的事。我那時候的感覺是，要存活下去，就非得這麼做。

威廉斯：　尼爾森 ABC 食品公司沒那麼糟，不過有些基本的東西還是得知道一下，免得有人跟你玩起政治來你都渾然不覺。

溫謝爾：　有哪些是該注意的事呢？

威廉斯：　嗯，有一件是非常明顯的。如果有人拍你馬屁，你要能不為其所動，還要反過來詰問對方想從你身上得到些甚麼。在辦公室裡，多疑一點會比較好。

澤崎：　像那樣的情況，你能怎麼做？

威廉斯：　如果你認為某人在跟你玩把戲，那你得當面質問他。你的態度可以溫和一點，但還是得問。這種作法在任何情況都能適用。

Lesson 43   Office Politics (3)

Words and Phrases

glory-seeker	追求名譽地位的人	survive	存活
agency	(廣告)代理行; 代理商	flatter	阿諛; 諂媚
client	客戶	skeptical	懷疑的
boring	令人厭煩的	confront	與…當面對質

Vocabulary Building

● **be thrown into**   投身於…; 熱衷於…

Olaf got thrown into a class of students much more advanced than he was in the study of Spanish.

(歐雷夫整個人都投到他的西班牙文課上去了, 他班上學生的西班牙文造詣個個都比他強得多。)

● **bunch of**   一群…

The people working for me are a real bunch of shirkers.

(我手下工作的那些人簡直是一群懶鬼。)

● **fight for**   爭奪…

Everybody in this office is fighting desperately for recognition from the boss.

(在這個辦公室裡, 每個人都使出渾身解數要爭取到老闆的賞識。)

● **that goes for**   適用於…

What you say about dressing for success goes for women as well as men.

(你所說的關於利用衣著來求取成功之道, 不只適用於男人, 女人也是一樣。)

▶ **Exercises**   在下列例句中，每句各有四個劃線部分，
其中一個的文法有誤，請將之選出。   （解答見 269 頁）

1. <u>Speaking generally</u>, <u>most</u> companies are <u>bloated</u> <u>by</u> 20 to 25 percent.
　　　　A　　　　　　B　　　　　　　C　　D

2. Gil and <u>his</u> friends like to eat Chinese food <u>most</u> everyday <u>at</u> the restau-
　　　　　A　　　　　　　　　　　　　　　　B　　　　　C

   rant <u>on</u> campus.
　　　D

3. <u>Sometime</u> car manufacturers need to <u>recall</u> certain <u>models of cars</u> be-
　　　A　　　　　　　　　　　　　　B　　　　　　C

   cause of design <u>defects</u>.
　　　　　　　　D

◆◆◆◆◆◆◆◆◆◆◆◆◆◆ 簡短對話 ◆◆◆◆◆◆◆◆◆◆◆◆◆◆

Sawasaki: You never mentioned that experience on your first job to me before, did you?

Winchell: Probably not. It wasn't exactly the happiest time of my life, so I've done my best to banish it from my memory. At least I try not to talk about it too much.

Sawasaki: Oh, I'm sorry to hear that. I wanted to ask you more. You know, as part of my education into the ways of American business in various organizations.

Winchell: You loosen up my tongue with a beer or two after work, Shoichi, and I'll tell you anything you want to know.

Sawasaki: It's a deal.

---

banish 排除；忘卻　　**loosen up someone's tongue** 使某人透露消息　　**It's a deal.** 就這麼說定了。

Office Politics (4) (辦公室內的政治活動)

預習 — *Sentences*

· I can't believe that politicking is good for a company.
· Not all office politics is automatically bad, Shoichi.
· It will certainly do you no good to make political blunders.
· You don't want politics to get out of control.
· Involve all parties in open discussion as much as possible.

Vignette

Sawasaki: I can't believe that politicking is good for a company. Isn't there any way to stop it?

Williams: Not all office politics is automatically bad, Shoichi. As I said, sometimes you're in a battle for resources, and if you're working on something important, it will certainly do you no good to make political blunders.

Sawasaki: For example?

Williams: Oh, openly complaining about your boss, for instance. Or keeping information from him or her. You've got to be more tactical than that. On the other hand, you don't want politics to get out of control.

Sawasaki: But what can you do if politics are so inevitable?

Williams: Oh, it's not too mysterious. You can set the tone in your own unit by creating an atmosphere of openness and trying to tell the truth.

Winchell: That's a pretty tall order right there.

Williams: Yes, but it's important to make the effort. You should ignore gossip. Break up cliques within the department so that there's no "us against them" mentality in the office. And maybe the most important thing is to keep information and disputes in a public forum as much as possible. Always involve all parties in open discussion as much as possible. Politics thrives on secrecy.

　　雖然不能整個地否認辦公室內的政治活動，但可以避免的還是要盡量避免。重要的是要能營造出坦誠開放的氣氛，所以一定要讓閒言閒語自生自滅，並努力消除部門內的派系關係。

澤崎：　我無法相信這樣子搞政治對公司會有甚麼好處。難道就沒辦法阻止嗎？

威廉斯：昭一，並非所有辦公室內的政治活動都會導致不良結果。就像我剛剛所說的，有時候你會置身於一場經營資源的爭奪戰之中，如果當時你手頭上的事正好很重要，那麼，一些政治策略上的失誤對你而言是絕對沒有好處的。

澤崎：　比方說？

威廉斯：呃，舉例來說，像是公然抱怨你的上司，或是不把某些消息告訴他。這都是不行的，你必須更加懂得如何善用策略。另外一方面，你也不會願意看到這種政治活動搞到失控的局面。

澤崎：　可是，如果政治活動是這樣地無可避免，那你能怎麼辦？

威廉斯：噢，這也不是那麼無法理解。在你自己的組裡頭，你要營造出一種開放的氣氛，試著在凡事上坦誠，而藉以樹立起行事的風氣。

溫謝爾：這可是件相當困難的工作。

威廉斯：是沒錯。不過重要的是要去努力。不要去理會閒言閒語。要打破部門內的派系關係，這樣辦公室裡才不會有「敵我」的情結。而且，也許最重要的，就是盡可能地使消息和爭執都擺在公開的討論會中。總要盡量把所有相關的人都找來，大家一起公開討論。政治活動只有在暗地裡才會生長壯大。

Lesson 43　Office Politics (4)

Words and Phrases

automatically	自動地; 不自覺地	break up	打散
tactical	善用策略的	clique	朋黨
inevitable	無可避免的	"us against them" mentality	
mysterious	不可理解的	有「敵我之分」的心態	
ignore	忽視; 忽略	dispute	爭論
gossip	閒話; 閒言閒語	thrive on	成長繁茂; 孳生

Vocabulary Building

- **make a blunder**　犯錯
  Butch made a blunder that cost the company its most important client.
  (布奇犯了個粗心的錯誤, 結果使公司丟掉了一個最重要的客戶。)

- **get out of control**　失控
  The rivalry among the divisions of this company is starting to get out of control.
  (這個公司裡頭部門與部門之間的敵對狀況開始有點失控了。)

- **set the tone**　樹立風氣
  George tries to set the tone for his staff by never gossiping.
  (喬治嘗試著不說閒話, 用以身作則的方式來給他的下屬樹立辦公室內的風氣。)

- **tall order**　困難的工作; 不合理的要求; 難應付的工作
  Finishing the report by Friday is a tall order, but I'll do my best to fill it.
  (要人在星期五之前把報告完成是個不合理的要求, 不過我會盡我所能地去做就是了。)

1. <u>Although</u> I tried as <u>hardly</u> as I <u>could</u>, I didn't <u>win</u> the tournament.
    A   B   C   D

2. <u>Learners</u> should use <u>both</u> textbooks <u>and</u> drills, as well as <u>attending</u> class,
    A   B   C   D
to learn new computer skills.

3. <u>Seldom we saw</u> homeless people <u>on</u> the street <u>before</u> the bad <u>times</u>
       A   B   C   D
started.

◆◆◆◆◆◆◆◆◆◆◆◆◆◆ 簡短對話 ◆◆◆◆◆◆◆◆◆◆◆◆◆◆◆

Sawasaki: Tell me, Clarence, how did you come to be such an authority on office politics?

Williams: Oh, I wouldn't call myself an authority, exactly. But I think that my ghetto upbringing may have something to do with my feel for the subject.

Sawasaki: You learned office politics there?

Williams: No, I mean that I learned to be alert to what was happening around me. Had to stay alive. The environment here in the office is different, to put it mildly, but I've found that the same type of alertness pays off here too.

---

authority 權威   **ghetto** 城市中少數民族居住的區域   **upbringing** 養育
have something to do with 跟…有關係   **alert** 警覺的   **environment**
環境   **to put it mildly** 說得含蓄一點   **pay off** 成功

Lesson 43

Office Politics — 總結

在 *Winning Office Politics* (by Andrew J. DuBrin, Prentice Hall, 1990) 這本書中, 有個饒富趣味的章節叫做 "Measuring Your Political Tendencies"; 它列舉了一百個問題, 若照實回答 mostly true (=mostly agree) 或 mostly false (=mostly disagree), 那你就可以測得自己的「政治化」程度了。

我們來看看其中幾個代表性的問題。

- The boss is always right. (老闆永遠是對的。)
- I would ask my boss's opinion on personal matters even if I didn't need the advice, just to show I respected his or her judgment. (為了表示尊重老闆的判斷, 縱使沒有必要, 我也會問問老闆對我私人問題的看法。)
- I would invite my boss to a party in my home even if I didn't like that person. (我就算討厭老闆, 也會邀他參加家裡的宴會。)
- I would go out of my way to develop an interest in a hobby I knew that my boss preferred. (我會刻意培養和老闆相同的興趣。)
- If a customer was very pleased with the way I handled his or her account, I would ask the customer to write a complimentary note to my boss. (若有某客戶對我的服務非常滿意, 那我會請他寫封褒獎我的信給我老闆。)
- I would stay late in the office just to impress my boss. (我會為了給老闆留下好印象而刻意在辦公室待到很晚。)
- While on vacation, it's a smart idea to pick up a small gift for your boss. (休假出去玩的時候, 幫老闆買份小禮物是個不錯的點子。)
- I laugh heartily at my boss's jokes even when I think they are not funny. (只要是老闆講的笑話, 縱使不好笑, 我也會笑得很開心。)
- I would be careful not to hire a subordinate who might outshine me. (我會留意不要找個會搶我光彩的人進來當我下屬。)

怎麼樣? 有哪些問題你會回答 "mostly true" 呢?

Personal Vision

（個人先見）

◆ Lesson 44 的內容 ◆

　　傑出的領導者不論身處何種世代，總是心懷「遠見」。他們在心中描繪自己的目標，並確信其終要完成。帕克之所以會問澤崎：「你想做甚麼？為甚麼想做？還有你是用甚麼樣的價值觀和信念來衡量你每日的思考和行為？」就是希望澤崎能胸懷遠見，好好想想日後若擔任尼爾森 ABC 食品公司日本分公司的總裁，要如何來訂定公司未來的路。不管情形如何，澤崎都得要持續不斷地學習，因為這是要具有遠見所不可或缺的要素。

Martin Luther King showed his in his "I have a dream" speech.

Personal Vision (1) (個人先見)

●預習 — *Sentences*

- It's been a long time since we've had time to chat like this.
- I must admit that I wanted to get you out of the office.
- It would mean relocating to Tokyo, of course.
- You don't have to make a decision right this minute.
- You're the most logical choice for the job.

●*Vignette*

Sawasaki: This is a great place, Gil. Thanks for asking me to lunch today. It's been a long time since we've had time to sit down and chat like this.

Parker: Well, I must admit that I wanted to get you out of the office because this is more than just a chat.

Sawasaki: Yes?

Parker: As you know, there have been some changes recently in our Japan operation. Alex has been looking closely at Japan and has decided that the person in charge there should be someone who knows the company well but also understands the Japanese language and business climate. He mentioned your name. How would you feel about being head of Nelson ABC Foods Japan?

Sawasaki: Me? For that job?

Parker: Yes. It would mean relocating to Tokyo, of course. Anyway, relax, Shoichi. You don't have to make a decision right this minute. But Alex has decided that the company will do better in Japan if someone like you is directing our efforts. You're the most logical choice for the job.

Sawasaki: I really don't know what to say, Gil. This is so unexpected.

Parker: You don't have to say anything today, Shoichi. I know it isn't easy to relocate, and you may not want to so soon after getting settled here in Chicago.

　　帕克很難得地邀澤崎出來吃飯。他的目的是要問澤崎是否願意擔任尼爾森 ABC 食品公司日本分公司的總裁。由於這是澤崎始料未及的事，所以他一時間也不知該如何回答。

澤崎: 吉爾，這地方棒極了。謝謝你今天找我出來吃午餐。我們已經好久沒有像這樣坐下來聊聊天了。

帕克: 嗯，我得向你承認一件事，我找你出來的目的不只是聊天而已。

澤崎: 哦?

帕克: 你知道的，我們公司在日本方面的營運近來有些變動。亞力士一直在密切注意日本的動態，他決定，那裡的負責人不僅要很瞭解公司狀況，而且也要懂得日文並清楚日本當地的企業情勢。他提到了你的名字。如果說要你做尼爾森 ABC 食品公司日本分公司的總裁，你意下如何?

澤崎: 我? 做那個工作?

帕克: 是的。當然了，這也意味著要調回東京。不管怎樣，昭一，放輕鬆點，你不用立刻就做決定。不過亞力士已經決定了，日本那邊要有個像你這樣的人來主導，這對公司會比較有利。而你是這個職位最合理的人選。

澤崎: 吉爾，我真的不知道該說些甚麼。這太突然了。

帕克: 昭一，你今天不用說甚麼。我明白，要搬到另一個地方並不是甚麼容易的事。而且你才在芝加哥定下來沒多久，你可能也不太想再搬家。

Lesson 44 Personal Vision (1)

Words and Phrases

Yes?　(在聽了對方的話之後)繼續詢問對方語意的用詞	relocate　遷徙
	right this minute　當場; 立刻
in charge　管理; 負責	unexpected　不期然的
head　長官; 首領	get settled　落腳; 安定下來

Vocabulary Building

- **chat** *v.*　聊天; 閒聊
  Have you got a minute to chat? I've got something I'd like your opinion about.
  (你有沒有些時間可以聊聊? 我有事情想要問問你的意見。)

- **business climate**　企業動向; 業務情勢; 企業情勢
  In the current business climate, it would be folly to invest heavily in new manufacturing facilities.
  (以現在的企業情勢來看, 把錢大量投資在新式生產設備上會是件愚蠢的事。)

- **direct**　指揮; 主導
  Eileen did an excellent job of directing the reorganization project.
  (艾琳在主導重組計畫的事上做得好極了。)

- **logical choice**　合理的選擇
  Pete's experience in France makes him a logical choice to head our Paris office.
  (彼特在法國的經驗使他成為主導公司在巴黎辦事處的當然人選。)

1. Nancy has to develop common sense <u>on</u> <u>money matters</u> as she <u>tends to</u>
A   B   C

purchase <u>everything</u> she sees.
D

2. One of the most interesting <u>subjects</u> in my school days <u>was</u> history and
A   B

<u>the other</u> <u>was</u> geography.
C   D

3. Many <u>new</u> books have a great <u>number of</u> <u>information</u> <u>about</u> computers.
      A   B   C   D

◆◆◆◆◆◆◆◆◆◆◆◆◆◆ 簡短對話 ◆◆◆◆◆◆◆◆◆◆◆◆◆◆◆

Sawasaki: Gil, you really know how to surprise people. From the serious look on your face when you asked me out to lunch, I never would have guessed you were going to spring something like this on me. Frankly, you've floored me.

Parker: Did I really look that grim? I wasn't trying to trick you or anything.

Sawasaki: One possibility that crossed my mind was that you were going to advise me to update my résumé. With all the downsizing that's been going on, I think we're all a little nervous on that score.

Parker: I know what you mean.

---

ask someone out to lunch 找某人出來吃午餐　　**spring** *v.* 冒出來　　**floor** *v.* 令人困惑；把人打倒　　**grim** （表情）嚴肅的　　**trick** *v.* 欺騙　　**cross one's mind** 想到　　**update one's résumé** 把履歷表的資料翻新　　**on that score** 在那個點上

Lesson 44

Personal Vision (2)（個人先見）

預習 —Sentences

- I also think it's a hell of an opportunity for you.
- What do you want to do, and why do you want to do it?
- What are your governing values and beliefs?
- But you still have a lot to learn, as we all do.
- Personal vision goes beyond simply taking care of business.

Vignette

Parker: But I also think it's a hell of an opportunity for you. Anyway, you'll have to decide what's best for you.

Sawasaki: Do you think I'm ready for that kind of responsibility?

Parker: From a technical perspective, yes, absolutely. And, of course, from a cultural perspective, you'll do far better than anybody else from the head office would in the same position. The thing you may not have yet— and it's time to begin thinking about it— is a sense of personal vision. What do you want to do, and why do you want to do it? What are your governing values and beliefs?

Sawasaki: I'm not sure I understand what you mean by a personal vision, Gil.

Parker: You have good business instincts, Shoichi. You think in terms of the company's future. You care about your coworkers. And I've noticed that you're constantly looking for ways to improve your skills. You're good at what you do and you can make a good business leader, but you still have a lot to learn, as we all do. What I call personal vision goes beyond simply taking care of business. People like Alex, for instance, don't get where they are simply by working hard or being ruthless. They always have a picture in their mind of what they want, and they always feel sure that they will get it. That's vision.

Sawasaki: Yes, but Gil, you know I'm not like Alex, and I have no great desire to be like him.

　　帕克正在說明擁有個人先見的重要性。它不僅攸關業務的成敗，還深深影響個人的價值觀和信念。

帕克： 可是我也覺得這對你是個千載難逢的好機會。不管怎樣，你得做個對自己最有利的選擇。

澤崎： 你覺得我可以勝任那樣的職責了嗎？

帕克： 以技術面而言，你絕對可以。而若以文化面來看，總公司也沒有任何人會比你更勝任這個職位。有一點可能是你還欠缺的 —— 現在也該是好好想想的時候了 —— 就是個人先見的意識。像是說，你想做甚麼？為甚麼要做？還有你經營管理的價值觀和信念為何？

澤崎： 吉爾，我不是很清楚你對個人先見的解釋。

帕克： 昭一，你有很好的商業直覺。你為公司的未來著想。你也關心你的同事。我還注意到你不斷在探尋方法，以求改良個人技巧。你很稱職，而且會是一個相當好的事業領袖。但就像我們一樣，有很多東西你仍有待學習。我所謂的個人先見並不只限於把事情辦好而已。我打個比方，像亞力士這樣的人，他們若單憑著努力工作，或是冷血無情，還達不了今天的地位。在他們心中有一幅畫，裡頭是他們想要的東西，而且他們總是篤定：自己會得到這東西。這就是個人先見。

澤崎： 吉爾，這麼說是沒錯，可是你也知道我不像亞力士。我更沒甚麼多大的慾望想要變得跟他一樣。

Words and Phrases

hell of a	〔口語〕絕佳的…	coworker	同事
responsibility	職責	constantly	不斷地
head office	總公司	look for	尋求
governing	支配的	ruthless	冷酷無情的

Vocabulary Building

● **from a technical perspective**　　以技術面而言；從技術觀點來看
The idea sounds good, but from a technical perspective I'm afraid it may not be practical.
(這個案子聽起來不錯，可是從技術面來看，我怕它會行不通。)

● **values and beliefs**　　價值觀和信念
You should have your own clear values and beliefs, but you mustn't force them on others.
(你自己本身是應該要有明確的價值觀和信念，但你不該把這些東西強加在他人身上。)

● **business instinct**　　商業直覺；商業本能
Louise had never held a position of such responsibility before, but she proved to have good business instincts.
(露薏絲以前從來沒有擔任過需要承當這樣職責的位子，但是事實證明，她有相當好的商業直覺。)

● **go beyond**　　超過
Oliver's devotion to the job goes beyond the call of duty.
(奧利佛對於工作的獻身超過了職務本身的要求。)

▶ *Exercises*   在下列例句中，每句各有四個劃線部分，其中一個的文法有誤，請將之選出。   (解答見 269 頁)

1. Japanese schoolchildren are <u>so</u> busy with <u>schoolworks</u> that it is difficult for them to find time for sports.
           A   B
<u>for them</u> to find <u>time for sports.</u>
C   D

2. The <u>motor</u> journalist was <u>looking for</u> <u>special kinds of</u> car <u>at</u> the auto show.
    A   B   C   D

3. Did you receive <u>a permission</u> <u>for</u> <u>a fortnight</u> <u>off?</u>
          A   B   C   D

◆◆◆◆◆◆◆◆◆◆◆◆◆ 簡短對話 ◆◆◆◆◆◆◆◆◆◆◆◆◆

Sawasaki: I thought being a successful leader was largely a matter of charisma. Certainly the leaders you just mentioned had or have more than their share of it.

Parker: Oh, sure, charisma helps, but a charismatic leader without a constructive personal vision is nothing more than a demagogue. People like that may be able to whip their followers into a frenzy, but once they're gone, the movements they led generally fizzle out, leaving nothing behind but a lot of damage.

Sawasaki: You're right, I guess, but I still can't help wondering whether I have leadership potential.

---

charisma 領袖氣質　　　**demagogue** 煽動家　　　**whip into** 煽動；激起
frenzy *n.* 狂熱　　　**fizzle out** 無疾而終　　　**potential** 潛能

Lesson 44

Personal Vision (3)（個人先見）

- John F. Kennedy definitely had his own share of it.
- He said he'd send a man to the moon by the end of a decade.
- When you have to do it, I think you'll be ready.
- Alex DeMarco's vision would be more important than mine.
- Vision is not just a matter of inventing the future.

● *Vignette*

Parker: That's all right, Shoichi, but clarity of vision isn't just something for Alex or people like him. It's what makes all true leaders stand out. Martin Luther King showed his in his "I have a dream" speech. John F. Kennedy definitely had his own share of it when he said he'd send a man to the moon by the end of a decade. Nobody's asking you to lead a nation or a civil rights movement, but having a clear vision of where you want to go— or where you want a company to go— will help you sort through all the conflicting messages and problems of daily life.

Sawasaki: It's hard to imagine myself steering a course for a company.

Parker: Don't worry about it. When you have to do it, I think you'll be ready.

Sawasaki: I must admit that having the future of Nelson ABC Japan in my hands is a rather exciting prospect. But it seems logical that Alex DeMarco's vision would be more important than mine.

Parker: That's true. In business, vision is not just a matter of inventing the future, but of enrolling other people in it or convincing everybody else to come along for the ride, as it were. You'll have to share Alex's vision, and you may have to convince Alex to share yours. Fortunately for you, part of Alex's vision is a corporate culture that allows individual managers a great deal of autonomy.

　　能將尼爾森 ABC 食品公司在日本的未來掌握在手中，這對澤崎而言，光是想像就令人興奮。但帕克提醒他：「先見不只是用來創造未來，還得用來讓其他人也加入我們的行列」。

帕克： 昭一，那並沒有關係，可是，清楚的先見並不是只有亞力士或是像他那樣的人才應該要有的。這種先見是使所有真正的領袖可以超人一等的原因。我們在金恩牧師那篇「我有個夢想」的演說中看見了他對事情的洞察力。而當約翰・甘迺迪說到他要在十年內送人上月球的時候，也表現出了他的先見。並沒有人要你去領導一個國家或是帶領民權運動。但是，你若能清楚的看見自己所想達到的目標──或是你能明確知道，自己要公司發展成甚麼樣子──那會有助於你釐清日常生活中所碰到的矛盾訊息和問題。

澤崎： 真是很難想像我要來替一家公司掌舵。

帕克： 這你別擔心。船到橋頭自然直，到時你就可以了。

澤崎： 我得承認，想到尼爾森 ABC 食品公司日本分公司的未來會掌握在自己手中，這個前景相當令人興奮。不過，想當然爾，亞力士的先見會比我的先見要來得重要。

帕克： 沒錯。在事業上，先見還不只是用來創造未來而已，它還得用來招募其他的人，或是好比說叫人信服而加入我們的行列。你會得要顧及到亞力士的先見，不過你很幸運，因為在他的先見之中，也包括了一個賦與各個主管相當自主權的企業文化。

＊　　＊　　＊

Words and Phrases

stand out　　傑出；突出

Martin Luther King　　馬丁・路德・
　金恩牧師〈黑人解放運動的主導者〉

civil rights movement　　（特指黑人
　的）民權運動

sort through　　整理

conflicting　　相矛盾的；相抵觸的

logical　　合邏輯的；合理的

enroll　　使加入；徵募

convince　　說服

as it were　　好比是

corporate culture　　企業文化

autonomy　　自主性

Vocabulary Building

● **have one's share of**　　在…上也有某人的一份
Like everyone, I have my share of faults.
（就像每個人一樣，我也是有缺點的。）

● **steer a course**　　決定前面的路程；行進
Try to steer a course between recklessness and excess caution.
（在莽莽撞撞和過度謹慎之間，你要試著找出一個中庸之道。）

● **prospect**　　展望；前景；可能的客戶
We're preparing a business pitch for a new prospect.
（我們正在為著某個可能的新主顧籌畫商業廣告活動。）

● **come along for the ride**　　一起搭車前往
I'm going downtown to do some errands. Want to come along for the ride?
（我要到市區去辦點事。你要一道去嗎？）

1. Most of foreign students realize that Japan as a nation is rich, but the
   　　A　　　　　　　　　　　　B　　　　　　　　　　C
   average Japanese citizen isn't.
   　　D

2. It was John F. Kennedy, not his brother, who was the youngest person
   　　　　　　　　　　　　　　A

   to be elected president in the United States.
   　　B　　　　　C　　D

3. My friend was greatly influenced from his brother who wanted him to
   　　　　　　　　　　　　A　　　　B　　　　　　　　　C

   be a lawyer.
   D

◆◆◆◆◆◆◆◆◆◆◆◆◆◆ 簡短對話 ◆◆◆◆◆◆◆◆◆◆◆◆◆◆◆

Sawasaki: Well, I don't know what to say. I'm not sure whether I'll be
able to whip up a personal vision that'll be adequate for the purpose.

Parker: I'm not suggesting you need to "whip up" anything. I just think
it's an area you'd do well to devote some thought to.

Sawasaki: I read you. Let me sleep on it, OK?

Parker: No great rush. Alex would probably like to know how you feel
about the offer without too much delay, but you can take a few days to
think it over. And as for this personal vision business, it's an ongoing process, not something to be completed by some deadline and then forgotten.

---

whip up 迅速地準備　　**devote some thought to** 好好想想某事　　**I read
you.** 我瞭解你的意思了。　　**sleep on it** 過一晚再決定 (此事)　　**No great
rush.** 沒有很急。　　**without too much delay** 沒有拖太久地　　**think it over**
考慮一下　　**ongoing process** 持續進行的事　　**deadline** 截止日期

Lesson 44

Personal Vision (4) （個人先見）

●預習 — *Sentences*

- Well, I wish I were as certain about that as you are.
- Vision is not a magic ability that you're born with.
- I think you'll just keep right on learning.
- You have to ask yourself a set of questions.
- A lot of it is nothing more than plain common sense.

●*Vignette*

Williams: That's about it for the paperwork, Shoichi. You know, I'm very happy for you, but I must say I'll be sorry to see you go.

Sawasaki: Thank you, Clarence. I'm going to miss you too. It was a tough decision, but I decided I'd be crazy not to go.

Williams: I'm sure you'll do a good job at that, Shoichi.

Sawasaki: Well, I wish I were as certain about that as you are. After talking with Gil, I've been trying to think in terms of personal vision, trying to organize my thoughts about the company and where it's going. I still don't understand fully.

Williams: Vision is not a magic ability that you're born with, Shoichi. You can learn to shape your personal vision, and you can learn to make it come true. Stop worrying. I think you'll just keep right on learning, which is a key element of being visionary.

Sawasaki: I still don't feel very "visionary."

Williams: Well, let's look at it this way then. You have to ask yourself a set of questions: Is the vision possible? Is it worth the time, energy, and resources that it would take to complete it? Is it in alignment with my personal values? And more important, am I willing to commit myself to it? In other words, you have to distinguish between real vision and impractical dreams of glory. Of course, a lot of it is nothing more than plain common sense.

Sawasaki: Thanks for your words of wisdom, Clarence. I'm really going to miss your advice.

威廉斯: 昭一,這就是所有的文件了。你知道的,我很替你高興,但我得說,我捨不得看你走。

澤崎: 克雷倫斯,謝謝。我也會想念你的。這是個相當為難的抉擇,不過我已經想清楚了,我若不去就是瘋了。

威廉斯: 昭一,我相信你會勝任這份工作的。

澤崎: 這個嘛,要是我能像你那麼有把握就好了。在跟吉爾談過話之後,我一直試著要用個人先見的角度來思考,試著把我對公司和公司未來走向的看法理清頭緒。不過,我還是沒有完全瞭解。

威廉斯: 昭一,先見並不是一種你生來就有的神奇能力。你可以學習塑造出自己的個人先見,並學習如何落實。不要再去擔心。我認為你只要不斷學習就可以了,而「不斷學習」就是能「有先見」的關鍵因素。

澤崎: 我還是不覺得自己很「有先見」。

威廉斯: 嗯,我們這樣來看好了。你得要問自己一些個問題:這個先見有可能落實嗎?它值得投入所需的時間、精力和資源以將之實現嗎?它跟我個人的價值觀是否相結合?更重要的是,我個人願不願意為此傾力以赴?換句話說,你得要會分辨,甚麼是實際的先見,甚麼是不實際的空中樓閣。當然了,我講的這些有很多都只是普通的常識而已。

澤崎: 克雷倫斯,謝謝你的睿智之語。我絕對會懷念你所給的建議。

Words and Phrases

paperwork	文書事物; 事務處理	worth	值得的
miss	想念	in alignment with	與…相結合
tough decision	難下的決定	distinguish between	在…之間作
magic ability	神奇的能力		區別
shape	塑造出來	impractical dream	不實際的夢想
visionary	adj. 有先見的	glory	榮耀
	n. 有先見的人	nothing more than	只不過是…
Let's look at it this way.	我們這	plain common sense	普通常識
樣來看好了。		words of wisdom	智慧的言語

Vocabulary Building

- **That's about it.**　就是這樣了; 這就是全部了; 全都在這兒了。
  That's about it. Can you think of anything I missed?
  (就是這些了。你還想得到我漏了甚麼嗎?)

- **would be crazy not to**　若不…的話就是瘋了
  Gil suggested I'd be crazy not to accept the offer.
  (吉爾示意說, 我若不接受這樣的職務, 就是有點不太正常了。)

- **organize one's thoughts**　理清思緒
  When I have to make a speech, I organize my thoughts and jot down a few notes, but I don't write out a complete draft.
  (當我要演講的時候, 我會先理清自己的思緒, 作一些摘要, 可是我不會把整篇草稿都擬出來。)

- **come true**　實現
  It started out as my dream, but it was your work that made it come true.
  (這本來只是我的一個夢想, 但你的努力卻使它成真了。)

1. My <u>lawyer</u> suggested <u>to sue</u> the company <u>for</u> <u>violation</u> of safety.
　　　A　　　　　　B　　　　　　　C　　D

2. I usually have some <u>toasts</u>, <u>fried</u> eggs, and coffee <u>early</u> <u>in</u> the morning.
　　　　　　　　　　A　　　B　　　　　　　　　C　　D

3. I wonder <u>if</u> you would <u>tell to</u> me <u>which</u> French school to go to <u>for</u>
　　　　　　A　　　　　B　　　　C　　　　　　　　　　D
lessons.

◆◆◆◆◆◆◆◆◆◆◆◆◆◆ 簡短對話 ◆◆◆◆◆◆◆◆◆◆◆◆◆◆

Williams: All in all, I think you'll make a great head for the Japan operation.
You used to work there, right?

Sawasaki: Yeah, though that was before the merger, of course. I'm not
sure how much has changed there since.

Williams: Still, you're familiar with the people and setup both over there
and here in Chicago. Plus you're completely bilingual and bicultural.

Sawasaki: I wouldn't say that. I still sometimes have trouble understanding
people and expressing myself in English.

---

all in all 大體而言　　**setup** 組織；編制　　**bilingual and bicultural** 懂得
兩國語言又熟悉兩國文化的

Lesson 44

Personal Vision —— 總結

■ ■ ■

　　在本課中，帕克以 Martin Luther King 和 John F. Kennedy 這兩位 visionary leaders 為例，來說明懷有明確先見的重要性。

　　"I have a dream" speech 是金恩牧師於 1963 年 8 月 28 日在 Lincoln Memorial 之前，對著萬名 civil rights marchers (民權運動大遊行的參加者)所作的演說。

　　金恩牧師在那場演說中，曾數度提到"I have a dream"，那就是他的 vision。他深信，人類終有一天將不再因種族或膚色的不同而歧視他人。翌年，金恩牧師獲頒諾貝爾和平獎，但不幸地，在 1968 年 4 月 4 日，他被暗殺於田納西州的孟斐斯。

　　而甘迺迪總統則是不顧 NASA 專家的反對，於 1960 年發表了他的 vision：「我要在 60 年代結束前，將人類送上月球」，並積極推動阿波羅計畫。終於，在 1969 年 7 月 20 日，Apollo II 順利發射升空，Neil A. Armstrong 等人因此為人類的登月史寫下劃世紀的一頁。

　　以下是一些追求先見的經營者的特徵 (摘自 *Creating Excellence*)。

　Visionary Executive:

- Makes contact with employees at all levels (與各階層的員工都有所接觸)
- Is receptive, expressive, supportive and "hot" (people and ideas ignite him) (感受性敏銳、表達能力強，願意支持他人，而且「熱情」(即能與他人和一些想法觀念產生劃擦)
- Pays attention to strengths (所注重的是他人的長處)
- Talks about future goals (談論將來的目標)

Farewell to America

（再會了！美國）

◆ Lesson 45 的內容 ◆

　　今天是尼爾森 ABC 食品公司位於芝加哥的新式工廠要開放給外界參觀的日子。這間工廠可說是世界上最先進、生產設備最符合生態要求的工廠之一。受邀參觀者除了有當地的政治人物、企業家、地方政府官員、教育工作者、工廠員工及其家屬之外，電視台和報社也在邀請的名單之列。另一方面，澤崎返國擔任總裁的日子也即將到來。這回連一向愛挖苦人的溫契爾都極為罕見地說道，「我會想念你的。」晚上大家預定要在帕克家裡為澤崎舉行歡送會。

That's great!
This should be
some party!

Lesson 45

Farewell to America (1) （再會了！美國）

預習 — *Sentences*

- It's obvious you've put in a lot of work on this open house.
- The people here at the plant have all done a lot of work too.
- I saw a local reporter interviewing the plant manager.
- We've taken such a bruising in the media over the layoffs.
- Alex is very proud of this place, as well he might be.

Vignette

Murphy: Shoichi, over here! Here, put this on.

Sawasaki: What? A name tag?

Murphy: It may not really be necessary, but we're putting them on the headquarters' staff just in case any of the visiting VIPs are looking for someone to talk to.

Sawasaki: That's a good idea, Patti. I also thought the invitations you sent to the local media and politicians were very nicely done. It's obvious you've put in a lot of work on this open house.

Murphy: Why, thank you, Shoichi, I'm really going to miss your giving credit where credit is due. Actually, though, the people here at the plant have all done a lot of work too.

Sawasaki: I saw a local reporter and photographer interviewing the plant manager on my way in, so it looks like we'll get some coverage, at least in the local press. It's important that we get some good publicity on the opening of this plant because we've taken such a bruising in the media over the layoffs elsewhere.

Murphy: I know. Alex is very proud of this place, as well he might be. It's state-of-the-art in all respects and it's actually added jobs to the community.

Winchell: Hi, kids. Patti, this is really some party. Isn't this place great?

Sawasaki: We were just talking about how impressed we are with the advanced technology in the plant.

　　這間工廠在許多方面都是最先進的，而且也為當地製造了許多就業機會。不過，雖然它有很先進的電腦一貫作業系統，但更受大家注目的還是工廠在環保方面的成就。這兒幾乎算得上是世界上生產設備最乾淨的工廠之一了。

墨菲：　昭一，在這兒！來，把這個戴上。

澤崎：　這是甚麼？一張名牌？

墨菲：　可能也不是那麼必要啦，可是我們讓總公司的每個職員都戴上名牌，這樣的話，若來訪的要人想找個人說說話，就會方便得多。

澤崎：　派蒂，這個主意不錯。還有你們寄給本地媒體和從政者的邀請函，我也覺得你們做得很好。顯然地，在這個開放參觀的活動上，你們是花了不少心血。

墨菲：　哦，謝謝你，昭一，我以後鐵定會懷念像你這樣歸功於有功者的做法。不過，事實上工廠這裡的人也都相當費心。

澤崎：　我進來的時候看到一個本地記者和攝影師在採訪廠長，這樣看來，至少有本地新聞會報導我們的事。我們這次的工廠開放真的是需要點好宣傳，因為公司在其他地方的裁員事件被媒體批評得很慘。

墨菲：　我知道。亞力士對於這個工廠當然是相當引以為傲的。這裡在各個方面都很先進，而且，對於增加社會上的工作機會更是不無幫助。

溫謝爾：　你們好啊！派蒂，這真像是在開派對。這地方棒極了，不是嗎？

澤崎：　我們才正在讚嘆這間工廠裡的先進科技呢！

Lesson 45 Farewell to America (1)

Words and Phrases

put on	戴上; 穿上		重要人物
name tag	名牌	coverage	報導
headquarters' staff	總部的人員	get publicity	得到注意 (宣傳)
just in case	以防萬一	layoff	裁員
visiting	來訪的	state-of-the-art	最新式的
VIP (very important person)		advanced technology	先進技術

Vocabulary Building

- **open house**　開放參觀; 開放參觀日
  How about holding an open house to let people in the community see the new research center?
  (我們來個開放參觀, 好讓社區民眾進來看看我們新的研究中心如何?)

- **give credit**　讚揚; 認可某人的功蹟
  Don't forget to give credit to the support staff, without whom this project couldn't have succeeded.
  (別忘了要讚美那些幕後工作人員, 沒有他們, 這個計畫是不會成功的。)

- **due**　應歸給的; 當然的
  Lloyd thought he was due for a raise, but his boss disagreed.
  (勞埃認為他該加薪了, 可是他老闆卻不同意。)

- **take a bruising**　受到打擊
  Our consumer electronics division has taken a bruising from foreign competition.
  (我們公司的家電部門受到國外競爭廠商的嚴重打擊。)

▶**Exercises**　在下列例句中，每句各有四個劃線部分，　　　(解答見 270 頁)
其中一個的文法有誤，請將之選出。

1. Japan's trade <u>with</u> the United States has <u>improved</u>, but it <u>is getting</u> more
　　　　　　　A　　　　　　　　　　　　　B　　　　　　　C

　and more <u>complication</u> with other countries.
　　　　　　　D

2. <u>Even if</u> I <u>submitted</u> my college application, I haven't <u>yet</u> <u>decided</u> to go
　　A　　　　B　　　　　　　　　　　　　　　　　C　　D

　to Australia to study.

3. I hope that we <u>will</u> have <u>better</u> <u>weather</u> tomorrow <u>at</u> the baseball game.
　　　　　　　　　A　　　　　B　　　　C　　　　　　　　D

◆◆◆◆◆◆◆◆◆◆◆◆◆◆ 簡短對話 ◆◆◆◆◆◆◆◆◆◆◆◆◆◆

Murphy: I want to thank you for arranging this assignment for me. I've learned a lot from it, and I've really enjoyed it too.

Sawasaki: Also, it's given you a chance to get away from the routine of working for me, right?

Murphy: Oh no, that's not it at all. This may sound a bit corny, but I really find it inspiring to work for you.

Sawasaki: Wow, that's the first time I've heard that line from anybody. Let me tell you, though, ever since the news of my transfer came out, I've been getting all this unsolicited praise. It's really been going to my head.

---

routine *n.* 例行公事　　　**corny** 重感情的；傷感的　　　**inspiring** 鼓舞人心的
line 話；台詞　　　**unsolicited praise** 他人自動給與的讚美　　　**go to one's head**
使人開始自命不凡起來

Lesson 45

Farewell to America (2) （再會了！美國）

●預習 — *Sentences*

- This must be one of the cleanest production facilities.
- Alex takes the company's responsibilities seriously.
- What I'm going to miss is all those conversations.
- The balloon man is running short on balloons.
- It's very nice of Gil to give a party for me at his own house.

●*Vignette*

Winchell: But I've heard more people talking about the environmental aspect of the plant than about CIM. This must be one of the cleanest production facilities in the world.

Sawasaki: Gosh, it seems like just yesterday I was talking with Peter and Sally about Nelson ABC Foods' new commitment to the environment. It's obvious that Alex takes the company's environmental responsibilities very seriously.

Winchell: Yes. You know, what I'm especially going to miss about working with you, Shoichi, is all those conversations. Instead of talking about last night's football game or whatever, I've been learning useful stuff. The office has been like an ongoing seminar.

Murphy: I feel the same way, Shoichi. It's been fun, but it's also been very informative around the office. Anyway, I have to go now. The balloon man is running short on balloons, and I was on my way to restock him when I saw you. If I don't run into you again, I'll catch you tonight at Gil's house.

Sawasaki: See you, Patti. It's very nice of Gil to give a party for me at his own house.

Winchell: He and his wife love to throw parties. His place looks more like a country club than a house, anway.

Sawasaki: I'm really going to miss the spacious housing here in the U.S.

248

溫謝爾：　不過據我所聽到的，談論工廠環保設施的人，要比談論工廠 CIM 的人來得多。這裡一定是世界上生產設備最乾淨的工廠之一了。

澤崎：　老天，我想起上回跟彼得還有莎莉談到尼爾森 ABC 食品公司對環境保護的承諾，那好像才是昨天的事而已。顯然亞力士十分重視公司的環保責任。

溫謝爾：　對啊。你知道嗎，昭一，我以後會特別懷念和你共事這一段日子中的所有對話。我們所談的並不是前晚的足球賽或其他有的沒有的，但我卻藉此學到了不少有用的東西。這個辦公室就像是個持續不斷的研討會場。

墨菲：　昭一，我也是這麼覺得。這裡一直都很有趣，而且也相當富有知性。不過，我現在得走了。那個負責弄氣球的人氣球快用完了，我剛剛看到你的時候就是正要去給他補貨。假如我沒再碰到你的話，今晚我會到吉爾家去跟你碰面。

澤崎：　派蒂，再見。吉爾真好，還為我在他自己的屋子開派對。

溫謝爾：　他跟他太太都很喜歡開派對。他那間房子看來不像個家，反倒有鄉村俱樂部的味道。

澤崎：　我真的要懷念美國這裡寬大的住屋空間了。

Lesson 45　Farewell to America (2)

Words and Phrases

environmental aspect	環保層面	informative *adj.*	能獲得知識的
CIM (computer integrated manu-facturing)	電腦一貫作業	balloon	氣球
		restock	補充存貨
It seems like yesterday.	似乎還是昨天的事。	run into	碰到
		throw a party	開派對
environment	環境	country club	鄉村俱樂部
environmental responsibilities	環保的責任	spacious housing	寬廣的住宅

Vocabulary Building

● **commitment**　承諾; 約定
These are just sales goals, not commitments.
(這些只是銷售目標而已, 不是甚麼承諾。)

● **or whatever**　或是任何東西
Tell me about your "golden handcuff" program or whatever you call it.
(告訴我一點關於你的「金手銬」〈為慰留優秀員工而給的優渥待遇〉計畫的事, 不管你是怎麼稱呼它的。)

● **ongoing**　持續進行的; 持續不斷的
We conduct performance evaluation not just once a year but as an ongoing process.
(我們公司的人事考核不是一年做一次, 而是隨時都在進行。)

● **run stort on**　…不夠了
cf. Leonora has lots of good ideas, but she's a bit short on the ability to translate them into reality.
(莉奧諾拉有不少好點子, 不過她有點缺乏付諸施行的才幹。)

1. Marie said <u>she'd</u> never <u>set foot in</u> this house <u>again</u> unless you <u>stopped to</u>
      A   B   C   D

   <u>smoke</u>.

2. If you met my <u>family</u>, you would <u>surprise</u> that all of <u>them</u> <u>are</u> very thin.
                    A   B   C   D

3. Although the <u>amount</u> of information <u>available on</u> India <u>are</u> tremendous,
                  A   B   C

   many people <u>still</u> know little about it.
                  D

◆◆◆◆◆◆◆◆◆◆◆◆◆ 簡短對話 ◆◆◆◆◆◆◆◆◆◆◆◆◆

Winchell: You know, Shoichi, when I first met you, I thought you were really uptight—a super serious type.
Sawasaki: Maybe I am.
Winchell: You certainly have your serious side, but the funny thing is that I've really gotten to appreciate it.
Sawasaki: Spare me the kind words, will you, Brad? You're the last person I expect them from.
Winchell: Oh, don't think I'm praising you or anything. Me? Praise? But I'm going to miss you, old buddy.

---

uptight 拘謹的   **spare** 使人免受某事   **old buddy** 老搭檔；老朋友

Lesson 45

Farewell to America (3) （再會了！美國）

●預習 — *Sentences*

- I do hope to get back to Chicago on a regular basis.
- It was a very good idea on someone's part.
- That may be a good idea, both for her and the company.
- But she may feel differently now that you're leaving.
- We should get her to think some more about her future.

●*Vignette*

Sawasaki: I'm looking forward to going home, but I know I'm going to suffer a heavy dose of reverse culture shock.

Winchell: Seriously, Shoichi, we're going to miss having you around.

Sawasaki: Well, that's mutual, you know. Leaving you and my other friends here is the downside of this assignment. Still, I do hope to get back to Chicago on a regular basis.

Winchell: You'll probably be working so hard you'll forget where Chicago is. Oh, here's Clarence. Hi there.

Williams: Hi, guys. I got roped in working with the volunteers from our adopt-a-school program, but I must admit I'm having fun. We have a table set up out by the day-care center on the plant and we're signing people up for local volunteer efforts. It was a very good idea on someone's part.

Sawasaki: Probably Patti's. She's shown some good skills on this project, and one last thing I want to do before I leave here is recommend her for some sort of promotion.

Williams: That may be a good idea, both for her and the company. The last time I talked to her, she said she was happy doing what she was doing and not particularly interested in moving up the ladder. But she may feel differently now that you're leaving. We should probably get her to think some more about her future.

Sawasaki: That's exactly how I feel.

雖然威廉斯說他是被拉去幫忙「認養學校」計畫的義工們，不過他看來可一點兒沒有不高興的樣子。他們在工廠托兒所外面架設了一張桌子，來招募員工加入地方自願工作的行列。

澤崎：　我期盼著能夠回到本國，不過我也知道自己會遭到一記重重的逆向文化衝擊。

溫謝爾：　昭一，說正經的，我們都會懷念有你在這兒的日子。

澤崎：　嗯，你也知道這種感覺是相互的。這項任命的缺點就是，我得要跟你以及我其他在這裡的朋友分別。不過，我真的希望能定期回到芝加哥來。

溫謝爾：　你可能會埋首工作，而忘了芝加哥在哪。噢，克雷倫斯來了。嗨！

威廉斯：　嗨，你們好！我才被拉去跟「認養學校」計畫的義工們忙著，不過我得承認自己是樂在其中。我們在工廠的日間托兒所外面架設了一張桌子，來招募人加入我們地方自願工作的行列。有人給我們出了這麼個好主意。

澤崎：　這可能是派蒂想出來的。她在這次的策畫上表現出相當優秀的技巧。我在離開之前想做的最後一件事，就是向上級報請給她擢升。

威廉斯：　這對她和公司本身可能都有好處。我上回跟她聊天的時候，她說她對自己現在所做的事覺得很滿意，也不會特別想要升官。不過現在既然你要離開了，她的感覺可能會不一樣。也許我們該讓她多想想關乎自己未來的事。

澤崎：　這正是我的感覺。

Lesson 45   Farewell to America (3)

Words and Phrases

that's mutual	這是相互的		供義務性支援而與學校建立起新關係
assignment	任務		的計畫
on a regular basis	定期地	have fun	有樂趣
Hi there.	嗨!	day-care center	日間托兒所
"adopt-a-school" program	藉提	move up the ladder	升遷

Vocabulary Building

- **dose**　一次痛苦的經驗

  Jocelyn has had a dose of hard luck since her business started going under.

  (喬瑟琳在她的事業開始走下坡之後，嚐到了霉運當頭之苦。)

- **reverse**　逆轉的

  John claimed that, as an Anglo-Saxon white American, he was a victim of reverse discrimination.

  (約翰聲稱，身為一個盎格魯撒克遜白種美國人，他成了逆向種族歧視的受害者。)

- **rope in**　拉某人加入; 說服原本不情願的人加入; 誘騙

  I let myself get roped in serving as chairman of the fund-raising drive.

  (我接受了他們的說服加入這個募款活動，擔任活動的委員長。)

- **sign up**　參加; 立約加入

  More than 100 people signed up to take part in the volunteer tutoring program.

  (有一百多人要加入這個自願家教服務計畫。)

1. Tom, I'd rather that you don't call me at midnight.
          A   B C   D

2. My nephew said that he'd rather studying in Europe than in America.
             A   B   C   D

3. Tom was surprised to see his baby crawled on the floor in six months.
        A   B   C   D

◆◆◆◆◆◆◆◆◆◆◆◆◆◆ 簡短對話 ◆◆◆◆◆◆◆◆◆◆◆◆◆◆

Sawasaki: I do hope you'll follow up with Patti on the idea of taking on a position with more responsibilities.

Williams: I will, I promise. Also, it wouldn't do any harm if you had a few words with her yourself before you leave. She respects you an awful lot. In the final analysis, of course, she has to make up her own mind about where she wants to be headed. But some strategic words from you may be just what it takes to get her thinking about it seriously.

Sawasaki: Gotcha, Clarence. I'll make a point of talking to her about it.

---

wouldn't do any harm 不會有害   **in the final analysis** 總之；終究
strategic 戰略性的   **Gotcha.** (=I got you.) 我瞭解你的意思。   **make a point of** 一定會…

Lesson 45

Farewell to America (4)（再會了！美國）

●預習 — *Sentences*

· Anyway, I've got to get back to that volunteer desk.
· Sally, you're looking very nice for the occasion.
· I bought this suit a couple of months ago.
· Why don't you get DeMarco to send Brad somewhere?
· Maria Cortez and her husband Geoff are coming too.

●*Vignette*

Williams: Anyway, I've got to get back to that volunteer desk. I'll be seeing you at Gil's tonight.

Sawasaki: You're coming? Great. See you there.

Winchell: Hey, there's Gil and Sally. Let's go say hello.

Parker: Well, well, the office odd couple.

Sawasaki: Hello, Gil. Sally, you're looking very nice for the occasion.

Egler: Why, thank you Shoichi. See, Gil? Someone noticed. I bought this suit a couple of months ago and I've been waiting for a chance to wear it. Do you think it's too severe?

Sawasaki: Not at all. I think you strike the perfect balance between "fashionable" and "dressed for success."

Winchell: A cross between Cinderella and her stepmother.

Egler: Thanks, Brad. Listen, Gil, why don't you keep Shoichi here and get DeMarco to send Brad somewhere? Don't we need someone to head our operations in Siberia?

Parker: That's a thought.

Winchell: I don't mind. The wind-chill factor couldn't be much worse than Chicago in the winter.

Egler: Oh! I just remembered I have to pass on a message. Peter called just as I was leaving. He said he's coming tonight.

Parker: And Maria Cortez and her husband Geoff are coming too.

Sawasaki: That's great! This should be some party!

　　會出席今晚派對的人不僅有澤崎現在的同事，還有上個月才離職的彼得‧史瓦布利克，而以前在紐約共事過的瑪莉亞‧古岱茲和她先生也會到場。這場派對看來似乎會很精采。

威廉斯：　不過，我現在得回到那個招募義工的檯子去了。晚上吉爾家見。

澤崎：　你也會去？那太好了，到時候見。

溫謝爾：　嘿，那是吉爾和莎莉。我們過去跟他們打個招呼。

帕克：　哇，看我們辦公室裡這對奇特的組合。

澤崎：　哈囉，吉爾。莎莉，妳在今天這樣的場合看起來很漂亮。

艾格勒：　真的！謝謝昭一。吉爾，看到了嗎！有人注意到了耶！這套衣服是我幾個月前買的，只等合適的時機亮相。你覺得它會不會太樸素了點？

澤崎：　一點也不會。我覺得妳在「流行」與「為成功而穿著」之間取得了極佳的平衡。

溫謝爾：　也就是介於灰姑娘和她繼母之間的一種穿著。

艾格勒：　謝謝你哦，布雷。聽著，吉爾，你為甚麼不把昭一留在這兒，讓迪馬哥把布雷調到別的地方去呢？看看我們在西伯利亞的廠房需不需要有人去領頭？

帕克：　這個主意不錯。

溫謝爾：　我是無所謂。那裡冬天的風速冷卻效果應該不會比芝加哥糟到哪裡去。

艾格勒：　噢，我想起來了，我還得傳個話呢，我剛剛要離開的時候彼得打過電話，他說他今晚會過去。

帕克：　還有，瑪莉亞‧古岱茲和她先生傑夫也會到場。

澤崎：　太好了！這個派對一定會很棒。

Lesson 45 Farewell to America (4)

Words and Phrases

I'll be seeing you.　再見。
say hello　打招呼
odd couple　奇妙的二人組
fashionable　流行的
Cinderella and her stepmother
　灰姑娘和她的繼母

Siberia [saɪˈbɪrɪə]　西伯利亞
wind-chill factor　風速冷卻效果
　〈皮膚表面在風力吹襲下放出熱量而
　造成身體冷卻的效果〉
pass on a message　傳個話

Vocabulary Building

- **severe**　樸素的；樸實的
  The severe lines of the house were a dramatic contrast to the Victorian architecture of the rest of the neighborhood.
  (這棟屋子的樸實線條與鄰近的其他維多利亞式建築形成了強烈的對比。)

- **strike the perfect balance between**　在…之間取得完全的平衡
  It's almost impossible to strike the perfect balance between flexibility and the maintenance of strict standards.
  (又要能變通，又要能維持嚴格的標準，在這二者之間幾乎不可能取得完全的平衡。)

- **cross between**　介於…之間的中間物
  The "mook" is a cross between a magazine and a book.
  (「雜誌型書籍」是一種介於雜誌和書本之間的出版品。)

- **That's a thought.**　這個主意不錯。
  That's a thought. Why didn't it occur to me?
  (這個主意不錯。我怎麼會沒有想到？)

1. If you <u>knew to use</u> a modem, I <u>would</u> let you use <u>mine</u> <u>while</u> I'm away.
          A   B   C   D

2. Your stereo is <u>too</u> loud <u>that</u> I can never <u>hear</u> your voice <u>on</u> the tele-
               A   B   C   D

phone.

3. Flight 663 <u>for Moscow</u> is now ready <u>for</u> <u>boarding</u> <u>on</u> Gate 6.
              A   B   C   D

◆◆◆◆◆◆◆◆◆◆◆◆◆ 簡短對話 ◆◆◆◆◆◆◆◆◆◆◆◆◆◆

[*At Gill Parker's that evening*]

Parker: People, could I have your attention for just a moment? Shoichi, on behalf of your colleagues and friends, I'd like to give you this token of our appreciation and best wishes in the hope that it will serve as a memento of the time you've spent with us.

Sawasaki: For me? You shouldn't have.

Parker: Go ahead, open it. I hope you like it.

Sawasaki: What can it be? The package is certainly much too big for a gold watch . . . A view of the Chicago skyline from Lake Michigan! This is stunning! It'll be the first thing I put up in my office in Tokyo. Thank you all so much.

---

people 各位   **on behalf of** 代替…   **colleague** 同事   **token of ap-preciation** 表示感謝的東西   **memento** 紀念品   **stunning** 十分漂亮的

Farewell to America ── 總結

一年前，澤崎在飛往尼爾森總公司所在地芝加哥的途中，內心充滿著疑懼與不安。

「這是個競爭激烈的新公司，我有辦法與那些美國同事共事嗎？」

「對於這些急劇的變化，我有足夠的應變能力嗎？」

「企業的存在是以『物慾』為其目的嗎？」

但是，這些現在都已無需擔心了。來美的第二年，澤崎的才能已得到大家完全的認同，所以他現在要回去當日本分公司的總裁，可說是「衣錦還鄉」吧！

三十八歲就能當到總裁，在日本可說是絕無僅有。在美國，就算深具實力，也少有這樣的際遇。而澤崎身處企業購併的變動期間，不僅能屹立不搖，還獲得了上司如此的肯定，不免令他覺得有些自豪，自信心更是大為提升。所以，他在回到日本之後，不管會碰到甚麼樣的困難，都可以認定自己是經歷過大風大浪的人，而不會被輕易打倒。

此外，我們也充分瞭解到，人類的能力、創意和潛能是無限的。所以，學習美國新消費動向，或是高齡化社會的相關知識，是絕對有用的。而澤崎本身就是個學習能力很強的人，擺在他前面的道路委實難以限量。

不過，澤崎至今仍無法理解的一點是，何以美國企業一面汲汲於利益之爭，一面卻又要大量投資於幾無利益可言的環境保護？何以他們在大幅裁員之際，卻又同時大做社區公關、獎勵員工參與自願活動？最令人訝異的還是那個為維護自尊而選擇離去的彼得・史瓦布利克，我們暗祝他能在小眾市場行銷顧問一職上，找到自己的路。

現在縈繞在澤崎腦海裡的，也許就是尼爾森 ABC 食品公司在日本未來的走向了。在此，我們或可預見他的成功。

再見了，澤崎昭一。

Answers to Exercises

Lesson 32
(1)
1. A n examination committee informed the students who failed the exam.
2. A Having forgotten his notes, Jim winged his pesentation to management.
3. C Not until Ned's wife left him, did he realize how much he loved her.

(2)
1. D To balance this year's budget, the task force proposed laying off half the personnel.
2. B I thought living in a city would be rather exciting but now I am completely fed up.
3. A There were quite a few people who could make themselves understood in Chinese.

(3)
1. B You must wash a wool sweater by squeezing water through it.
2. A Not having been given instructions, the demonstrator was unsure how to handle the new car.
3. B There was much confusion among the people who lost their houses in the earthquake.

(4)
1. C When Bill was in grammar school, he dreamed of being a doctor.
2. B The audience should listen to Lisa's lecture in silence so as to show respect.
3. D Few persons showed any interest in playing the market.

Lesson 33
(1)
1. D What we have to have at camp is fire for cooking, water for drinking, and tents for shelter.
2. D The management had to cut the budget in order not to lay off workers.
3. D The high school soccer tournament will be held every day enen if it rains (or if it is rainy).

(2)
1. A Can you point to (or point out) the exact spot on the map where you live?
2. A Our new design software enabled us to create the graphs for next week's presentation in just under an hour.
3. A Tomiko wanted to go abroad so she could practice speaking English.

(3)

1. A Even when driven carefully, the motorcycle is a very dangerous mode of transportation.
2. C If you had spent less money on cards, you wouldn't have gotten in trouble.
3. C "I want you to know I cannot be bought off," Andy said refusing to accept the bribe.

(4)

1. B People spend more time at the office these days than they did in the past.
2. B Times have changed— and time flies like an arrow.
3. C Please come to my house on Sunday for a surprise birthday party for James.

Lesson 34

(1)

1. A Some teenagers do not respect the elderly and behave rudely toward them.
2. A Most people think that Chinese is a very difficult language to master because it has a great many hard-to-memorize characters.
3. B Mozart is one of the greatest composers who ever lived.

(2)

1. D The zoo fire was a terrible tragedy. A number of exotic and rare animals died.
2. A Yoshiro committed suicide in the traditional Japanese fashion by disemboweling himself.
3. D I try to tailor my remarks to suit the particular audience I'm speaking to.

(3)

1. D The best way to find yourself is to lose yourself in our hotspring.
2. D You just don't have to be perfect. Just do your best and you will improve gradually.
3. C Almond and vanilla are natural essences available at most health food shops throughout the nation.

(4)

1. D The Japanese have refined the art of living in a small world. Everything can be at your fingertips.
2. A It is best to store flour in the bag in which it is sold, and keep it in a cool, dry spot.
3. B Students of English should listen to as much authentic English language as possible.

Lesson 35

(1)

1. A "What a great idea!" Arthur told his secretary, who was helping him write the script.
2. A Dave baked the muffins from scratch, but most people now use a commercially prepared mix.
3. C The experts say that the health benefits of body massage are numerous.

(2)

1. A Do you think we can get away with that scene? Won't the censors object?
2. C Whenever I was baffled by a reader's complicated inquiry, Rosemary always came to the rescue.
3. B Although numerous mosquitoes buzzed around him, Bob slept like a log.

(3)

1. C I accepted the position in Ethiopia, but I am beginning to have second thoughts about it.
2. D Just when we were about to give up, we began to see the light at the end of the tunnel.
3. D Shortly after arriving in Buenos Aires, Alice wondered what she had come for.

(4)

1. A Never leave alcohol anywhere near Thomas because he drinks like a fish.
2. D Since I took the opposite side on this issue, our relationship is on the rocks.
3. A When we reached Los Angeles, we had to look for an apartment in the newspaper.

Lesson 36

(1)

1. C My supervisor said I deserve a raise, but I just wanted a pat on the back.
2. D The port city suffered a major earthquake in early 1995.
3. A The group thinks putting in long hours at work will enable them to complete the assignment on time.

(2)

1. B You should look around before you check out of a hotel room. I once forgot my expensive watch in a hotel in Paris.
2. B Ralph gave many history lectures this year at the university.
3. D You should take better care of your finances, or you'll never be able to afford retirement.

(3)

1. D You just can't wait for Lady Luck to come; you should go out and find her.
2. A In the old days, my father had a short fuse when I didn't complete my work.
3. B My family will lose face if I don't get accepted by Yale.

(4)

1. B Because of your poor preparation, you failed the test.
2. B From now on, we advise that you try to study (or studying) harder or you may flunk out of school.
3. D I'm afraid I'll have to take a rain check on your dinner invitation.

Lesson 37

(1)

1. C Kim should not be chain smoking during her pregnancy, but she just can't seem to kick the habit.
2. B It is not advisable to say something in the staff meeting that you don't want the entire company to know about.
3. B The key to success, I think, is to have not only modern equipment, but also capable staff.

(2)

1. A I'm sick and tired of beating around the bush with her.
2. B John is buttering up customers in hopes of selling more products than his colleagues do.
3. A TV news, shown almost hourly, keeps viewers up-to-date on world events.

(3)

1. A If Anita had read the instructions before starting the machine, she wouldn't have encountered so many problems.
2. C Our president made up his mind to postpone releasing (or the release of) the results of the climate survey.
3. C Tommy used to work for a trading house, but he was let go after criticizing its lack of leadership.

(4)

1. C The refugees were troubled by the hardships of war which lasted more than two years.
2. A To hear Bette tell it, she's the best French speaker in her entire class.
3. C The researcher's discoveries in genetics brought him success in the academic community.

Lesson 38

(1)

1. B Professor Smith goes over his students' papers with a fine-tooth comb.
2. A As far as I am concerned, normal body temperature is 36 degrees centigrade.
3. D Mr. Burns attributes his company's success to working diligently.

(2)

1. D When Kathy saw that the audience was enthralled by her superb performance, she felt dazzled by her success.
2. D I was so shocked to hear the news of my company's bankruptcy that I didn't feel like going out.
3. B People have largely refused to listen to the government's request for water conservation.

(3)

1. D McIntyre Enterprise just completed a big deal with an Indian semiconductor company.
2. D Robert's taste in clothing has never suited Tim.
3. C When you start working, you should join the corporate pension plan for the financial security it will provide during your retirement.

(4)

1. A On Guam, while enjoying its wonderful climate, we should take care to avoid overexposure to the sun.
2. A To estimate how much it will cost to visit chile, add the total cost of air fare, hotels, meals, and ground transportation.
3. A This old cabin, which I have been using every summer since I was in kindergarten, was originally built by my uncle.

Lesson 39

(1)

1. D I'm still in the middle of talking to my father on the phone, but I'll be ready to go in ten minutes.
2. B Mr. Adams has been surveying the travel business for the past half-year and has concluded that it has a great future.
3. C Chuck is very knowledgeable about vital political and economic issues the nation now faces.

(2)

1. D It is said that space is the last frontier for man to explore.

2. B Mike tried to avoid taking the final exam with the excuse of a death in the family.

3. D This chart gives us a dramatic representation of the rapid rise in drug use among teenagers.

(3)

1. C After speaking with the human resources manager, Sara was no longer fascinated with job prospects in the company.

2. C Patricia will have a difficult time telling which of these two used cars is in better condition as both look brand new.

3. A Should there be a need to make changes in our plan for tomorrow, please call me as soon as possible.

(4)

1. D Top corporate management usually interprets workforce needs by asking about them on the shop floor.

2. B Because of the economic recession, at least five companies have gone bankrupt.

3. B We have been busy discussing cost-cutting measures for the last month or two.

Lesson 40

(1)

1. A Charles agreed to my suggestion to relocate his corporate headquarters to Osaka.

2. D If there's anything Pat doesn't need, it's more unwanted advice.

3. B Sports trainers agree that concentration is the key to building strength, not long hours of exercise.

(2)

1. A Let's not go out tonight. It looks like a snowstorm is on its way.

2. A The data in this newsletter are usually trustworthy, but there were a lot of errors in the last issue.

3. A Sally looks a bit cold, but actually she is a warm-hearted person.

(3)

1. D Thomas has had time to get in contact with us from Geneva, hasn't he?

2. A We hope the new equipment on order from your company will be sent to us without delay.

3. D By this time next year, we will not only have moved to a new city, but will have built our house.

(4)

1. D I told Jack that he had to finish the unfinished job completely before he went home.
2. B How many journalists you know is not so important as how you are known to them.
3. C Today's newspaper carried many news items about the impending airline strike.

Lesson 41

(1)

1. B If you have time, Tom, please take this letter to the post office and mail it for me.
2. A Mary will go to a four-year college after she graduates from high school.
3. B The majority of the residents will have moved to other places by May of next year.

(2)

1. A Henry can hardly run since he broke his leg playing baseball.
2. B All students must either write a term paper or present an oral report to the class.
3. A Yesterday I asked Mr. Roberts which day he sent the postcard and he said he was not sure that he sent it at all.

(3)

1. C The exam results stunned the math teachers because none of the students could answer the basic equations.
2. C The guest of honor, sitting with his wife and three children, was introduced at the state dinner.
3. B If one does not sleep soundly at night, one cannot expect to work effectively the next day.

(4)

1. D Millions of people use computers, but most would not consider themselves to be computer literate.
2. B Compare the cost of housing in Japan with that of other countries to get a real sense of the value of money.
3. B According to some researchers, the sea level appears to have risen around the world throughout the last decade.

Lesson 42

(1)

1. D This computer is capable of storing millions of pieces of information.
2. A My uncle always tells lots of jokes and funny stories when he gets drunk on wine.
3. A I have laid your keys under the door mat so that you won't miss them.

(2)

1. B The cost of living has risen over 15 percent in the past six years.
2. B David asked the caller to repeat because he did not catch him the first time.
3. A The duties of school teachers are to teach their subjects, to grade their students, and to give them guidance.

(3)

1. C Every man and woman 18 years of age or older is eligible to have a driver's license.
2. D I majored in statistics in college and am interested in its application to technology.
3. A Many Japanese marvel at the cost of Japanese products overseas because they are cheaper than in Japan.

(4)

1. B Neither the United States nor the countries of Europe require vaccination against any kind of illness.
2. C Everyone who majors in archaeology or anthropology has to study sociology in order to understand humanity.
3. D There have been several objections raised about the new Supreme Court judge concerning his past personal scandals.

Lesson 43

(1)

1. A The Class of 1944 consisted of only 98 students, but no less than 300 students will graduate this year.
2. D It may be difficult to understand the true Japanese spirit unless you have lived in Japanese society.
3. B It is an accepted custom in some cultures for men to let women go first into the elevator.

(2)

1. A According to the news, some mammals are no longer on the endangered species' list.

268

2. A Each of the partners needs to draw the same salary regardless of his experience.

3. B For the last couple of years, the hiring freeze has been on to cut down on
overhead costs.

(3)

1. A Generally speaking, most companies are bloated by 20 to 25 percent.

2. B Gil and his friends like to eat Chinese food almost everyday at the restaurant
on campus.

3. A Sometimes car manufacturers need to recall certain models of cars because
of design defects.

(4)

1. B Although I tried as hard as I could, I didn't win the tournament.

2. D Learners should use both textbooks and drills, as well as attend class, to learn
new computer skills.

3. A Seldom did we see (or We seldom saw) homeless people on the street before
the bad times started.

Lesson 44

(1)

1. A Nancy has to develop common sense in money matters as she tends to purchase everything she sees.

2. C One of the most interesting subjects in my school days was history and another was geography.

3. B Many new books have a great amount of information about computers.

(2)

1. B Japanese schoolchildren are so busy with schoolwork that it is difficult for
them to find time for sports.

2. C The motor journalist was looking for a special kind of car at the auto show.

3. A Did you receive permission for a fortnight off?

(3)

1. A Most foreign students realize that Japan as a nation is rich, but the average
Japanese citizen isn't.

2. D It was John F. Kennedy, not his brother, who was the youngest person to be
elected president of the United States.

3. B My friend was greatly influenced by his brother who wanted him to be a
lawyer.

(4)

1. B My lawyer suggested suing (or that I should sue) the company for violation of safety laws.
2. A I usually have some toast, fried eggs, and coffee early in the morning.
3. B I wonder if you would tell me which French school to go to for lessons.

Lesson 45 ————————————————————

(1)

1. D Japan's trade with the United States has improved, but it is getting more and more complicated with other countries.
2. A Even though I submitted my college application, I haven't yet decided to go to Australia to study.
3. D I hope that we will have better weather tomorrow for the baseball game.

(2)

1. D Marie said she'd never set foot in this house again unless you stopped smoking.
2. B If you met my family, you would be surprised that all of them are very thin.
3. C Although the amount of information available on India is tremendous, many people still know little about it.

(3)

1. B Tom, I'd rather that you didn't call me at midnight.
2. C My nephew said that he'd rather study in Europe than in America.
3. C Tom was surprised to see his baby crawl (or crawling) on the floor in six months.

(4)

1. A If you knew how to use a modem, I would let you use mine while I'm away.
2. A Your stereo is so loud that I can never hear your voice on the telephone.
3. D Flight 663 for Moscow is now ready for boarding at Gate 6.

Key Words and Idioms
單字片語一覽表

課文中出現的主要單字及片語依字母順序檢索如下。
括弧內的數字表示該單字出現的頁數

271

出; 被擱置一邊　　(54)

false 虛偽的　　(104)

fashionable 流行的　　(256)

fax machine 傳真機　　(10)

fellow professional 其他同為專家的夥
　　伴　　(18)

fiancé 未婚夫　　(58)

fight for 爭奪…　　(216)

figure out 解決; 想出來　　(190)

financial handshake 一次領完的退休
　　金或獎金　　(122)

financial incentive 金錢誘因; 金錢獎
　　勵　　(40)

fine arts performance 藝術公演
　　(162)

fire 解雇　　(76)

fire away 投射; 投籃　　(68)

first thing in the morning 早上第一
　　件事　　(148)

flattened pyramid 扁平了的金字塔
　　(18)

flatter 阿諛; 諂媚　　(216)

flower power 權力歸花朵 (60 年代由嬉
　　痞所號召的和平運動, 愛情與非暴力為
　　其訴求)　　(54)

focus group discussion (銷售)討論
　　小組會議〈從潛在的消費者中選出一些
　　人來組成討論小組, 然後由一位市調人
　　員主導討論會的進行, 目的是要令與會
　　者能發表其對公司、產品、以及宣傳廣
　　告的感覺和看法〉　　(64)

focus on 集中於…　　(162)

food aisle 食品區的通道　　(112)

foolproof 極簡單的; 愚人也會的; 相當

安全的　　(184)

foot the bill 付帳　　(18)

for one thing 其一　　(122)

forceful 強勢的　　(90)

foster 培養　　(94)

foursome 四人組　　(208)

free agent 不受契約限制的職員〈棒球
　　的「自由契約選手」〉　　(94)

from a technical perspective 以技術
　　面而言; 從技術觀點來看　　(230)

frustrating 令人沮喪的　　(46)

fuzzy 不明確的; 模稜兩可的; 乏晰
　　(108)

G

gather 推測; 考慮　　(118)

gather dust on the shelf 在架上蒙灰;
　　被束之高閣　　(108)

gay 男同性戀者　　(58)

generous 寬大的; 慷慨的　　(202)

get along (與人)相處　　(180)

get along with 與…相處　　(136)

get back on the track 言歸正傳
　　(126)

get in trouble 有麻煩了　　(22)

get out of control 失控　　(220)

get publicity 得到注意(宣傳)　　(244)

get settled 落腳; 安定下來　　(226)

get smashed 醉倒　　(22)

get the impression 得到某種印象
　　(194)

get-together 會議〈非正式用語〉
　　(82)

give credit 讚揚; 認可某人的功蹟
　　(244)

if necessary 必要的話　　(194)

ignore 忽視；忽略　　(220)

illegal 非法的　　(100)

immense 龐大的　　(184)

impractical dream 不實際的夢想
　　(238)

in a way 就某種意義而言；或多或少
　　(190)

in alignment with 與…相結合
　　(238)

in charge 管理；負責　　(226)

in essence 在本質上；重點上　　(112)

in other words 換句話說　　(90)

in part 部分　　(28)

in the hope of 期待著…　　(158)、
　　(208)

in the meantime 同時　　(148)

individual 個人的　　(190)

inevitable 無可避免的　　(220)

inflated 誇大不實的　　(112)

information battleground 資訊戰場
　　(184)

informative 能獲得知識的　　(248)

inner-city 市中心 (的)　　(144)

instant results 立即效果　　(158)

instinctively 本能地　　(90)

in-store exhibit 店內展示　　(166)

interfere with 干擾…　　(28)

intersection 十字路口；交叉口　　(10)

interview 面試　　(130)

introduction 介紹　　(180)

irons in the fire 攬事太多　　(140)

irrelevant 不相關的；不適切的　　(82)

It seems like yesterday. 似乎還是昨天
的事。　　(248)

It's much more than that. 還不只是
那樣呢!　　(18)

J

Jekyll and Hyde personalities 雙重人
格〈出自 R. L. Stevenson 所著的 The
Strange Case of Dr. Jekyll and Mr.
Hyde〉　　(194)

job massacre 大量裁員　　(122)

jobless 失業者　　(122)

joiner 喜歡參加社團活動的人　　(190)

juicy 有趣的　　(208)

jump into 躍入　　(184)

jump ship 逃離；辭職　　(140)

just in case 以防萬一　　(244)

K

KC Kansas City 的簡稱　　(118)

keep abreast of 與…並駕齊驅　　(90)

keep an(one's) eye on 留意；照顧；監
視　　(176)、(194)

keep on top of it 掌握；走在前端
　　(58)

kid 小孩；開玩笑　　(166)、(190)

kind of 有點　　(194)

know for certain 確實知道　　(104)

know no boundaries 沒有國界之分
　　(28)

know the picture 知道那個狀況
　　(154)

L

labor laws 勞工法　　(126)

"ladies first" 「女士優先」　　(54)

land in 陷入…；著落於…　　(208)

landfill 垃圾掩埋場　　(32)

last 支持；耐久 (176)

lavish 浪費的；奢侈的 (100)

lawsuit 訴訟案件 (122)

lay off 裁員 (194)

layer 層 (18)

layer of management 管理階層 (94)

layoff 裁員 (244)

lean and agile 沒有贅肉，活動靈活自如 (18)

let someone go 解雇某人 (194)

Let's look at it this way. 我們這樣來看好了。 (238)

line manager 部門經理；生產線經理 (208)

line up 安排；預備 (144)

litigious 好訴訟的 (108)

living arrangement 生活形態 (58)

lock the doors 關門大吉 (126)

log 記錄 (100)

logical 合邏輯的；合理的 (234)

logical choice 合理的選擇 (226)

look after 照顧 (198)

look for 尋求 (140)、(230)

look into 研究；探討 (76)

loosen one's grip on the reins 放鬆控制權 (94)

lose faith in 對…失去了信心 (140)

loser 輸家 (144)

low-fat 低脂肪的 (72)

low-key 低調的；不顯眼的 (166)

M

magic ability 神奇的能力 (238)

mail basket 信件籃 (100)

maitre d' 服務生領班 (68)

majority 大多數；大部分 (54)

make a blunder 犯錯 (220)

make a dent 大幅降低；使減少 (32)

make sure 確定 (176)

make tracks （快速）離去 (100)

marketplace 市場 (82)

Martin Luther King 馬丁‧路德‧金恩牧師〈黑人解放運動的主導者〉 (234)

mass market 量販市場；大量市場；大眾市場 (154)

master's degree 碩士學位 (158)

match with 與…配合 (198)

match wits with 與…鬥智 (148)

matching grant program 同額補助捐款計畫 (202)

materialistic pleasure 物質享受 (176)

matter of …的問題 (136)

matter of life or death 攸關生死的問題 (28)

"me decade" 「以自我為中心的十年」（70 年代的口號） (54)

media 媒體 (136)

medical complaint 病痛 (112)

meditate 沈思；冥想 (76)

membership 會員的資格 (18)

mental health 心理健康 (144)

mercilessly 無情地 (194)

mergers and acquisitions M&A、企業購併 (82)

messenger 使者；信差 (136)

messy 複雜的 (108)

279

micro marketing 小眾市場行銷〈將商品所針對的消費者加以區隔，瞄準單一的消費者族群，而予以各個擊破的行銷手法〉 (148)、(154)

middle management 中層管理階級 (94)

Midwestern 中西部的 (14)

miff 使惱怒 (46)

minimize 使最小化 (32)

misconduct 違法行為 (108)

miss 想念 (238)

mock 嘲笑 (172)

modify 修改 (54)

morale 士氣；工作意願 (130)

motivated 受到激發的 (22)

mount (數量、程度、費用)增加 (76)

mouthful 長而難唸的字 (104)

move up the ladder 升遷 (252)

moving expenses 搬家的花費 (64)

much ado about 大驚小怪；白忙一場 (46)

mysterious 不可理解的 (220)

N

name names 指名道姓 (208)

name tag 名牌 (244)

narrowcasting 窄播〈與傳統的 broadcasting (廣播)相對，是以限定地區內的特定族群為其視聽對象〉 (166)

natural resources 自然資源 (32)

negative 否定的；負面的；消極的 (194)

network television 電視廣播網〈像是 ABC, NBC, CBS 等大型廣播電視公司〉 (158)

night spot 夜總會 (104)

no more right than 不比…來得正確 (136)

nominal 微少的 (100)

noncommittal 不明確的；模糊的 (172)

nonmanagerial type 非主管階級的人 (118)

non-media marketing 非媒體的市場行銷 (172)

nonprofit organization 非營利團體 (190)

not much of 不是甚麼了不起的… (198)

note 摘記；注釋 (194)

note pads 拍紙簿 (122)

nothing more than 只不過是… (238)

O

observe 遵守 (112)

obvious 清楚的；明白的 (172)

odd couple 奇妙的二人組 (256)

office politics 公司內部的政治活動 (208)

on a regular basis 定期地 (252)

on file 存檔 (104)

on one's way home 回家途中 (158)

on sabbatical 在有薪休假中 (82)

on that count 就這方面來說 (58)

on top of 在…之上 (82)

ongoing 持續進行的；持續不斷的 (248)

save money 儲蓄；省錢　　(40)

save the whales 反對捕鯨 (運動)　(190)

say hello 打招呼　　(256)

scale 標準　　(72)

scapegoat 代罪羔羊；替罪者　　(22)

Scout leader 童軍領隊　　(194)

scratch the surface 只涉及事件的表面 (皮毛)　　(198)

self-esteem 自尊心　　(136)

self-esteem counseling 為提高個人自尊心所作的諮商　　(130)

self-respect 自尊心　　(46)

sell 說服　　(162)

sense 感覺；察覺　　(76)

sense of …的感覺；…感　　(54)

sense of humor 幽默感　　(68)

sense of self-worth 自我價值感　(144)

set the tone 樹立風氣　　(220)

settle the dust 使塵土沈澱　　(76)

severe 樸素的；樸實的　　(256)

sexual harassment 性騷擾　　(108)

shape 塑造出來　　(238)

share of the action 責任的擔當　(136)

shelf display 商品架上的陳列　(172)

shoot up 快速上升　　(162)

shop floor 工廠的作業現場　　(18)

show 出現　　(46)

show up 出現　　(10)

Siberia 西伯利亞　　(256)

sign up 參加；立約加入　　(252)

sink 投資；投入　　(158)

skeptical 懷疑的　　(216)

skepticism 懷疑論　　(32)

skill 技巧　　(198)

skip 省掉；略過　　(22)

snob appeal 以消費者的虛榮心為訴求　(172)

soap opera 連續劇　　(158)

someplace else 別的地方　　(162)

something 了不起的人或物　　(172)

something like 約　　(36)

sort through 整理　　(234)

spacious housing 寬廣的住宅　(248)

spare time 空暇時間　　(190)

speak highly of 對…評價甚高　(154)

specialize in 專門做…　　(162)

sponsor 贊助；支持；發起　　(172)

spring up 長出；萌芽　　(162)

stand out 傑出；突出　　(234)

standard 標準的；普遍的　　(166)

state-of-the-art 最新式的　　(244)

stay "on top" of things 掌握狀況　(94)

steer a course 決定前面的路程；行進　(234)

stint 任期　　(72)

stop short of 沒有達到…　　(112)

strangle 將…絞死；悶死　　(76)

stressed out 精疲力盡　　(72)

strike the perfect balance between 在…之間取得完全的平衡　　(256)

subordinate 下屬　　(212)

sue 控告　　(108)

suit 訴訟　　(126)

supplier 上游廠商　　(104)

Surprise, surprise. 真令人驚訝！〈這是個反語，說話者其實是要表示，這根本不是甚麼新聞，更沒甚麼好驚訝的〉(82)

survive 生存；存活　　(82)、(216)

survivor 倖存的人　　(130)

switch on 打開 (電器等的開關)　　(166)

T

tactical 善用策略的　　(220)

take a bruising 受到打擊　　(244)

take a lead role 居領導地位　　(82)

take a look around 四周看一下　　(212)

take advantage of 利用…　　(22)、(176)

take the load off someone's mind 減輕某人心中的擔子　　(130)

talk someone out of 勸某人不要做…　　(162)

tall order 困難的工作；不合理的要求；難應付的工作　　(220)

target 對象　　(172)

target audience 收視對象；針對的觀(聽)眾　　(162)

tax implications 稅金的牽連　　(126)

technically 就現實面而言；規則上　　(144)

technological advances 科技進步(82)

territory 領土　　(208)

that goes for 適用於…　　(216)

That's a thought. 這個主意不錯。(256)

That's about it. 就是這樣了；這就是全部了；全都在這兒了。　　(238)

that's mutual 這是相互的　　(252)

There's life before death. 人只要還沒死，日子總是得過。〈與 life after death (死後) 相對應，是特意要表示幽默的講法。一般較常使用 There's life after . . . 的形態。例如：There's life after work. (下班後還有生活要過。) There's life after Nelson ABC Food.〉　　(68)

these days 近來　　(122)

things like that 像那類的事情等的(10)

think much of 看重…　　(144)

thrive on 成長繁茂；孳生　　(220)

throw a party 開派對　　(248)

to death 至死；到極點　　(212)

to some extent 在某種程度上　　(172)

toothpaste 牙膏　　(166)

top brass 高級主管 (官員)　　(90)

top-of-the-line 最高級的　　(176)

total ban 全面禁止　　(112)

tough decision 難下的決定　　(238)

toxic emissions 有毒排放物　　(36)

traditional 傳統的　　(172)

transfer 調任　　(118)

transformational 轉型的　　(90)

traumatic 創傷的；屬於精神上衝擊的(76)

trick 祕訣；技巧　　(50)、(72)

troops 一般職員；士兵 (常用複數)(18)、(94)

tube 電視　　(154)

tune in to 收看 (158)

turn down 拒絕 (136)

turn over 移交 (90)

turn-away 被拒入場的; 拒絕; 謝絕 (10)

tutor 家庭教師 (198)

tycoon (實業界、政界的)鉅子; 大亨 (180)

U

ugh (表示厭惡的聲音)哎; 呀; 啊 (64)

underdressed 穿著簡單的; 樸素的 (68)

underestimate 低估; 小看 (136)

undo 摒棄; 取消 (94)

under-30 crowd 三十歲以下的人士 (172)

unethical 不道德的 (100)

unexpected 不期然的 (226)

union-busting 破壞工會的 (126)

up side 正面 (22)

up to a limit of 到…的限度 (202)

urgency 迫切 (90)

"us against them" mentality 有「敵 我之分」的心態 (220)

V

values and beliefs 價值觀和信念 (230)

variation 變化 (172)

VCR (video cassette recorder) 錄影 機 (166)

veteran 老手; 有經驗的人; 老資格 (126)

violate 違反 (108)

VIP (very important person) 重要人 物 (244)

visionary 有先見的; 有先見的人 (238)

visiting 來訪的 (244)

volunteerism 自願活動 (190)

vulnerable 易受攻擊的 (208)

W

wad 揉成一團 (68)

walk away 離去 (140)

waste management 廢棄物管理 (40)

waste time and energy 浪費時間與精 力 (212)

watch the big picture 縱觀全體 (176)

wave a flag 表明自己的意思 (212)

what in the world 到底是甚麼 (136)

what's going on 怎麼了 (64)

What's up? 甚麼事; 發生甚麼事了? (126)

wherever they might be 不管他們有可 能在哪裡 (162)

wield the ax 揮動斧頭; 砍別人的頭 (118)

wind down 慢慢地停下來 (126)

wind-chill factor 風速冷卻效果〈皮膚 表面在風力吹襲下放出熱量而造成身體 冷卻的效果〉 (256)

winery 釀酒廠 (22)

wing it 臨場發揮 (58)

women's liberation 婦女解放 (54)

Wonderful. 真不可思議。 (50)

Y

讀後心得

讀 後 心 得